Secrets of the Stream

Elizabeth A. Miller

Elizabeth A Miller

Innovative Writing Works
St. Louis, Missouri

For my parents,
Stephen and Ellen Miller,
with love and gratitude.

Chapter One

July 1880

A cloud of dust encased the stagecoach as it skirted the center of town and pulled up outside the Overland Stage Lines office. Hitches and harnesses squealed with the strain of four powerful horses as they were brought to a halt. The heat of the day had worked up a lather on the over-worked beasts and generated enough sweat on the passengers' brows to make all the grit in Missouri stick to their clothes.

"Copper Creek," the driver announced. "End of the line."

A stocky fellow, with muscles to spare, Hank Wilson hopped down from atop the coach to open the passenger door.

Relieved the endless jostling of the trip from St. Louis had finally ended, Thomas Mason looked out his window to observe the hubbub on the street. All the buildings and porches were decorated with festive buntings. He saw several long tables laden with food and casks of beer. A small group of men with fiddles, banjos, and other sundry instruments were tuning up close by.

The door to the stagecoach had been left ajar and Thomas realized he was the last one still on board. He collected his small valise from under the seat and stepped down from the coach. A sudden wind scooped up dust from the street and tugged at his suit coat. He looked down to the far end of the road and then back up the other way, carefully assessing everything he saw. Then, as he turned, he noticed a young woman coming around the corner. She was dressed in a white blouse trimmed with lace. Her skirt was a rich, cobalt blue and her hair was the color of wheat. It was pulled back from her plain, but gentle, face with a simple, black ribbon. But it was the size and depth of her warm, brown eyes that captured his attention. They were fixed upon him in awe or perhaps suspicion. He couldn't be sure which. He smiled at her and spoke.

"Good afternoon."

His words seemed to break the trance she was in because she hastily averted her gaze. Bobbing her head in acknowledgement of his greeting, she hurried away. Thomas made a mental shrug at the inscrutability of females and walked around the stagecoach to collect the rest of his luggage. The woman, who'd sat beside him during the trip, was animatedly bellowing orders to the station agent for faster service. Her harassed husband looked on in silence as the station agent tossed down their bags. Realizing he'd have to wait his turn, Thomas approached the driver, who was standing beside the porch wiping his face with a dingy bandanna.

"What's going on in town there?" Thomas asked, gesturing towards the festivities.

"It's the Randolph's annual summer party."

"I'm supposed to be meeting a Mr. Michael Randolph," Thomas replied. "Is that the same fellow?"

"Sure is. Every July the whole town turns out to enjoy Michael's hospitality."

"Sounds as if he's a friend of yours."

"Michael Randolph is one of those men who's everybody's friend and nobody's."

Thomas gave him a puzzled look.

"Hell. He's lived here for near on to twenty years and in all that time I don't hardly think we've ever conversified proper like. He can be the most standoffish of fellas. I guess he can afford to be with his kind of money. But he don't put on airs like a lotta rich folks do. And when you've got a free pint of beer in your hand, regular like, it sure is hard not to feel friendly toward the fella that done give it to ya."

Thomas smiled. "I see."

"What's your business with Michael anyway?"

"I'm can't really say."

Hank's brow wrinkled in suspicion at Thomas' evasive reply.

"That is to say I'm here to help Mr. Randolph with a personal matter," Thomas clarified. "You see, he and my father are old friends…"

"And you've come for a visit?" Hank interpreted.

"Something like that."

"Well, there's no use waitin' round here then. Everybody at the Randolph's will be too busy today to come for ya, what with the party and all. But if you like, I'll take you over."

"Are you sure it won't be an inconvenience?"

"A what?"

"A bother," Thomas explained.

Hank scowled. "I know what it means."

"I'm sure."

"I'm just not used to such formal talk's all."

Thomas nodded to appease the older man's obvious indignation.

"Shall I collect my luggage then, so we can start?"

"Never mind that."

"But I can't leave my trunks…"

"No such a thing. George there'll keep 'em in the office till later."

"Won't they be in the way?"

"Will they still be here later is what ya mean, isn't it?"

"No I…" Thomas paused to sigh; fully aware arguing wouldn't get him anywhere. "Look," he continued, "I'm sorry. I didn't mean to offend you. If you'll accept my apology, I would be very grateful for your help."

Hank eyed him momentarily, and then held out his hand. Relieved, Thomas gratefully accepted the stagecoach driver's gesture of friendship.

"I'd be glad to let George watch over my bags until I can return for them with a wagon," Thomas added.

"Good. Now let's get going before the Lester brothers have all the beer guzzled down. All this talk's only increased my thirst."

Hank slapped Thomas on the shoulder and stepped away from the porch. "Hey, George," he yelled. "Put those last two trunks in the office fur me then lock up and come along."

"Sure thing, Hank."

"This one too," Thomas added, setting his small valise down outside the office door. Hank looked at him in surprise until Thomas explained, "Then I'll have two hands to hold the beer."

Hank laughed. "Now you're thinking straight." He turned to attract George's attention again and point out the extra bag.

"Come on now, young fella," Hank said. "Say, what is your name anyway?"

"Thomas Mason."

"I'm Hank Wilson. Glad to know ya."

"Likewise," Thomas replied. "Now, tell me a little more about these Lester brothers...."

Hank and Thomas moved off, too engrossed in their conversation to notice they were being watched. Jane Randolph shrank back into the shadows where she had waited and watched since the stranger startled her with his unexpected greeting. Flustered by her audacity to spy, she hoped her impropriety hadn't been witnessed by any of her neighbors milling about for the party. She peeked around the corner to check if it was safe to move on. Thomas Mason had progressed far enough down the street that he was well out of view. Relived, Jane gathered her skirt and set off in the opposite direction, unsure why the sight of that strange man had sent her spine tingling. She had never been one to swoon over an attractive face. Yet, in this instance, there was something about that face, and the man behind it she just couldn't ignore.

Over the many years Michael Randolph lived in Copper Creek, he had earned a reputation as a generous man. Being a success in business had not made him forget his poor beginnings or his less fortunate neighbors. He and his wife, Ruth, ran the town's general store with fairness and friendliness, extending their hospitality to the townspeople of Copper Creek every year. Their annual Independence Day celebration was a social gathering anticipated by everyone for miles around. And today was no exception.

By five o'clock, the town was becoming so crowded Jane had trouble making her way through the throng to her Uncle Michael's store. She needed to find her Aunt Ruth before she started welcoming their guests. As she came into the store, Jane noticed her uncle sitting in his office. She hurried back to ask him about Ruth's whereabouts.

"Uncle Michael, have you seen Aunt Ruth?"

"Ah, Jane. So nice to see you," an unexpected voice replied.

Startled to discover her uncle was not alone in his office, Jane smiled in recognition of the silver-haired gentleman sitting across from him.

"Hello, Mayor Winston," she said. "I hope you'll forgive me for interrupting. I thought Uncle Michael was alone."

James Winston smiled. "Think nothing of it, Jane. I wish I could enjoy such lovely interruptions more often."

"Thank you, Mr. Winston," Jane replied, then looked to her uncle. "Have you seen Aunt Ruth?"

"I believe she's upstairs helping Rachel with her dress," Michael said. "Is anything wrong?"

"No. Sarah and I just had a few questions about her preferences for displaying those special lanterns you ordered. We wanted to hang them up before it gets dark and it's already getting crowded outside. So, I'd better hurry along. Goodbye, Mr. Winston."

"Goodbye, Jane, and be sure you don't keep yourself too busy today. I'm sure there are plenty of young men looking forward to a dance with you tonight."

Jane bobbed her head in deference to the mayor. Politeness required her to agree with him though she could hardly believe anyone would even notice her presence. No one ever did. After she had gone, the mayor asked Michael, "Why is that girl always in such a rush?"

"It isn't that she is so terribly busy," Michael replied. "She just isn't comfortable around people. Her father was like that. In fact, I don't rightly know how my brother managed to court any women let alone get married. But then, Dorothy was a very patient woman. Gentle too, just like him. I expect that's why she and Matthew weren't hearty enough to survive out here."

"They went bust?"

Michael nodded. "Only in the sense that the hardships of keeping up a homestead killed them. Jane was only a tot when it happened and she's lived with Ruth and me ever since."

"Tragic."

"We try not to dwell on it."

"I understand."

The two men exchanged a sympathetic look before the mayor added. "Was there any other business you needed to discuss?"

"No. Not especially. I had word from George Mason just yesterday. His son should be here anytime now."

"Splendid."

"I think you'll all be quite pleased with the plans the young man has drawn up. But then I'm not surprised. He always was a bright boy," Michael added.

"Have you known him long?"

"I've only met him a few times. But his father and I have been friends for years. We blazed a trail all the way from Texas together before I finally decided to settle down here."

"Two young bucks on a tear, eh?" the mayor teased.

"George certainly was," Michael replied. "He had more ambition than anyone I've ever known...though he refused to apply it in any sort of respectable endeavor. Still, I owe more than I can say to him."

"I expect you look on this deal as your chance to repay him, then?"

"Not at all. His son doesn't need any favors from me to get ahead. Thomas Mason graduated the top of his class and he's gone on to become one of the most sought after architects in the country. He's already had commissions in New York, Washington, and even abroad. We are very lucky to have him."

"I'm inclined to agree. I think you know how much your endorsement means to me and I look forward to hearing his full proposal."

Michael nodded and stepped around his desk. "In the meantime," he began, "I hear there is a party going on out there and I think it's high time we joined in. Don't you?"

"Lead on," the mayor smiled.

Jane found Ruth in Rachel's room. They were standing in front of the long looking glass Rachel kept in the corner. Ruth was positively beaming at the loveliness of her daughter. Jane halted in the doorway at the sight of her cousin. The sheen in Rachel's raven tresses glowed as she spun in front of the mirror. The fine, elegant lines of her new dress showed off her petite figure to advantage. Deep down a small part of Jane resented the fact she was so tall and plain and unlikely to ever look so delicate and alluring.

"Oh, Jane," Rachel cried, noticing her. "Isn't it gorgeous?"

Rachel held out her skirt and spun around again.

"You look beautiful," Jane admitted.

"Lavender does flatter you, my dear," Ruth added. "But I think we must give Jane the credit for choosing the dress pattern."

Jane shrugged. "You made the dress, aunt."

"Well, don't I get any credit for wearing it so well?" Rachel said.

Ruth laughed. "That goes without saying, my dear."

Jane bit her tongue at Rachel's show of vanity. Lately, it had become a new facet of her character that Jane could not abide. She hated the fact Rachel's sweetness and sincerity were slowly giving way to more superficial interests.

"I've taken the last of the lanterns out to Max," Jane said. "And Sarah has a few questions for you about the food before the party begins. Was there anything else you needed done?"

Rather startled by Jane's abruptness, Ruth thought a moment then said, "No. No, I'll see Sarah and then I think she and Max should be able to handle the rest, especially with the helpers she'll have in the kitchen."

Jane smiled inwardly at the notion of their irascible cook voluntarily accepting help. She usually barred everyone from her culinary domain. More likely than not, Sarah knew nothing about Ruth's plans to open up the kitchen to a passel of green girls. As a result, Jane decided it might be best to avoid that part of the house for the rest of the day.

"C'mon then, Jane," Rachel said, grabbing her hand. "Let's get downstairs before the music starts."

"Just a minute," Ruth called after them. "There is one more thing you girls should know. We are expecting a guest soon and I trust you both will welcome him when he arrives."

"Who is he, mother?"

"The son of one of your father's oldest friends. The town council engaged him at your father's recommendation to help draft plans for improvements to the town."

"What sort of improvements are they planning, Aunt Ruth?"

"I'm not quite sure, Jane. But I have no doubt Mr. Mason will share the details of his work during the course of his visit with us."

Jane's eyes widened at the mention of the architect's name. "Mason?" she repeated.

"Yes...a Mr. Thomas Mason," Ruth recalled. "Do you know him, Jane?"

"No," Jane lied. "I...where would I meet an architect from back East?"

"Look, mother. Jane is blushing."

"Jane?" Ruth's face colored with concern.

"I don't know him, Aunt Ruth, truly. I just happened to be passing when the stage arrived this afternoon and I noticed a young man when he got off. I thought I heard him say his name was Mason, but I could be wrong."

"That's all, Jane?" Ruth pursued.

"Yes."

"I don't believe her," Rachel said teasingly.

Jane felt weak and slightly sick. She was sure it showed on her face. "There's nothing else to tell."

"Nonsense," Rachel insisted. "There are a million things to tell."

"Such as?" Jane asked.

"Such as...was he handsome?"

Jane visibly balked.

Rachel smiled. "Ooh, he must be or you wouldn't be acting so spooked."

"I am not spooked," Jane asserted.

"Girls! I won't have any more of that kind of talk, particularly while our guest is here."

"Here, mother?"

"Yes," Ruth explained, "Mr. Mason will be living with us until his job in Copper Creek is completed and I trust while he is under our roof you will both conduct yourselves with more decorum and act like proper young ladies."

"Yes, mother."

Jane seemed caught in a daze at the news Mr. Mason would be living with them.

"Jane?"

"What...oh. Of course, Aunt Ruth."

"Good," Ruth said. "Now, enough scolding. You two get downstairs and have a good time."

As Ruth instructed, the girls headed down to join the party. Rachel was full of high spirits and giddy anticipation as they went. Her chattering was so constant, it more than amply compensated for Jane's contemplative silence. *How strange*, Jane thought, *to be struck by the appearance of a stranger one moment and discover in the next that he was to become an intimate member of one's household.*

A strange mix of panic and delight possessed Jane at that realization. She feared the presence of Mr. Mason in her home and longed for it at the same time. In truth, she found the company of most men intimidating and, judging by her earlier encounter with Mr. Mason, he would be no exception. Still, the friendly, relaxed atmosphere of home might make it easier to forge a friendship. Then again, she wondered if there was something sinister about Thomas Mason or his business in Copper Creek. Why else would Aunt Ruth and Uncle Michael have been so secretive about their plans to invite him? Before today, Jane had been blissfully unaware of his existence, let alone her uncle's association with anyone named Mason.

Jane took a deep breath and tried to calm her frantic thoughts. Thomas Mason was a man like any other. He was going to be a guest of her family and both duty and reason insisted she stop worrying and trust her uncle's judgment. However, she never expected to have to adopt her resolution quite so quickly. As Jane and Rachel stepped out the front door, they were amazed to find Mr. Thomas Mason greeting his host on the porch of Randolph's General Mercantile.

Chapter Two

Though he was still somewhat dusty from his travels, Thomas Mason had none of the hallmarks of toil or dirt so common among most men in Copper Creek. His youth and strength were at once recognizable. That he was a gentleman of high education was apparent in his speech. The longer his conversation flowed, the more Jane delighted in the dulcet tones of his voice. His hair was thick and dark as molasses. The contours of his face were decidedly masculine, well-defined, and in every way pleasing. But it was the spark of mischief in his intense, blue eyes that most enthralled Jane.

Her pulse quickened under his gaze as the introductions finally came to her.

"And of course this is our niece, Miss Jane Randolph."

Jane made a small curtsey.

Thomas grinned. "Miss Randolph, I am delighted to see you again."

"Again?" Michael Randolph said.

"Jane, what's this? I thought you told me you didn't know Mr. Mason," Ruth added, concerned by the young man's familiarity with her niece. Rachel looked smug as though her suspicions of Jane's impropriety had just been confirmed.

Thomas leaned in and said to Jane conspiringly, "Shall we keep them in suspense, Miss Randolph? Or should I tell them our secret?"

"Jane?" Michael pressed.

"I assure you, sir, there is no cause for alarm," Thomas said.

"It's true, Uncle Michael," Jane added. "And we have no secret…really. It's just as I told you, Aunt Ruth. I saw Mr. Mason getting off the stage this afternoon and we met… only in passing."

"Yes, Jane told us *all* about him. Don't you remember, mother?" Rachel giggled. Mortified, Jane glared at her with murderous intent.

"I'm glad to hear I made an impression," Thomas offered.

"You certainly did," Rachel replied.

"Then may I return the compliment, Miss Jane?"

Jane tried to muster a smile.

"I must confess, Mr. Randolph, I had my doubts about coming to Copper Creek," Thomas said. "But seeing your niece upon my arrival was a most compelling endorsement of your town. And now to discover you have two more lovely ladies under your roof makes me feel most fortunate to have come to a place filled with such natural beauty."

"What a charming sentiment," Ruth replied.

"Yes," Michael agreed. "And you are of course most welcome."

"Thank you. I am just sorry my arrival coincided with today's festivities. I hope it won't create any added burden or inconvenience."

"Not at all," Ruth assured him.

"We've been expecting you for some time," Michael added. "Though you must have had an arduous trip from New Orleans."

"Yes," Ruth added, "You must be tired."

"A bit," Thomas admitted. "But the pleasant company and high spirits of a party is just the thing to revive me."

"Excellent," Michael replied. "There are quite a few people here I'd like you to meet. Mostly other members of the town council and of course, the mayor, Jim Winston."

"Naturally, Mr. Randolph. But this is a party isn't it?"

"Yes…"

"Well, I make it a policy to keep business and pleasure separate. And right now, it would be a great pleasure if your daughter would consent to dance with me."

Jane was stunned and supremely irritated. Rachel seemed to beam with pleasure.

"Will you dance with me, Miss Rachel?"

"Why, yes," Rachel cooed. "Thank you, Mr. Mason."

Thomas took Rachel's hand and led her down the porch steps out to the street where other couples were already dancing. Ruth and Michael followed them and joined in the dancing as well, leaving Jane alone on the porch. She looked on, wounded by the slight, especially after Thomas made such a fuss over their passing this afternoon. Some part of her hoped he would think of her favorably, but apparently, she was only good for a joke.

Jane kept her eyes fixed on Rachel. The way she twirled in Thomas' arms made her look like a picture of femininity and fashion. *No doubt, that was the reason for Mr. Mason's preference*, Jane thought. She continued to watch and brood as the pattern of the dance drew Rachel and Thomas close. Then, he leaned in to whisper in Rachel's ear. She said something in reply that made him laugh. Rachel began to laugh too and the mingled sounds of their mirth stung. Jane turned away and hurried off the porch. She had seen enough. She headed around to the back of the store and set out across the dry patch of grass that lead to the woods beyond.

Spiteful, self-recriminating thoughts seemed to be chasing Jane as she went. The faster she walked, the more furiously they came. She could not stop remembering the way things were when she and Rachel were children. Then they had been inseparable, sharing every secret, every confidence. But since Rachel's sixteenth birthday, that closeness had begun to erode and was being replaced by mistrust and competitiveness.

Jane worried at times their division was her fault for being too serious and demanding. Then it could be because Rachel was too thoughtless and frivolous. The only satisfying conclusion Jane could reach was that they weren't interested in the same things anymore – *except Thomas Mason* – a nasty, inner voice reminded her.

Whatever the reason for the state of their present relationship, Jane hated the fact she and Rachel were becoming strangers. Jane had always loved her younger cousin and imagined she always would. But that love did not prevent her vexation at the world's preference for Rachel's exuberance and self-interest over her quiet sense and dignity. Thomas Mason's partiality tonight was just another incarnation of this phenomenon and for Jane it was the last straw. She couldn't stomach the bitter taste of being overlooked or dismissed anymore.

Before Jane realized it, she was in the heart of the woods. She hurried past shrubs and familiar trees, moving on to her favorite spot near the creek. When she finally emerged from the trees, the sultry sounds of evensong were flooding the canopy above. Warm from her exertions, Jane sat on a large, smooth rock embedded along the bank of the stream and dipped her hand beneath the ripples running past. It felt cool and wonderfully soft. She drew out her handkerchief and dampened it to wipe her face. Then she sat very still, reveling in the serenity of her placid surroundings.

A smile tugged at Jane's lips at the sight of a dragonfly as it skimmed the glassy surface of the water only to speed off into the dazzling crimson sunset. She closed her eyes to quiet the noise inside her head, but she was soon jarred out of her peaceful contemplation by the sound of rustling in the willows. Jane watched as concentric rings of water spread out towards her from the opposite bank. Expecting to see a deer emerge, she was disturbed to see a man instead.

His face was difficult to discern in the fading light, but he appeared to be in his mid-thirties. He wore a white shirt that was open at the throat. His shirtsleeves were cuffed to the elbow and his feet were bare. In one hand, he held his boots and in the other, a fishing pole. Jane noted how smooth and well-defined his hands were. The sort of hands a doctor or an artist might have. He stopped short at the sight of Jane and she stood up, uncertain what to do next.

"Pardon me," he said. "I didn't mean to startle you."

Jane nodded in acceptance of his apology.

He moved a little closer and said, "I wasn't expecting to see anyone. I thought the whole town would be at that party tonight."

"I was," Jane confessed. "But I left."

"So I see. Whose shindig is it anyhow?"

"The Randolph's," Jane replied.

"You know them?"

"I should. I'm a Randolph."

The stranger turned sharply and gaped at her.

"Sorry," he said. "I didn't…"

"You needn't be sorry. It isn't my party anyway. My Uncle Michael is the host."

"*Michael Randolph?*"

Jane nodded. "Yes. Do you know him?"

The stranger grimaced. "The name does sound familiar. How is it you said you were related?"

"He's my father's brother."

"I see…" His words seemed to trail away as he studied her for a moment and then retreated into his own thoughts.

"And you are?"

"Tired," he replied, resting his fishing pole against a nearby tree. "Now, if you don't mind. I'd like to sit down. My feet hurt."

"That's no answer," Jane persisted.

"Well, it will have to do."

"I don't understand you at all."

"Why should you? We're strangers aren't we? So let's keep it that way."

The stranger lowered himself to the ground and began to brush the grit off the bottom of his left foot.

"It might help your feet more if you actually wore your shoes," Jane observed.

He looked over his shoulder at her. "I was. I only took them off so they wouldn't get wet when I crossed the creek."

"Oh."

He busied himself pulling on his left boot and reached for the right one when Jane added, "Do you live around here?"

"I haven't decided."

"Then where do you come from?"

He finished pulling on his right boot and turned to face her.

"Are you always this nosy?"

Jane bristled. "Are you always this rude?"

The stranger smirked and got to his feet.

"Aren't you going to answer me?" Jane persisted.

"No," he said. Then he smiled.

Jane crossed her arms in frustration and watched as the stranger walked away to collect his pole.

"Now don't be irritable," he added, turning to face her again. "Just run along home to your uncle now, before it starts to rain."

"You're condescending too," Jane replied.

"Am I?"

"Yes. Who are you to order me about like I'm a child?"

"I am the voice of experience telling you that *nice* young girls shouldn't be out alone in the woods at night."

"And why not?"

In her anger, Jane had unwittingly narrowed the gap between them. She stood close enough to the stranger now to be captivated by his clever, green eyes. In an instant, his expression changed from amusement to frustration and then to something far more disconcerting that Jane could not identify. The way he gazed into her eyes made her feel quite vulnerable, as if he could read her thoughts. Finally, he spoke.

"The fact you don't know *why* is precisely the reason."

Jane took a step back. The stranger took one last look. "I think I'd better be going now. You'd better get going too. That storm is coming fast." He started to walk away.

"Wait. Won't you tell me who you are?"

He paused to consider her request and shook his head.

He moved on again and Jane shouted after him. "Stubborn!"

He continued to walk away.

"And it isn't going to rain," Jane added.

The stranger spun around momentarily and smiled at her. "Good night, Miss Randolph." With that, he vanished among the darkening trees.

Jane mumbled under her breath. "I can stay here as long as I like. Doesn't the fool know we're in a drought?" Satisfied she had put the stranger in his place, she reclaimed her seat upon the rock. She looked around and reaffirmed, "It isn't going to rain," as if repeating it would confirm its veracity. However, the words had barely escaped her lips when she heard the low rumble of thunder. Her chest tightened as the rumble grew louder. The moon was beginning to be obscured by fast moving clouds.

"It *won't* rain," Jane asserted.

She settled back upon the rock, determined to remain, when a flash of lightning tore across the horizon.

Rain began to speckle the dry ground. Jane cursed under her breath and scrambled to her feet to take cover beneath the trees. She waited briefly for the storm to break, but was forced to run for town. By the time she reached home, she was soaked through and her spirits were just as damp. The party had been forced to an abrupt ending by the storm and those who wished to continue celebrating had moved down the street to the hotel. So there was no one around to question Jane as she went up to her room and changed into her night dress. It was a little past quarter to nine as she fell into bed and doused her lamp, determined to forget the whole miserable day.

Lying in the darkness, Jane listened to the sound of rain dripping from the gutter outside her window. It seemed to be tapping out "I told you so" with such irritating persistence she wasn't able to relax. She couldn't get her mind off the vexing stranger she'd met in the woods. When she finally succumbed to sleep, her dreams were fraught with rainstorms, fishing poles, and the melodious laughter of a man she could never quite see.

By the time early morning sunbeams carpeted the floor in Jane's bedroom, she was up and on her way down to the kitchen. She was anxious to begin the day's work and escape the aura of the dreams still plaguing her thoughts. Since the Randolph's lived above their store, there was an endless list of chores that needed tending to before the shop opened for business each day. Jane was certain the party last night only increased the number of tasks that needed attention today.

She sought out Sarah to learn what duties she might undertake, but when Jane found the family's faithful cook and housekeeper, she was grumbling to herself in a most foreboding manner.

"If I told her once, I told her a thousand times I didn't need any flighty girls in my kitchen!"

"What's the matter, Sarah?" Jane asked passing through the kitchen door.

Sarah pursed her lips in disgusts. "Plenty's the matter," she replied. "Just look at this."

She held out a large silver pot.

"Burnt to a crisp," Sarah went on. "And it was my favorite pot, too. I used it for everything! And now look at it, because some fool girl couldn't keep her mind on her work."

Jane clicked her tongue. "I'm so sorry, Sarah. But I'm sure Uncle Michael can get you another one."

"That is beside the point. There are larger principles at stake here."

Jane raised an eyebrow. "Oh?"

"I told your aunt I could mind my own kitchen, but she completely ignored me."

"I'm sure Aunt Ruth was only concerned you might be overwhelmed by so much extra work."

"That may be. But she should have listened to me when I said I didn't want any help. I tell you, Jane, I don't know why I put up with her sometimes!"

Jane hurried over to Sarah and placed her hands on the older woman's shoulders to quell the diatribe she felt coming on. "Now, Sarah. You're just overwrought. Aunt Ruth isn't all that bad. She was just distracted by all the details for the party and allowed her zeal to overcome her better judgment."

Sarah grimaced. "Maybe."

"I'm certain of it," Jane insisted. "Now, tell me what I can do."

"Set right down and have some breakfast."

"But Sarah, surely there must be some chores you need…"

"I'll have no more help for the present, thank you," Sarah replied. "Now sit."

Jane was disappointed and it showed on her face.

"No thanks, Sarah." Jane said. "I'm not hungry."

"Nonsense."

"I honestly couldn't eat a bite. I'll just head out to the Crawley's to pick up that order for Uncle Michael."

"That's a long ride to make on an empty stomach."

Jane shrugged.

"What's troubling you, child?"

"Oh, I guess you'd just call it growing pains."

Sarah frowned. "Didn't you have a good time at the party last night?"

Jane gave her a look that emphatically stressed she did not. "I don't seem to have Rachel's knack for socializing."

"Ah, well no one expects you to."

"I'm not so sure."

"Now, Jane. Anyone who truly cares about you wouldn't want an imitation. Just be yourself and that's enough."

Jane forced a smile.

"This sudden urge to be more like Rachel wouldn't have anything to do with that Mr. Mason would it?" Sarah pursued.

"Of course not, Sarah."

"You can't fool me. The minute I saw him, I knew he'd cause trouble between you and Rachel." She paused to tap Jane on the cheek. "Mind, he's just a man and not worth the fuss no matter how handsome he is. But by the same token, don't you let Rachel run off with him neither."

"Sarah!"

"No use in scolding me, Miss Jane. I'm old enough now I can speak my mind and my mind's made up that you're just as good as your cousin and better."

When she finished, she smiled at Jane.

Touched by Sarah's kindness and loyalty, Jane returned the smile. "Thank you, Sarah"

"Aww. You can thank me by eating up some of those biscuits I made."

Jane nodded and allowed Sarah to serve her. Once she began eating, Jane realized she had more of an appetite than she thought. She ate heartily, and then headed out to the stables feeling far more optimistic about the day ahead than she had when she awoke.

Jane's palomino mare pawed anxiously in the stall as she entered, signaling its eagerness to be out. Jane quickly set about saddling up the mare and in her distraction was caught off guard by the sound of a masculine voice behind her.

"You certainly aren't easy to pin down, Miss Jane."

She looked up, surprised to see Thomas Mason.

"Why would you want to do that, Mr. Mason?"

"I thought perhaps we could get better acquainted."

"Oh?"

"Yes. I looked for you last night, but you seemed to disappear and then of course the rain put a damper on the rest of the evening."

Jane circled round her horse to check the right stirrup. "You seemed well occupied with my cousin when I last saw you, Mr. Mason. I hardly expected you'd miss my company."

Thomas walked towards Jane. "Miss Rachel is a lovely girl. But she is young."

Jane raised her brow. "And I'm old?" she replied, pausing in her work.

"That's not what I meant at all."

Jane nodded and went back to her work.

"Miss Jane, couldn't we start over?"

"What do you suggest?"

He was standing opposite her with his hands on the mare's back. "Let me ride with you this morning?"

She paused to look at him and tried to discern any subterfuge in his features.

"If you wish," she said, satisfied he was sincere.

"Splendid."

"There is an extra mount in that last stall," Jane added.

Without another word, Thomas set about saddling the horse and, within a few minutes, they rode out at an easy pace on the main road for the Crawley's farm.

Chapter Three

Everything seemed fresh and renewed from the evening rain. Jane could smell the fragrance of clover and wild honeysuckle as she urged her palomino onward. The scent was a pleasant distraction from her uneasiness in Thomas' company. She couldn't understand his interest in *getting to know* her, as he had said, unless it was to get closer to Rachel by ingratiating himself with those nearest to her.

An awkward silence accompanied them from the stable until Thomas asked,

"Where are we headed?"

"The Crawley's farm. I have to pick up some lace goods from Mrs. Crawley for the store."

"Is it far?"

"Another two miles or so," Jane replied.

"Do you go there often?"

"Every month or so. Whenever Mrs. Crawley has enough pieces made to make a trip worthwhile."

"I'm surprised, but happy to learn that such niceties as lace are in demand out here."

"I'm so glad you've discovered Copper Creek isn't the backward community you obviously expected it to be."

"On the contrary, Miss Randolph, I've heard nothing but good things about your town and I'm delighted to find it's all true."

"And whose been telling you about us?"

"My father," Thomas replied casually. "He lived here for a while with your uncle and then continued prospecting alone once your uncle decided to marry."

"Oh, I hadn't realized. Uncle Michael never talks much about himself or his past."

"Really?"

Jane nodded. "Sometimes I feel he'd like everyone to believe he was born a rich, respectable businessman."

Thomas grinned. "You suspect him of having a checkered past?"

"No, not really. It's just, somehow it seems...well, less than human to ignore half a lifetime."

"Perhaps the recollection of his youth is something he prefers to forget. Often youthful indiscretion can be a painful memory...so I'm told."

Jane couldn't repress a smile. "I gather, then, you have no such foibles you'd rather disregard?"

"I very well may...I'm just not old enough yet to realize it. How about you, Miss Randolph?"

"Me?"

"Yes, is there any error in judgment you've buried deep within your subconscious?"

Jane visibly tensed. "I hardly think so," she said softly. "I've led a very quiet life."

"You'll probably think me a lout for admitting it, but I guessed as much."

Jane pulled back on her reins to look at him and he stopped beside her.

"But before you hurl daggers at me with your eyes," Thomas continued, "let me clarify that I don't mean to infer that living a quiet, respectable life is in anyway negative. On the whole, I find it very refreshing. The places I've lived and the company I've kept in my work has never permitted me to spend much time with anyone who was really *good*, Miss Randolph. And if you'll forgive me for saying so, I find your goodness captivating."

The uncomfortable implications of Mr. Masons' flirtatious remark caused Jane to straighten her spine.

"I don't like to play games, Mr. Mason."

"No?"

"No. And I think considering you are a guest in my uncle's home it is quite rude of you to tease me in this fashion."

"I didn't intend to tease you, Miss Randolph. Only to compliment you. But if I have offended you, please accept my apology."

Jane was embarrassed to look at him now, yet in the few furtive glances she dared to take, she guessed his remorse was sincere. She inclined her head as a sign of truce and they rode on with a renewed silence overshadowing them.

"Do you mean to punish me by not speaking to me?" Thomas asked a few moments later.

"No. I just have nothing to say. What would you like to discuss?"

Thomas shrugged. "Anything…the weather, the town, any points of interest we're passing along the way…"

"I'm afraid there aren't any points of interest, as you put it, Mr. Mason."

"Come now. There's got to be something." He paused to think for a minute. "My father mentioned once that there were rumors of a rich copper mine in this area. There must be some truth to the legends."

"What makes you so sure?"

"The name of the town for one," he replied. "How else did Copper Creek get its name if there isn't any copper around?"

"Most folks figure the name can be attributed to wishful thinking on the part of some early settlers who hoped to strike a rich vein of ore to make their homesteads go."

"And you? What do you think?"

"That some member of the first town council probably appreciated the beauty of the nearby stream and decided to identify the town by the coppery color of the stones glistening beneath the ripples."

"That's not a very practical explanation."

"It is when you consider that stream also provides all the water for the town. Without it, there'd be no town at all."

"True," Thomas conceded. "Still, there had to be something besides the scenery that kept a community thriving here for so many years. Commerce and profit, Miss Randolph, are the cornerstones of civilization."

"Perhaps in New Orleans, Mr. Mason. Not here," Jane corrected him.

"Even here a man has to earn money to feed his family."

"Of course. But there are many ways to earn a living."

"Agreed. But for some men just *earning a living* isn't enough. They want more. They want the comforts and power they can only get with money and what better way is there to get lots of money than by owning a rich mine?"

"And are you such a man, Mr. Mason?"

Thomas shrugged. "I suppose any man could be under the right set of circumstances."

"Such as?"

"Such as discovering a hidden copper mine."

"I'm afraid you'll have to keep on searching then, Mr. Mason. Because the only copper you're liable to find around here is among the hardware at my uncle's store."

"How unfortunate."

"Not really," Jane replied. "Copper Creek is a beautiful place because there are no mines around here to spoil the land or corrupt the people."

"You sound as if you're proud of that fact."

"I am, Mr. Mason. Copper Creek is my home. But more than that, its serene setting and kind people have created a sort of haven for me since my parents died. I'd hate to see it ever change."

"You can't imagine how sorry I am to hear you say that, Miss Randolph."

"Why?" Jane asked incredulously.

"Because I'm here for the sole purpose of brining change to Copper Creek and I had so hoped we could be friends."

"Friends?"

"Does that word offend you so much or is it just the idea of being friends with me?"

"I don't know you, Mr. Mason."

"That is precisely what I want to change."

"To what end?" she asked.

"You are the most suspicious woman I ever encountered."

"That's doesn't answer my question, Mr. Mason."

"No. It doesn't."

"Well?"

"Well, Miss Randolph, to put it plainly and simply, I like you. I think you're a woman of rare talents and virtues whose friendship would be worth earning and I genuinely hope you'll give me a chance to prove I have certain qualities that might enrich your life too."

Jane didn't know what to say. She was flattered by his compliments but wary of his sweeping claims since they had such a tenuous acquaintance.

"Perhaps with time, Mr. Mason," she replied.

"That's all I ask. But in the spirit of friendship, don't you think we can dispense with formality."

"I don't understand."

"I've always been of the opinion friends should be on a first name basis. It's Thomas from now on."

"If you wish."

Thomas reached for her hand. "I do..., Jane."

At his touch, Jane raised her eyes to meet his. An irrational surge of pleasure rose from some unknown corner of her being as he smiled at her and she wondered how it was possible for any one person to be such a paradox.

After Jane had completed her errand at the Crawley's, Thomas insisted she take him down to see the town's namesake. At first, Jane hesitated because a detour to the creek would mean a serious delay in returning to the store. After her family's reaction over her foreknowledge of Thomas at the party, she didn't like the idea of having to explain why she was alone with him again for so long.

There was also a vague concern in the back of her mind that they might run into the brash stranger she'd encountered last night. She still couldn't fathom who he was or what he was doing fishing when everyone else for miles around was at her uncle's party. The memory of how he'd looked into her eyes was still disconcerting and she didn't want to run the risk of repeating the experience.

But between Thomas' ceaseless urging and the horses' genuine need for water, she gave in and led the way to the stream. However, she avoided going to her usual spot to diminish the chances of seeing anyone *unfriendly*. They both dismounted while the horses drank. Jane stayed close by the horses, while Thomas looked around.

Jane ensured their stay was brief by reminding Thomas of her other responsibilities in town. He finally agreed to leave, but only if she promised to ride with him again tomorrow to explore more of the stream. Jane gave her word, though she was baffled by his interest.

Her mind was a riot of contradictory thoughts as she tried to understand Thomas Mason. She wanted to trust him and she had no reason not to. Yet something about him still troubled her. When Copper Creek finally came into view, her inner conflict was suspended long enough to bid Thomas farewell. He had been invited to the mayor's house for lunch. As he left her, she watched him pensively for a moment before continuing on to the post office to pick up the mail for the store.

She was in an agitated mood when she finally arrived home. A fact that Ruth noticed the moment Jane greeted her and set down the packet of lace from Mrs. Crawley on the counter.

"Something troubling you, Jane?"

"No. Why do you ask?"

Ruth shrugged." If you had any more wrinkles in your brow, I wouldn't be able to see your eyes at all."

Jane quickly relaxed her face and turned away from Ruth.

"It's nothing, Aunt Ruth. I was only thinking about something."

"Well, please don't think so hard, Jane." Ruth stepped around the counter and brushed Jane's cheek. "It spoils the sweetness of your face."

Jane nodded.

"Anything you want to tell me about?"

"I'm not sure I can," Jane replied.

"I see," Ruth said softly. "It wouldn't have anything to do with our guest would it?"

Jane nodded. "But it's not what you think."

"Oh?"

"I'm afraid I can't help feeling suspicious about him."

"Why? I think he's a perfectly charming young man."

"Yes...he is," Jane admitted. "Perhaps too charming. But his personality isn't what bothers me."

"Isn't it?" Ruth teased.

"No," Jane insisted. "Why didn't Uncle Michael ever mention him or the council's plans to make drastic changes to the town?"

"Perhaps you should ask Michael that yourself."

"Don't you know?"

"I wouldn't presume to speak for your uncle, Jane. Besides, he's been waiting to see you anyway."

"What about?"

"The party last night. You disappeared on us and then snuck back in without a word."

Jane looked down at her shoes. "Yes. I'm sorry about that, Aunt Ruth. I didn't mean to worry you. I just went out for some air. But I'm sure no one noticed I was missing. Especially since the rain broke up the party."

"That is beside the point. Your uncle and I are very worried about you."

"There's no reason..."

Ruth raised her hand. "You'd better not keep Michael waiting any longer. Now, hurry along and give him your arguments. I have work to do."

The brusque tone in Ruth's final words only added to Jane's qualms. She would have easily abandoned her doubts with one word of reassurance from her aunt. Instead, she'd been met with evasion and mild hostility. As a result, Jane couldn't help feeling resentment. It wasn't like her aunt and uncle to keep her in the dark and she didn't like the implications of such a development.

She headed for her uncle's office without another word, irked further by the notion of being called on the carpet like a naughty child. She was twenty-six years old and her uncle had no right to reprimand her for discreetly suiting her own preference last night rather than his. She had a good mind to tell him just that and demand a full explanation for Thomas Masons' sudden arrival. But when she reached Michael's door, the reality of venting such hostile thoughts shocked her.

A wave of guilt and ingratitude crippled her anger. She couldn't deny how loving and patient Michael and Ruth had been all these years. More than once, Jane had blessed her aunt and uncle for helping her to recover from the shock of her parents' death by providing her with such a good home. Jane realized if it hadn't been for their kindness, she might be living a very different life; one overshadowed by the hardship and stigma that usually accompanied a childhood spent in an orphanage. She had no right to be cross with them or to question any guest they saw fit to bring under their roof. The strain of the last few days and the summer heat had allowed her emotions to get the better of her. So, as she raised her hand to knock on Michael's door, she resolved to meet her uncle with respect and decorum.

At the sound of Jane's tap, Michael called from inside his office.

"Come in."

Jane entered calmly and quietly closed the door behind her.

"Aunt Ruth said you wanted to see me."

"Yes, Jane. Sit down."

"Uncle Michael, before you begin, I think I can guess what you wanted to talk to me about…so let me apologize for any trouble I caused you or Aunt Ruth last night. I know it was most inconsiderate of me to wander off alone without a word. I promise you it won't happen again."

Michael gave her an appraising look.

"Thank you, Jane. I appreciate your candor. However, that doesn't change the fact you've been repeating these kinds of wayward behaviors and it is most disturbing."

"What do you mean, uncle?"

"For months now, Jane, you've been sulking. Going off alone, isolating yourself from the company of others."

"Have I?"

"You know you have. And I want it to stop."

Jane's posture grew rigid and she felt her self-control being eroded by a new wave of frustration. Misinterpreting Jane's silence, sadness touched Michael's face and he placed a hand on his niece's shoulder.

"I don't mean to hurt you," he went on. "But I wouldn't be doing my duty if I didn't say something to you about it."

"Oh? Then by that reasoning, why didn't you say something about your plans to change the town and invite a strange man into the house?"

Michael blinked at her in astonishment. "I don't see what that has to do with what we're talking about."

"No?"

"No, Jane. And I must say I don't like that accusatory tone in your voice."

"Well, I don't like secrets."

"I don't know what you're talking about, Jane. I haven't been keeping any secrets…"

"Then why didn't the family know about Mr. Mason until just before he arrived?"

Michael scoffed as he tried to think of an answer. "I thought it would be a nice surprise," he finally said.

"That's all?"

"Certainly. Jane, you're overreacting."

"That may be. But I'd stop easily enough if someone would give me a straight answer."

"What is it you want to know?"

"Why is Thomas Mason really here?"

"There's no great mystery about it. The town council has been discussing plans to improve the town for some time. I was aware of Thomas' reputation as an architect and I thought he could help. Since his father and I are old friends, I contacted him and asked if Thomas would be interested in the project. I didn't talk about what I'd done at first because I didn't want to get anyone's hopes up until Thomas wrote back about my inquiry with a definite answer."

"And when he did?"

"I told the mayor and the other council members immediately."

"But not your family?"

"The mayor thought it would be best to keep our intentions quiet until Thomas drafted a final plan. He thought it would be nice to have a celebration to unveil the proposal to everyone at once. That way it'd cut down on any rumors or false impressions that could potentially derail the project. So as a member of the council, I respected his leadership authority in the matter."

"And that's all there is to it?"

"Certainly," Michael insisted. "For weeks I've wanted to tell everyone about the changes that have been proposed, but until Thomas reviews all the suggestions and the council votes on a completed proposal, I'm just not at liberty to say more."

"I understand," Jane uttered. "I'm sorry I..."

"Don't punish yourself about it, Jane. Your reaction was perfectly understandable. I know you aren't fond of change."

"No," she agreed.

"But change isn't always a bad thing."

"Isn't it?"

"No," Michael said smiling. "Just you wait and see."

Jane nodded her head. "I'll try."

"Good."

Michael bent to kiss her forehead. "Now, was there any post for me today?"

"Yes." Jane turned away from him to retrieve the letters from the pocket in her skirt. "Four letters and a telegram."

Michael wrinkled his brow. "I wonder who could be sending me a telegram."

Jane handed him the mail. "Mr. Hibbert said it came from Willow Springs. Isn't that where Reverend Porter went?"

"Yes," Michael confirmed. "He must have news for me about the new pastor for the church."

"If a new man has been appointed, wouldn't he wire the mayor about it?" Jane asked.

"He may have. But the council and Reverend Porter agreed I should be in charge of handling all the details to help the new reverend to settle in," Michael explained. But with all this excitement over Thomas' visit, I'd almost forgotten about it."

Michael set the letters down on his desk and ripped open the telegram.

HENRY KOHL SELECTED TO BE NEW PASTOR
COPPER CREEK CHURCH STOP DUE TO
ARRIVE JULY 14 STOP NOTIFY TOWN
COUNCIL OF HIS APPOINTMENT STOP
REVEREND JOSEPH PORTER

Michael's eyes grew wide as he read and re-read the telegram in disbelief.

"It can't be," Michael mumbled. "It couldn't be the same…"

"Uncle Michael?"

He had forgotten Jane was still there and the sound of her voice drew him out of his daze.

"Is anything wrong?" Jane pursued.

"What…oh…nothing, nothing, Jane. You go along now and help Ruth out front."

He waved her away and sank down in his chair to stare at the telegram.

"It just can't be him," Michael said again, when he was alone. He let the small bit of parchment fall from his hands and closed his eyes against the ruination he was convinced had found its way to his door.

Thomas Mason was eager to enjoy the modest tea spread out on the little coffee table in the Randolph's parlor. Jane sat opposite him in her usual chair beside the window. It had been several days since her outburst over his appearance in Copper Creek and, though she still couldn't feel completely at home in Thomas' company, she felt less wary in his presence. She was attentively mending some loose buttons on her favorite blouse, while Rachel poured some Darjeeling into a cup from her place on the settee. She handed it to Mr. Mason who was sitting beside her, watching her delicate movements with appreciation.

"I fear I shall be quite spoiled by the time I return home," Thomas commented, accepting the cup from Rachel's hand.

"That suggests you aren't spoiled now," Rachel teased.

Thomas smiled. "Am I so transparent?"

"Not really," Rachel simpered.

"Even so, the kindnesses of your family this past week already make me dread the thought of leaving Copper Creek."

"Don't say that," Rachel protested. "You've only just arrived. Besides, you never know. Something might change your mind about leaving."

Thomas looked at Jane, who was consciously trying to avoid his gaze, and then he drew his attention back to Rachel. "It might at that."

"I for one will be sorry to see you leave," Rachel pursued. "It's been so exciting having someone so fascinating at our dinner table every night."

Thomas scoffed jovially. "I'm sure my travelogues have been more of a cause for indigestion than interest."

"Not at all. You've been to so many amazing places…I can't help being jealous."

"You aspire to travel then?" Thomas asked.

"Not really. But I would like to see something of the world beyond Copper Creek."

"And you, Jane. Would you like to see far off places?" Thomas asked

"I've never really given it much thought," Jane answered, looking up from her work. "For the most part, I am quite content here."

Rachel sighed. "Is it any wonder I'm starved for good company with such dull surroundings?"

Jane gave her cousin a pained look, but chose not to reprove her in front of their guest. Sensing Jane's distress, Thomas cleared his throat and said, "Come now, Miss Rachel, I think you're being a bit harsh. I've found delights in every corner of your town."

"Give it time, Mr. Mason and the novelty will soon wear off."

"Ah, I think you'll be inclined to change your mind, Miss Rachel, once you hear about the changes the council has in store for Copper Creek."

"Uncle Michael told me that any details regarding the improvements were to be kept confidential," Jane said.

"True," Thomas acceded. "But that doesn't mean I couldn't be persuaded to confess a few secrets to…*a friend.*"

He looked at Jane pointedly.

"Spare me your secrets, Mr. Mason. I wouldn't want to get you in any trouble."

"Thomas," he corrected her. "Remember? And it is no trouble."

Jane inclined her head. "In that case, please, tell us what you can. We're both eager to hear what's in store for us."

"How do you feel about electricity?"

"I scarcely know a thing about it," Jane answered. "Why?"

"Because it may soon become a part of your daily life."

"You don't mean the council intends to use electricity in town?" Rachel interpreted.

"Could be by this time next year the length of Main Street will be ablaze with electric light."

Jane shook her head. "It's incredible. I can't believe..."

"It sounds wonderful!" Rachel exclaimed.

"Isn't electricity a rather dangerous thing?" Jane asked.

"It doesn't have to be with the right planning," Thomas replied. "After all, it's been a year since Mr. Edison perfected his light bulb and it's already gone into use all across the country. Why, just this March, streetlights were installed in Wabash, Indiana."

"Did you see them lit?" Rachel asked.

Thomas nodded. "I was an integral part of the project, from start to finish, which is another reason your father thought I could be of use here in Copper Creek. I tell you, I've never seen a sight like I did that night, when a whole town was brought out of the dark ages. It was magnificent."

"How is such a thing possible?" Jane pursued. "I mean, I understood that electricity has to travel along wires to reach the lights. Didn't that create a lot of mess?"

"The wires are thin and relatively light, so it isn't difficult to lift them out of the way or even hide them among the structure of a building. But it takes planning to do it right."

"And that's why you're here," Jane replied. "To *do it right* for us."

"Of course he is," Rachel protested. "And I have complete confidence in your genius, Mr. Mason."

"That's kind of you to say, Miss Rachel. But I'm hardly a genius."

"You're too modest," Rachel replied. "Isn't he, Jane?"

Jane offered a weak smile and looked away.

"Jane," Rachel pressed. "Don't you think Mr. Masons' news is exciting?"

"Yes."

"You don't act like it."

"I'm sure it will be very nice. Only..." she stopped and focused on her needle and thread once more.

"Only what, Jane?" Thomas asked.

"I just wonder if it's really necessary. From the little I've read about electricity, I think it's still too unstable to place it in the heart of a community."

"Superstition," Thomas assured her.

"I hope so."

Perturbed by Jane's negativity, Rachel abruptly slammed her teacup down on the table. "Why do you always have to spoil everything, Jane!"

"Rachel..."

"It is just possible that my father and the other members of the town council have enough brains to know what's best for our community without you to tell them what's right!"

"I'm sure your cousin meant no offense," Thomas interrupted.

"No. Only to show once again how superior she is to the rest of us."

"Rachel!" Jane admonished.

"It's true. You never miss an opportunity to belittle me and everyone else. But this is one time I won't allow it. I know you aren't as perfect as you'd have everyone believe! I've seen what's been going on between you two... riding out together, meeting in the barn and talking in secret; to say nothing of your mysterious acquaintance the day Mr. Mason first arrived."

"Miss Rachel, I assure you there is nothing going on between Jane and me."

"Really?" Rachel mocked. "Then why is she just Jane and I'm *Miss* Rachel? Why else would you talk to one another in such intimate terms and seek so much time to be alone if you weren't very *familiar*?"

Jane stood up. "Do you have any idea what you are saying?"

"That your reputation isn't as unspoiled as you'd have everyone believe," Rachel replied.

Jane's face grew solemn, as she looked her cousin square in the face. "I have never once overstepped the bounds of propriety, as you well know, Rachel. And I think instead of judging me, you should be more concerned with the sinful motives behind your own childish behavior."

Emotion began welling up in Rachel's eyes. "Don't try and turn this around on me. I'm not a fool. It's plain there's something between you two. So stop lying to me and just admit it!"

"Rachel, that's enough," Jane admonished, as she rose from her chair.

Rachel glared at her cousin, unaffected by Jane's stern countenance, until she noticed the look of consternation on Thomas Mason's face. Suddenly, mortified that her intention to flatter him had been subverted into a juvenile squabble, Rachel grew eerily calm in her anger.

"Forgive me," she replied. "I forgot it's impossible for you to ever be wrong about anything!" Rachel turned sharply and ran out of the parlor.

Jane closed her eyes and crossed her arms in exasperation. Then she turned to Thomas.

"I'm sorry about that."

"I feel I should rather apologize to you."

Jane shook her head. "It isn't really your fault. Rachel and I haven't been able to get along for some time now. We just seem to grate on each other's nerves."

"It won't be that way forever."

"I hope you're right," Jane confessed. "You know. It wasn't always like this between Rachel and me. We used to depend on one another and now..." Jane gestured with helpless frustration. Thomas moved closer to her.

"I suppose it's my own fault," Jane went on. "Rachel is right about me, I guess. I do demand perfection and naively expect to be loved for it."

"I wouldn't consider it naive to desire love under any circumstances. I'd call it human."

Jane offered Thomas a weak smile.

"As my grandmother used to say to me," he went on, "We all have feet of clay, but we are all worthy of love."

Thomas' eyes drifted to Jane's mouth as he finished speaking. Slowly, he began to lean in to capture her lips. Jane braced her hands against his chest and turned her face away.

"Please," she said.

Thomas stepped back. "Are you afraid Rachel might be right about us too?"

For a moment, Jane looked as if she'd been struck. "You know she isn't."

"Of course," he replied. "I… forgot myself for a moment. Perhaps, I'd better go too. I have some drawings to finalize before my meeting with the town council tomorrow."

"Yes."

Thomas began to withdraw, but Jane called after him. "Thomas…I'm sorry."

"Think nothing of it," he replied. "We'll just forget it ever happened."

He offered a forced smile and continued out the door. Flustered, all Jane could do was stand alone and listen to the sound of his footsteps fade away down the corridor.

Chapter Four

Five men sat along one side of a narrow, battered table at the Copper Creek meeting house. Samuel Jenkins, Edward Hibbert, Marcus Graves, and Curtis Webber were all well-respected citizens of the community. They were men with businesses, families, and a greater interest in the prosperity of Copper Creek than most. They represented the town's bank, post office, hotel, and newspaper, respectively. Michael Randolph rounded out their ranks, but unlike his fellow members, he sat solemnly at his place with a haunted look on his face.

The ends of the table were occupied by Mayor James Winston and a very dapper, Thomas Mason. Unaccustomed to small town politics, Thomas sat quietly and observed the other men as they conversed animatedly about local affairs. He also took note of his surroundings. In his mind, he thought calling the space a meeting *hall* was a gross overstatement. It consisted solely of one small room adjacent to the church.

However, since the departure of the town's former minister, Joseph Porter, the entire structure served to house more political debates than Sunday services. As a result, both the church and the meeting space had become rather dilapidated from neglect; a fact which would only help to further Thomas' arguments. He was considering how to best use these circumstances to his advantage when the mayor rapped his gavel on the table.

"Gentlemen, I hereby call this meeting to order. As I'm sure you are well aware, a discussion on town improvements raised at the previous two meetings is our topic for discussion tonight. I know you must be just as eager as I am to hear Mr. Mason's appraisal of our proposal, so I will dispense with any further business and surrender the floor to him. Mr. Mason...."

Attention shifted to Thomas as he rose to his feet.

"May I say at the outset how grateful I am for your trust and confidence in me, gentlemen. I was quite excited to receive a commission to work here in Copper Creek and I will do my utmost to live up to your expectations. Having said that, I must tell you I've thoroughly looked over the proposed plans you submitted to me and I fear they are quite inadequate."

Sounds of consternation rose among the council members. Thomas raised his hand to quell their voices.

"It is my professional opinion," Thomas pursued, "that while the suggested modifications you've listed are quite acceptable, they aren't enough."

"Enough?" Mayor Winston echoed. "What do you mean?"

"Simply that I cannot recommend you proceed with any of the building you've requested so long as the rest of the town remains in its present condition."

"What's wrong with Copper Creek as it is?" Samuel Jenkins demanded. "Apart from a few drunks and rowdy trail hands."

"Nothing is *wrong* with Copper Creek," Thomas clarified. "It's a nice little town and that's the problem. It wouldn't be worth the expense of these improvements when you'd have to tear them all down in the long run."

"Tear them down!" the council members echoed.

"Why would you think we'd ever do such a thing?" Mr. Hibbert asked.

"Your problem, gentlemen, is infrastructure. You've come to me with ideas that suggest the beginnings of a city. But no means of supporting such a metropolis. You need to start thinking on a bigger scale...thinking about the future. Otherwise any investment you make in renovations will just be wasted."

"How do you figure that?" Samuel Jenkins asked.

"Well for one thing, this town needs to have paved streets and byways to simplify travel and cut down on dirt and disease."

"We thought of that," Mayor Winston reminded him. "That's why we included it in our list of suggestions."

"Yes, but you never thought about putting a sewer system beneath the streets or electric lights above them."

The men raised their voices in excited agitation.

"Really, Mr. Mason. You can't be serious," Mr. Winston shouted over the others.

"I am quite serious, Mr. Mayor. I have always believed progress to be a necessity. If we do not change, we die. The same is true of this town. The plans you submitted to me are proof that this body desires progress and prosperity in Copper Creek. I am here to see you get it with the right building plan."

"Surely, progress can be achieved gradually, Mr. Mason. We don't have to change Copper Creek over night," Mr. Webber said.

"I'm not suggesting you do. I'm merely pointing out that some forethought for the future should go into your plans."

"I can appreciate your point, Mr. Mason," Mayor Winston replied. "But I'm afraid the sort of changes you're proposing are a bit too grand for a rural community like ours."

"Indeed," Mr. Hibbert agreed. "We never intended to turn Copper Creek into a city. Most folks like our town the way it is."

"Most folks wouldn't cotton to using an electric light bulb or an indoor privy either," Curtis Webber pointed out. "I don't see the rush to force them into it."

"Forgive me," Thomas interrupted him. "But now *is* the best time to act. You're going to need things like sewers and electricity eventually anyhow. It only makes sense to put them in now. Otherwise you'd just have to tear up the streets again to put them in later."

"Maybe so," Samuel Jenkins noted. "But just how do you expect us to pay for all this additional *progress*? We haven't even managed to raise the full amount to construct the new meeting hall, hospital and school itemized in the original proposal."

"Mr. Jenkins, as a banker, you must be aware how most large ventures undertake financing."

"Loans or the sale of stocks or bonds," Mr. Jenkins replied.

"Exactly. I see no reason why Copper Creek couldn't do the same thing."

"You aren't suggesting the bank loan the town the funds?" Samuel replied. "Who would be responsible for repaying it?"

"Mr. Jenkins, my business is strictly architecture. I wouldn't presume to tell you how to finance this undertaking. But I'm sure a man of your considerable experience in the financial world could devise some way of enlisting your fellow citizens to invest in the future of Copper Creek."

Sam Jenkins fell silent and drew one finger across his mustache. "There might be a way," he said.

"Of course there is," Thomas encouraged. "As I said, I'm no expert. But it's been my experience that the more salient members of a town usually get the ball rolling on big projects like this."

"You mean all of us?" Curtis Webber interpreted.

"Well, you are among the most successful business owners in Copper Creek," Thomas replied.

"And for that we have to go bankrupt!"

"Not at all, Mr. Webber," Thomas said. "I was merely suggesting that if men such as yourselves were to invest in the future of the town, your neighbors might feel more confident in lending their dollars to the cause."

"With a few exceptions, the people around here need every spare cent they have to stay alive. They wouldn't pay for a project of this size. Even if they could be persuaded, it would be criminal to trick them out of their money for a development we can't justify."

"Always the editor," Marcus Graves replied. "Damn it, Curt! Why must you constantly look for trouble? You might sell more papers if you put some good news in them for a change."

"I won't varnish the truth," Curtis replied. "And that's why people around here trust me and my paper. I tell them what they need to know and if this proposed lunacy goes ahead, I'll tell them exactly why their children have to go hungry and who's responsible for it."

"I'm inclined to agree with Curtis," Mr. Hibbert put in. "More and more of my customers are struggling just to find the price of a stamp. I don't think it would be wise to overburden them with any further demands on their purse strings."

"You would, Ed." Marcus Graves said. "I never heard so many bleeding-hearts! You're all so busy worrying about the *poor people* you forget that what this man is suggesting would make everyone's life better. I admit it's a risk. But life is a risk. I built my business by taking chances and I for one think investing in our town is a risk worth taking. Hell, I'm not going to deny a bigger, better, Copper Creek means more guests in my hotel. But then it means more mail for the post office, more accounts in the bank, and more customers in the general store, not to mention more subscriptions for the newspaper."

"There is more to be considered here than personal profit," Curtis Webber insisted.

"Curt is right," Ed continued. "We were put on this council by our neighbors because they believed we would work for their best interests not ours."

"And are you suggesting that paved, well-lit streets wouldn't be safer for everyone? That clean water running into every home and business wouldn't make life easier and healthier? Or maybe wasting taxes on a school house and a hospital that will have to be torn down in a few years and rebuilt is in our neighbors' best interest," Marcus replied.

"No one is suggesting that," Mayor Winston interjected. "But we can't ask anyone to give what they don't have."

"Exactly!" Curtis Webber agreed. "Why build a city when there won't be anyone left who can afford to live in it."

"Gentleman, I fear you are over analyzing this problem," Thomas interrupted. "If your neighbors aren't able or willing to pitch in, there is also a distinct possibility you could interest outside investors in your town. Isn't that right Mr. Randolph?"

"Huh?"

"I say, isn't it possible that someone *outside* of Copper Creek might be interested in lending money to begin these improvement," Thomas repeated.

Michael looked around the table helplessly. "Well, I...that is I suppose so."

"Someone like my father, for instance," Thomas prompted.

"Yes," Michael replied. "Yes, George has always been very...keen on real estate and things like that."

"That would be most helpful," the mayor admitted. "But I confess, I don't understand why he would want to do something like that. Do you, Michael?"

Michael gave the mayor a puzzled look and stood mute before his peers.

Realizing Michael was about to fumble their opportunity, Thomas jumped in and explained, "As a business man, my father is always interested in the untapped potential of a burgeoning community. He's often told me that the future of our country is in the success of its rural towns. I feel sure with the right persuasion, he would agree that Copper Creek is exactly the kind of place that could benefit from his help and produce a handsome return on his investment for everyone involved."

"Sounds fishy to me," Curtis Webber mumbled.

"Shut-up, Curt," Marcus Graves warned. "I think its damn fine of this boy's pa to put up money for a town he doesn't even live in."

"I don't like the sound of the whole thing," Curtis persisted.

"No one asked you," Marcus replied.

"Gentlemen, please," the mayor intervened. "I can't say as I understand this completely myself, but I don't think we can turn down such a generous proposal off-hand. Mr. Mason, tell me realistically, do you think your father would invest in Copper Creek?"

"He's had a hand in helping several small towns to expand and I see no reason why Copper Creek would be any different."

"That' s fine. But we couldn't expect him to invest the full amount?"

"Well, no," Thomas agreed.

"Then the rest of us will have to put in our two cents," Marcus supplied. "How 'bout it?"

"Naturally the bank will lend all it can," Sam Jenkins replied.

"If it's what the council thinks best…," Mr. Hibbert added.

"You can count the paper out," Curtis snapped.

"We figured that, Curt," Marcus said. "How about you, Michael?"

Michael sat staring at the wall, deaf to the sound of his own name.

"Mr. Randolph!" Thomas prodded.

"Oh! Yes?"

"How do you vote about contributing to this new building fund?" the mayor asked.

"I'd be happy to put in my share," Michael said.

"Fine," Mayor Winston replied. "Then the only remaining question seems to be exactly how much money would be required."

"As to that," Thomas answered, "I've drawn up a complete list of expenditures for you all to review, along with a detailed description of all the suggestions I have for modernizing the town." He paused to pull out a folder from his portfolio and handed the pages out to all the council members.

Mayor Winston began to peruse Thomas' list and gently nodded his head.

"It seems you have been quite through, Mr. Mason," he said.

"I realize that the figures may seem a bit staggering at first," Thomas replied returning to his chair. "But you must remember what you'll be getting in exchange."

"Swindled," Curtis Webber drawled.

"Security in the future," Thomas replied.

"Well, it appears to me you've given us all a lot to think about, Mr. Mason," James Winston interjected. "Perhaps, it would be best if we were to adjourn for now to review all this new information before making a final decision. Agreed?"

The other council members nodded.

"Fine," the mayor went on. "Then in that case…"

"There is one more thing," Thomas interrupted him.

"What's that, Mr. Mason?"

"In order to make my final drawings for construction, I will require the council to give me carte blanche authority to conduct surveys in and around town."

"What sort of surveys?" Curtis Webber asked.

Thomas offered a subtle smile. "The usual kind, Mr. Webber. Measuring distances and terrain. Mapping out where important resources can be tapped and spots where building would be unsafe."

"I don't see why that couldn't wait until this council has made a final decision," Curtis replied.

"Of course, I'll do as you wish," Thomas replied. "But it would save a great deal of time if I could get my preliminary work out of the way. Then we'd be free to get started sooner. With the unpredictable fall and winter months ahead, time is precious."

"I see no reason why you cannot go ahead," the mayor replied. "Gentlemen. Any further objections?"

"Is it safe?" Mr. Hibbert asked.

"Perfectly," Thomas replied.

"Just a damn nuisance," Curtis added.

"I assure you I'll do my best not to inconvenience anyone."

"Then by all means begin, Mr. Mason," James Winston finished. Now, before we conclude, is there any further business?"

The mayor looked down the length of the table to Michael Randolph who slowly stood.

"Michael?"

"I received a telegram from Pastor Porter informing me a new minster has been appointed to our church. His name is... Henry Kohl and he is due to arrive on the fourteenth."

"Splendid," the mayor replied. "Mind you, Joseph Porter was a fine man of the cloth, not to mention a good friend. But it will be a relief to finally have the question of his replacement settled."

"Let's just hope this Mr. Kohl will be as capable," Sam Jenkins noted.

The mayor shifted his attention back to Michael. "I expect you plan to meet him at the stage?"

"I...no. That is I would prefer..."

"Michael are you all right?"

"I'm sorry, Jim. I haven't been myself lately. I expect I....excuse me."

Without another word, Michael hurried out the door.

"I wonder what's bothering him," Edward Hibbert said.

"He didn't say very much at all tonight," Graves noted. "That's not like him."

"How could he get the chance to talk with you grandstanding all evening?" Mr. Webber replied.

"I doubt Marcus was the deterrent," Sam Jenkins interrupted before his colleagues could come to blows. "Even before the meeting, Michael looked disturbed."

"Mr. Mason," the mayor began. "Since you've been staying with the Randolphs, have you been aware of anything that might be distressing Michael?"

"No."

"He hasn't said anything to you?" the mayor pursued.

"No. In fact, I haven't seen much of Mr. Randolph at all."

James shrugged. "Well, let us hope that whatever is troubling him will sort itself out. If all our business is complete, then we are adjourned." He banged his gavel on the table once more and the members of the council began to disperse.

A general chatter filled the room again as Thomas gathered his papers. As he reached for the last sheet, Curtis Webber took hold of it first.

"More proof of Copper Creek's yearning for progress, Mr. Mason," he said, handing Thomas the page.

"It's merely a sketch, Mr. Webber. Of little value until it actually becomes brick and mortar."

"I wonder how much value this sketch and the rest of your plans really holds for a man whose business is *strictly architecture*."

"I don't understand."

"Then let me put it bluntly. How much do you expect to pocket from this inflated proposal you made tonight?"

"Apart from my usual consulting fee, Mr. Webber, I assure you I don't expect a penny."

"You'll forgive me if I find that hard to believe."

Thomas glared at Curtis Webber.

"I can understand your skepticism, Mr. Webber. Having lived as you do, you've doubtless forgotten what it means when a gentleman gives his word."

Webber leaned in and scoffed. "In my experience, a gentleman's word is worth less than the air he breathes to utter it. The fact you group yourself among that class only confirms my instincts. I know there is more going on here than you'd like any of us to discover and I warn you, I intend to find out what it is."

Thomas' temper threatened to strangle him as he watched Curtis Webber walk out of the meeting room. All of the other members had gone except the mayor, who startled Thomas by coming up behind him.

"I trust everything is all right, Mr. Mason?"

"Fine," Thomas lied.

"Good. I'll look forward then to meeting with you again next week."

"The feeling is mutual," Thomas affirmed.

"And Mr. Mason, I would strongly urge you not to get too zealous with your designs. After all, Copper Creek is still a small town and we like it that way."

"Yes, of course."

The mayor slapped him on the back and then followed the path of the other council members out. Once he was alone, Thomas crumpled the paper in his hand. Copper Creek was headed for a shakeup whether or not its citizens approved. Of that Thomas was determined.

Still vexed, he began rummaging in his portfolio and extracted a blank sheet of paper. He reflected for a moment and then began writing to his father…

> *I've found everything just as you expected. Tomorrow I intend to begin phase two of our plan. However, Mr. Randolph did little to help me secure permission to begin my search. It seems news of a new minister's arrival distracted him from our purposes and may lead to trouble. Suggest that it would be wise to learn all you can about a Reverend Henry Kohl and as soon as possible….*

Rachel sat alone in her bedroom. Framed in her window seat by the late afternoon sun, she looked far more serene than she felt. Her tears had long since dried from yesterday's squabble with Jane, but her sweet face was still marred by the sorrow she felt deep inside. She watched the town bustling below her window and thought how much she hated being dismissed as the pretty, foolish child. Why must she always be overlooked for Jane?

The longer Rachel dwelled on Jane the more her envy roiled. Jane was always so smart, so sure, so good. She was always the one people sought in times of trouble. Her father frequently discussed store business with Jane and her mother constantly deferred to her judgment in matters concerning the household. Everyone in town knew it was Jane that kept the general store running efficiently. It was Jane that made the Randolph's parties such a success. It was Jane who orchestrated every detail of the Randolph's lives and Rachel had had enough. In her quiet, unassuming way, Jane had taken charge of everything, even the clothes Rachel wore.

At that realization, Rachel knew she had to escape. She couldn't allow Jane to stifle her any longer. Rachel had intelligence and talent of her own; gifts that would be appreciated, if only she could have the chance to use them. Determined to prove her worth, Rachel decided the best thing to do would be to leave town. But her grand scheme for escape was interrupted when she heard a knock at her door.

Ruth peeked in when Rachel didn't reply.

"Dearest, are you well?"

"I'm not sick, if that's what you mean," Rachel replied. "At least not physically."

Ruth came in and walked over to the window where Rachel was still sitting. She put a hand on her daughter's forehead. Relieved to feel no sign of a fever, she caressed Rachel's face.

"What's troubling you, Rachel?"

"I'm fed up with Copper Creek and everyone in it!"

"Everyone?"

"Well… of Jane."

Ruth smiled. "She told me you had quarreled. I must say I was disappointed to hear it was over Mr. Mason."

"Is that what Jane said?"

Ruth nodded.

"And of course you believed everything she told you."

"I have no reason to think Jane would lie to me."

"Maybe you should."

"Rachel. I'm surprised at you. What has Jane ever done to make you talk about her so maliciously?"

Rachel stood up and walked away in a huff. She stopped at the end of her bed and took hold of the bedpost.

"Rachel, I asked you a question," Ruth pursued.

"Why do you always go to Jane first?"

"I don't understand."

"Why did you talk to Jane about our argument first?" Rachel turned to look at her mother. "Why do you always ask her opinion about things before mine? Why does Jane help father run the store? Why is Jane always preferred over me?"

Ruth offered a wry smile then crossed the floor to embrace Rachel.

"Sweetheart, is that what's been upsetting you? You think your father and I prefer Jane over you?"

Rachel did her best to nod while her head rested against her mother's chest.

"You put that thought right out of your head because it just isn't so. I'll admit we do tend to entrust matters to Jane more often. But that's only because she's older than you. I imagine we also wanted to help instill some sense of purpose in her life."

Rachel looked up with surprise. "What do you mean?"

Ruth thought a moment, as she wiped a tear from Rachel's face. Then she said, "I know you were too small to remember, but when Jane's parents died she was broken-hearted. She seemed to retreat inside herself and, for months, she didn't speak. She wouldn't play and she barely ate. Things looked desperate. So, you're father decided to draw her out of herself by involving her in the store. At first, it was just little things like stocking the shelves or sweeping up. But it worked. Eventually, her work here gave her purpose and peace. I suppose over time we've just gotten used to delegating our responsibilities to Jane because she was so willing to undertake them."

Ruth paused and looked earnestly into her daughter's face.

"Jane's also been away to school," Ruth added. "Many of the things she learned have been of great help to all of us."

"Yes. I suppose so."

"I see now your father and I have been far too lazy and much too ignorant in letting things continue as they have. I'm sorry if our failings made you feel unwanted for even a moment."

She held Rachel close and stroked her hair gently, adding, "You are precious to us, Rachel. Your father and I wanted you so dearly, even before you were born. And since you've been with us, we've only loved you more each day."

"I know, mother. I love you both, too. But I've decided I can't go on living in Jane's shadow."

Ruth held Rachel at arm's length. Concern seemed to have transformed her expression.

"What do you mean, Rachel?"

"I want to leave Copper Creek."

"Leave? What a ridiculous notion. Where would you go?"

"Mother, couldn't I go away to school like Jane?"

Ruth was taken aback.

"I know it's sudden. But if Jane could go away to school, then why can't I? Maybe I'd learn something that could be of use."

Ruth could see the eagerness in her daughter's eyes and even though the thought of sending her daughter away to school terrified her, her better judgment told her it wasn't an unreasonable request.

"I can't say I find the idea agreeable," Ruth began. "But I'll discuss it with your father."

"Right now?" Rachel urged.

"Tonight," Ruth replied. "After he's had his brandy."

That evening Michael Randolph imbibed far more brandy than usual. Ruth expected his excess would make her task easier. However, instead of his usually tranquil demeanor following a drink, this binge had not softened his appearance. Rather, the distracted aura, which had consumed Michael Randolph for the past week, remained entrenched upon his visage. He didn't dare reveal the reason for his angst, nor would his mind let him forget it. He firmly believed his only hope for salvation now was to leave town. But he had not been able to devise an excuse to go, which would not arouse suspicion.

Amid his turmoil, he had barely heard a word Ruth said to him over dinner. He had just about given up all hope, when he realized she was talking about Rachel's desire to go away to school. A sense of relief coursed through his body at the notion. What better excuse could there be than chaperoning his daughter on a tour of schools?

"I didn't know Rachel was interested in attending school," Michael ventured.

"It seems she feels left behind. She knows Jane went and she thinks it's time she had her chance. Personally, I think Rachel is just having some growing pains. It isn't easy becoming a woman and I'm afraid her little worries have just been magnified since Mr. Mason arrived."

"What difference does that make?"

"Dear, I know you aren't a young girl, but certainly you've noticed he is a very attractive young man. It's only natural Rachel would want his attention."

"All the more reason she should go then."

"Michael, I hardly think it sensible to send our daughter off alone just because she has a little crush on our houseguest. She is still too young and inexperienced to leave home."

"Nonsense."

"It's not nonsense. I'm genuinely worried about her and I want her here where I can keep an eye on her."

"No," Michael replied more adamantly than he intended. He began to feel his means of escape slipping through his fingers and a renewed wave of panic urged him to argue his case.

"I mean… why not give Rachel a chance?" he continued. "I think you underestimate our girl. She's shown some real initiative and maturity with this request and I think we should encourage her."

"You really think this is a good idea?"

"I think it's an excellent idea! Rachel needs a challenge. A chance to stretch her wings and this could be just the thing."

"I don't know..."

"I promise you she'll be fine. I'll even go with her myself." He paused to allow the implied sacrifice of his offer to sink in. Ruth's face softened at the gesture.

"Would you?"

"Of course," Michael said gallantly. "Nothing is more important than our daughter."

"It would make me feel better about it."

"Then that's just what we'll do. Rachel and I can visit a few schools before she decides on one and then I'll stay on to help her complete the enrollment process. We can leave early tomorrow afternoon."

"So soon?"

"Why should we wait? You said yourself how keen Rachel was to go."

"I know. But I thought there'd be more time. You haven't even contacted any schools or made reservations. How will you..."

"There's no time like the present and I can send some wires before the stage leaves tomorrow."

"Yes, but where are you going?"

Michael thought a moment. "I see no reason why we couldn't start in New Orleans. I understand there are some very fine schools there. And I'm sure George Mason wouldn't mind returning the favor of hospitality."

"I suppose. But what about the store? If you're going to be gone, who will run things?"

"You and Jane of course."

"Michael, I don't think…"

"C'mon, Ruthie. There's nothing to it and I'll be back before you know it."

"Michael." A look of dread had soured Ruth's face.

He clasped her shoulders and gave her a stern look. "Now, no more arguments. This is for the best and we all have to do our part."

He kissed Ruth on the forehead.

"I'll go tell Rachel the good news," he said. "We both have a lot to do if we're going to be ready to leave in time."

As Ruth watched him go, she thought how very extraordinary it was that one conversation could so dramatically cause Michael and her to exchange moods. He seemed over the moon at the prospect of sending their only child away, when moments before he had been depressed. She wondered what delight he could see in this course of action she did not. Her heart sank at the sound of Rachel's excited exclamations echoing from above stairs. Whatever her doubts, she realized it was too late now to do anything about them. Michael and Rachel were determined, and Ruth would do her best to support their decision. But deep down, she could not deny the feeling that everything she knew was about to change forever and not for the better.

Chapter Five

Hank Wilson busily oversaw the loading of luggage and passengers on the stage. Two other men and one lady were waiting to travel with Michael and Rachel Randolph all the way to St. Louis. Rachel and Ruth had been inseparable all morning, while Michael had closeted himself with Jane after breakfast to give her instructions regarding the store. Now they all stood outside the stage office awaiting the call to board.

"Mr. Randolph. Miss Rachel."

The family turned to see Thomas Mason approaching with a small parcel.

"I'm glad I didn't miss you," Thomas said, as he reached them. "I want to wish you both a pleasant journey."

"That is most kind of you," Michael replied.

"I also hoped you'd be able to take this to my father," Thomas added, handing Michael the parcel. "And give him my regards."

"Certainly," Michael said, accepting the package.

"Miss Rachel, I hope you enjoy your journey and I wish you luck in your studies."

"Thank you, Mr. Mason. I'm looking forward to meeting your father."

"Well, don't tell him that," Thomas replied smiling. "The compliments of a pretty woman always go to his head."

"Then your father should be safe from me."

"Now you're the one being modest, Miss Rachel." Thomas took her hand and kissed it.

"I hope you'll permit me to write to you while you're away," Thomas added.

"Yes, I'd like that."

"I'll keep you well apprised of home and I hope you'll feel free to do the same for me?"

"With pleasure."

"I'll look forward to your first letter, then." Thomas squeezed her hand and smiled in such an appealing way Rachel couldn't help feeling regret she was about to leave. That look in his deep blue eyes made her keenly aware she was a woman and extremely grateful for the fact. But his spell over her was abruptly shattered by Hank Wilson's piercing yell.

"Everyone aboard!"

"Goodbye, Rachel."

"Goodbye...Thomas." She squeezed his hand, before turning to receive the farewell embrace of her mother. Her last words, though, were with Jane.

"I'll miss you, Rachel," Jane said. "But I know you'll have a wonderful time."

"Thank you, Jane."

Jane pulled Rachel into a hug.

"Goodbye...Take care of yourself."

"I will." Rachel whispered, "Goodbye."

The cousins stood arms length apart.

"C'mon now, let's go," Michael urged, pulling Rachel away.

Jane kissed him on the cheek. "I'm relying on you," he said to Jane.

"I know. Everything will be fine," she assured him.

He nodded and turned to get aboard.

Jane moved close to Ruth and wrapped her arm about her aunt's waist. They waved as they waited for Hank to mount the box.

"Jane," Rachel called from the window of the stage. "I'll miss you too."

Jane had just enough time to see the tears glistening in her cousin's eyes before Hank roused the team and the stage rolled away.

Ruth and Jane continued to wave until the stage was out of sight.

"I hope this isn't going to be a mistake," Ruth uttered.

"It won't be," Jane replied. "You'll see."

Ruth offered a weak smile. "In the meantime, we'd better get back and see to the store."

Jane nodded and Ruth started back.

"Are you coming?" Ruth asked.

"I'll be right along."

Jane watched the clouds of dust settle.

"They'll be back."

Jane turned, surprised to see Thomas Mason still standing beside her.

"Yes," she replied. "But I can't help feeling it was my fault they had to go at all."

"I can't see fault in this on anyone's part. Rachel's young and she wants to be young. You can't blame yourself because she felt the urge to see new things."

"I wouldn't if I thought that was the only reason she left."

"It is the only reason."

Jane shook her head. "You above all people know how we've been fighting with each other. No. I'm the one who should have left, not Rachel. I knew she'd been upset for awhile and I just never did anything about it."

"And where would you go?"

"I don't know. Somewhere. This is Rachel's home after all. Her parents. I'm just…"

"The orphan?"

"Well…yes."

"Do you know how ridiculous that sounds?"

"It's true."

"It's self-pity and there's nothing more useless."

"It is not!"

"Then what would you call it?" Thomas demanded

Jane thought a moment and, as she did, the indignation in her face softened. "Self-pity" she admitted. "Oh. You're right. What is the matter with me?"

"Apart from being stubborn and too smart for your own good?"

"It was a rhetorical question," Jane replied. "But I'm glad to know you're real opinion of me at last."

Thomas shook his head. "That's only a partial assessment."

"Well…what's the rest of it?"

"That in spite of your faults, you are exactly the sort of woman a man dreams of finding and fears that he will."

Jane turned away from him. "I wish you wouldn't flirt with me, Thomas. I'm no good at it and it only makes me feel you are mocking my inexperience."

"I'm not," Thomas insisted, as he forced her to turn and face him. "I am quite serious, Jane. By now you must realize how much I care about you. I've tried to tell you often enough."

"And every other woman you've met too, no doubt."

Thomas smirked.

"What are you so pleased about?" Jane asked.

"I didn't think it was possible. But you're jealous."

Jane's face flushed with temper. "I am not jealous. I just don't care to be made a fool of."

"Well, if you are a fool, it's your doing, not mine. Can't you see how special you are?"

Jane shrugged. "I'm sorry," she finally said. "I didn't mean to lash out at you. I'm just upset about Rachel." Jane looked down at her shoes.

"Don't get embarrassed now."

Her eyes flashed at him. "I'm not embarrassed," she lied.

"Good. Then you won't object to riding with me this morning. I've got some surveying to do and I could use a guide."

"I can't. Aunt Ruth needs me at the store."

"Tonight, then. After supper?"

Jane felt sure she should refuse. But something in Thomas' expression melted her resistance.

"After supper," she agreed.

He smiled and Jane couldn't help but do the same.

Jane was working at the counter late on Friday afternoon when James Winston came into the store. He seemed rather harried but was comforted to have found Jane.

"Jane!" he called rushing over to her. "What a relief."

"Is something wrong, Mr. Winston?"

"I'm under a great time constraint and I was hoping you and your aunt would help me."

"Certainly. I'm sure Aunt Ruth and I would be more than happy to help any way we can."

"I knew you'd feel that way."

"Well, what is it you need?"

"I don't know if your uncle mentioned it, but a new pastor has been appointed to Copper Creek."

"Reverend Porter did find a replacement then?"

"Yes, Jane, and he's due to come in on the stage tomorrow."

"That's wonderful. Isn't it?"

"It is, except with your uncle's abrupt departure, I'm afraid there is no one available to meet him when he arrives and, worse yet, there's nowhere for him to live."

"How could that be?"

"The church has fallen into disrepair since Reverend Porter left. The space for services can be put to rights easily enough, but the living quarters aren't fit for a hog."

"Then you need supplies?"

"A few, yes. Some men have already volunteered to do the work and I've set them to it. But more importantly, I need someone to meet Mr. Kohl when he arrives and share a little hospitality until the men are finished."

The mayor paused and looked expectantly at Jane.

She gaped at him momentarily, unsure what to say until he added,

"I wouldn't ask except your uncle had agreed to be responsible for the new minister once he arrived. For that reason, I can only presume Mr. Kohl will expect to meet a Randolph when he arrives. And with your uncle away…"

"Aunt Ruth and I are the only Randolphs left."

The mayor nodded. "Can I rely on you, Jane?"

"There would be no problem meeting the new minister at the stage, but as for accommodating him until the repairs are complete…"

"Yes, I know you already have a guest under your roof."

Jane nodded. "I'm not sure Aunt Ruth would want to house two men while my uncle is away, not to mention any family he might…"

"No. I've been informed the new minister is a bachelor."

"Even so. I can't speak for Aunt Ruth about the room."

"Is she here?"

"No. I'm afraid she stepped out to handle some business at the post office and then she was going out to pay a call on Mrs. Phillips. I don't know when she'll be back."

Mr. Wilson looked crestfallen. "I see."

Perplexed by his obvious anxiety over the matter, Jane decided to make the best offer she could.

"Look. Aunt Ruth and I will meet the stage and then invite the new minister home for dinner. I'm sure Aunt Ruth won't object to that. Then you should have at least a few more hours to make things livable at the church. And if by some chance the men don't make enough progress by then, perhaps Mr. Graves would allow the minster a free room at his hotel for a few nights?"

"Yes….Yes, I think that might work. Thank you, Jane."

He hurried around the counter and seized Jane's hand.

"Now, the stage is due to arrive at noon."

"And the minister's name again?"

"It's Kohl. Reverend Henry Kohl."

"Reverend Kohl. Noon," Jane repeated.

"Don't forget that now."

"No," Jane replied. "I won't."

A gentle breeze did little to relieve the heat of the afternoon as Ruth and Jane stood on the porch outside the Overland Stage Line office.

"I don't understand why Michael had to run off just when we are expecting a new pastor," Ruth said. Since her husband left, she had been more than a little exasperated and it showed.

"I imagine the surprise and excitement of Rachel's desire to leave home just threw it out of his mind."

"Piffle."

"Anyway, it's only going to be for a few hours," Jane added. "We'll meet Mr. Kohl and give him dinner and that will be it."

"Thank heaven for small favors."

"Don't you want to meet the new minister?"

"I suppose. But no doubt he's a pious, old codger just like most of the men in his profession."

"I'm sure Reverend Kohl will be a fine speaker or else Mr. Porter wouldn't have picked him to be his successor."

"Joseph Porter was a pompous, inflexible, poseur who was far too impressed with his own self-importance to do much good for anyone. I'm sure his arrogance wouldn't permit him to select anyone to take his place who did not match those characteristics."

"Aren't you being a little harsh?"

"Perhaps. But the fact we've been kept waiting for almost half an hour for Mr. Kohl has done nothing to endear him to me."

"Why don't you sit down? The stage is sure to be here soon."

"Not soon enough. But I do think I'll sit down...in my own parlor with a refreshing cup of tea."

Ruth opened the parasol she had brought with her and stepped off the porch. "I suggest you come too Jane or you'll have sunstroke."

"No. I promised Mr. Wilson a Randolph would be here to meet Mr. Kohl."

Ruth shrugged. "Very well. But if you aren't back in an hour I'll send Max to drag you home. Mr. Kohl or no Mr. Kohl."

Jane smiled. "Deal."

Ruth returned the smile and then made her way home.

Jane watched her aunt go and then settled back into the tedious chore of waiting. Another fifteen minutes went by with no sign of a stage and Jane decided to poke her head inside the office and ask George Lambert, the stationmaster, about the delay. Unfortunately, neither George nor anyone else was around. It was getting ridiculously late and promise or no, she was beginning to think she should go home too.

She decided to give it five more minutes and, as she turned to walk down the length of the porch again, she collided with a man who seemed to appear from nowhere. He put his arms around her to keep her from falling. As she righted herself, she got a good look at his face and was disgruntled to recognize two beguiling green eyes. It was the stranger from the woods.

"You?" Jane gasped.

" 'fraid so," he replied, grinning.

"What are you doing here?" Jane demanded, pushing his arms away from her waist.

"Isn't this where one usually waits for the stage?" he replied.

"I'm beginning to doubt it," Jane said.

"Huh?"

"Oh, nothing. I've been waiting here for ages and there's no sign of a coach."

"That's because it isn't due until one."

"I'm sorry, but I know for a fact it was due at noon."

"On weekdays. But this is Saturday. Saturdays it's due at one."

Jane didn't know how to respond. She only hoped her expression didn't reflect how stupid she felt. To her relief, the sound of a stage approaching filled the silence as it rounded the corner and pulled into view.

The stranger grinned again and tapped the brim of his hat before moving off. He stopped to wait just beside the stagecoach, as it came to a stop. After a few moments, the stage door opened and he smiled and swept one of the female passengers up in his arms. She looked older than he did. She was neatly dressed in a pale blue dress and her honey-blonde hair was swept up in a French roll. Her eyes mimicked the sparkle in the gaze of Jane's stranger and something about her smile was similar too. She heard him cry out as he embraced her.

"It's about time. I thought you'd never get here."

They hugged once again before stepping aside to wait for her bags to be unloaded from the roof of the coach.

Jane stepped forward, expecting to see an elderly man in black emerge from the coach, but no such person ever appeared. Confused, Jane looked around the other side of the stagecoach and still saw no one that would match the description of a minister.

"Pardon me," she said to Hank Wilson. "Did you have a Henry Kohl among the passengers?"

Hank scratched his head.

"No. But there was a Miss Kohl."

Jane's eyes widened in disbelief. "Miss Kohl?" She repeated.

"Yeah, right over there." Hank nodded in the direction of the stranger's lady. Dread engulfed Jane. Somehow she made her feet carry her over to the happy couple and tapped Miss Kohl on the shoulder.

"I don't mean to intrude," Jane began. "But the driver told me you might be able to help me."

"Oh," the lady said.

"You see, I was supposed to meet the new minister, Reverend Henry Kohl."

"And so you have," the stranger said.

Panic blanched Jane's features. "You're Henry Kohl?"

The stranger nodded.

"The new minister?"

"Do you find that so hard to believe?" he replied.

"I just wasn't expecting...."

"Of course you weren't," the lady interjected. "Henry, why must you always be so mischievous?" She turned to Jane and put a reassuring hand on her arm. "You mustn't take him seriously, my dear. For a minister, he is the most immature man you'll ever meet."

"A fine impression you're giving of me," Henry replied.

"I'm only confirming what this young lady must already think."

"Let's put it to the test then. Do you think me immature, Miss?"

Jane opened her mouth to speak.

"Don't embarrass her, Henry. Mind your manners and introduce me."

"Very well. Miss Randolph, I'd like you to meet my sister, Miss Olivia Kohl. Livy, this is Miss Jane Randolph."

Olivia Kohl gaped at her brother for an instant as a silent understanding passed between them. "Randolph did you say?"

"That's right," Jane answered.

Olivia managed to summon a smile and offered her hand.

"I am delighted to meet you, Miss Randolph," Olivia replied. "I do hope that now Henry and I will be living in Copper Creek we will be friends."

"Of course," Jane said. "But I must admit I am confused. I thought Mr. Kohl was coming in on the stage today."

"Change of plans," Henry said. "I arrived several weeks ago, as you must have realized."

"Yes, I do now."

"I thought it best to arrive early to make sure Olivia and I had a proper place to live before she made the long trip from home."

"So chivalrous," Olivia teased.

"Where is home?" Jane asked.

"Texas originally," Olivia replied. "Our family had a ranch there until...our father died."

A shadow fell over the siblings' faces once more. Henry squeezed Olivia's arm in what Jane thought was a warning.

"It was a long time ago," Henry finished.

"Yes," Olivia agreed. "Since then, we've been living in Ohio with our uncle and his family."

"Sounds familiar," Jane uttered. "I live with my aunt and uncle too."

"Well, if you'll excuse us," Henry interrupted her. "I'd like to get Olivia settled."

"I'm afraid you won't be able to go to the church yet," Jane said. "Mr. Winston tells me the men haven't completed repairs."

"They can take all the time they like," Henry replied. "As I mentioned, I've been fixing up a cabin a few miles away. It still needs a little paint and some more furniture, but otherwise it's ready and waiting…"

"I see. But, perhaps you should inform Mayor Winston of your plans. He's been so worried trying to fix up the living quarters at the church for you."

"I'm afraid I haven't met him or much of anyone from town yet. Would you be so good as to tell him for me?"

"If you wish."

"Thank you." Henry turned then to address his sister, "Olivia, are you ready?"

"Yes, if you are," she replied, taking her brother's arm. "I hope we'll meet again soon, Miss Randolph."

"I'm sure we will, Miss Kohl."

"You must call me Olivia."

Jane nodded.

"And may I call you Jane?"

"Please."

Olivia smiled. "I will look forward to our next meeting, *Jane*."

Jane offered a half-hearted smile. She was so befuddled she hardly knew what to think. But as she watched the Kohls walk away, she overheard Olivia say to her brother, "She seems such a nice girl."

"Looks can be deceiving," he replied. "Don't forget. She's a Randolph."

"Mrs. Randolph?"

Ruth looked up from the page of figures she was adding to see Mayor Winston standing in the entryway of the store. He had removed his hat and held it at his side. A friendly, hopeful expression animated his features.

"I'm surprised to see you tending to business," he went on.

"Why is that, Mr. Winston?" Ruth asked, setting down her pencil.

"I expected you would be entertaining your guest."

Ruth looked puzzled. "I believe Mr. Mason has been in Copper Creek long enough now that he can entertain himself for the afternoon."

"No." The mayor shook his head. "I did not mean to ask after Mr. Mason. I thought that Mr. Kohl, the new pastor, would be here. Jane promised me that the two of you would meet his stage this afternoon."

"Oh. Yes, I see. Well, I don't know how to tell you this...."

"You don't mean to say he didn't arrive?"

"I mean to say I have no idea where Mr. Kohl is at all. Jane and I waited at the stage office for quite some time and the stage never arrived. Finally, I had to leave to attend to the store. Jane remained behind, but she hasn't returned yet and, frankly, I'm beginning to worry. I can't imagine what's keeping her."

Mr. Winston's expression turned grave. "I hope the stage didn't run into any trouble."

Ruth shrugged. "I'm sorry I can't give you better news."

"There's no need to apologize. I'm just grateful you and Jane were there at all."

"I was just thinking I would go out and have a look around for her," Ruth replied. "Would you care to accompany me?"

Drawn out of his musings, the mayor nodded. "Thank you. I don't think we should waste another moment."

"Just let me fetch my hat."

Ruth hurried to remove her apron and then bustled into the store office to collect her hat. She had barely returned from the office when Jane came through the front door. She appeared somewhat preoccupied. So much so, she failed to notice her aunt and Mayor Winston watching her.

"Jane," Ruth called after her. "Where have you been?"

Startled by her aunt's voice, Jane stopped where she was and turned to look at Ruth.

"I was at the stage office."

"All this time?"

Jane nodded.

"Well, what kept you?" her aunt pressed.

"Did the new pastor arrive?" the mayor added.

A look of chagrin came over Jane's face. "Not exactly."

"Good heavens, Jane. Will you stop being so mysterious and explain yourself."

Jane crossed her arms and turned to face her aunt.

"It seems Mr. Kohl has been in Copper Creek for some time. It was his sister, Olivia, who arrived on the stage today. Which, for your information, arrives an hour later on Saturdays."

"What do you mean, several weeks?" Mayor Winston asked. "And what's all this about a sister? I wasn't aware provision would have to be made for a lady in...."

"Apparently you weren't supposed to know or make provisions of any kind," Jane replied. "From what I gather, our new minister is a man who prides himself on being self-reliant. He told me he already has a cabin for them to live in. He arrived on his own several weeks ago to begin the necessary repairs and preparations to the place in anticipation of his sister's arrival today."

"Then he doesn't intend to live in the pastoral residence?"

"Apparently not."

"Where is he now?"

"The last I saw of him, he was taking his sister home."

"Did he say where this *home* was?"

Jane shook her head.

"Gracious," Ruth commented. "What sort of man has Joseph Porter inflicted on us? I can't imagine any respectable man of God acting so secretive and high-handed."

"Perhaps he wasn't aware of the arrangements here," Mayor Winston offered.

"Certainly a man of his years and experience should know what is expected of a pastor."

"Jane, what was your opinion of him?" the mayor asked.

"He seemed sincere and most solicitous towards his sister. But he is also rather smug and abrupt. And as for his years of experience, aunt, I doubt he's had many."

"Why do you say that?"

"Because I don't think Mr. Kohl is as old as any of us expected him to be."

"You mean he is a young man?" the mayor said.

"I would guess he's isn't much older than me."

Ruth looked appalled. "Why on earth would Pastor Porter have entrusted his congregation to such a young man?"

The mayor shrugged. "I can only presume he has certain qualities, as yet unseen to us, which Joseph felt were worthwhile."

"Let us hope so," Ruth replied.

"In any case, I better tell the men to stop working on the house and do my best to find our new pastor to explain some of the expectations his congregation will have."

"But how will you find him?" Ruth asked.

"There are only two or three vacant homesteads in the vicinity he could have bought. I'll try them all until I find him."

"Why go to all that trouble? You and Ginny can come back and join us all for dinner tonight. You can converse with Mr. Kohl then." Ruth paused to look at Jane. "You did invite him to come, didn't you?"

Jane closed her eyes in frustration. "No. I forgot."

"Oh, Jane!"

"I'm sorry, Aunt Ruth. But with all the confusion over his arrival or rather his sister's arrival, it went right out of my head."

"Don't fret," Mr. Winston interjected. "I'll find him and issue the invitation to dine with us myself. Then both of you can join us for supper. I'm sure Ginny would prefer the extra company if Mr. Kohl is as troublesome as you say, Jane."

"Thank you," Ruth replied.

"I'm so sorry about all of this, Mr. Winston," Jane added.

"Forget it, Jane," he replied. "I have a feeling Mr. Kohl is the sort who will have us all turned inside out before he's through."

He smiled and replaced his hat. "Until tonight."

The mayor made his exit as hastily as he'd arrived. In the moments following his absence, Jane began to wonder just how many more surprises Mr. Kohl would have in store for all of them.

Chapter Six

James and Ginny Winston lived in a neatly-appointed house on the edge of town. Its style and décor reflected the elegant, gentle nature of its mistress. Ginny Winston was a lady in every sense, but still shrewd enough to meet the responsibilities of an aspiring politician's wife. She had extended her dinner invitation to include all of the town council members, as well as Ruth and Jane. When her guests arrived, she greeted them warmly and shared a keen, but cautious, curiosity with them regarding the guests of honor.

At half past six, the Kohls had not yet arrived and conjecture over their delay began to pervade the Winston's dining room. Whispered exchanges continued as all of the other guests took their seats around a long table adorned in white linen. The table was set with the Winston's best china. A simple, low-cut bouquet of wildflowers lent a dash of riotous color to the room.

James Winston sat at the head of the table, opposite the door. Ruth Randolph sat to his left, while Edward Hibbert and his wife were beside her. Samuel Jenkins was at the far end of the table to Ginny's left and Curtis Webber was to her right. Jane found herself pleasantly situated beside Mr. Webber, whose experience as a journalist always made him an engaging conversationalist. The two remaining chairs to her left remained empty for the Kohls.

When Jane and Ruth first arrived, there had been some talk that Jane would be seated beside the new pastor since she had already made his acquaintance. However, Ginny Winston managed to convince her husband that Henry Kohl should sit beside him, while Olivia Kohl might me more comfortable beside Jane. For that intervention alone, Jane was eternally grateful. After their first two encounters and his offhanded remark about her being *a Randolph*, Jane was more than disconcerted at the prospect of spending an entire evening in his company. On the other hand, meeting Olivia Kohl again would be a pleasure.

Jane had genuinely liked Miss Kohl, despite their brief introduction, and the thought of counting her as a friend seemed more appealing by the minute. To have a trusted, female confidant, in Rachel's absence, would be a great comfort as she struggled with the turmoil of recent events. Yet, she couldn't help but wonder if Henry Kohl would permit her to forge a friendship with his sister.

The memory of his whispered warning to Olivia rankled in her memory. *What did he mean? She's still a Randolph.* She realized good manners barred the possibility of asking him outright to explain such a statement, so she would have to try to infer a reason on her own. Her mind was engrossed in searching for just such a reason when Mr. Webber dared to comment upon the Kohl's tardiness.

"You don't suppose our new pastor just isn't coming because he's one of those religious fanatics who believe in living like a hermit?"

"Of course not," Mayor Winston replied.

"What do you say, Janey?" Mr. Webber pursued. "Does Mr. Kohl strike you as an ascetic?"

"Hardly. From what I've seen I'd say he's quite the opposite."

"Perhaps something has happened to them?" Ginny suggested.

"But what?" Sam Jenkins asked. "I doubt any danger could have befallen them on the ride into town. It's a most pleasant evening."

"Maybe they simply forgot or mistook the time," Mr. Hibbert suggested.

"Well, whatever the reason, I don't think it's fair to keep you all waiting any longer," James replied. He picked up a small silver bell on the table and rang it. A young man, smartly dressed, answered the summons. "Joseph, would you please serve dinner now. I think we've all waited long enough."

James looked down the length of the table to see if Ginny agreed. She nodded and within minutes a steaming bowl of soup was placed before each of them followed by plates generously laden with roast beef and potatoes. Friendly conversation about neighbors, mutual friends and town matters filled the room with a pleasant hum.

"Tell me, Jane," Mr. Webber asked. "How is your houseguest getting along? I haven't seen him around lately."

"Just fine, Mr. Webber. He's been very busy surveying the area."

"Yes, he mentioned he would be. Is he working anywhere in particular at the moment?"

"I couldn't say for sure, but he seems very interested in the creek."

"Oh?"

"I can't understand it myself," Jane continued. "I know I've always found it to be a lovely spot, but he seems obsessed about it."

"Why do you say that?"

"Well, on his first day here, he insisted I take him over there and at least three times since then, he's enlisted me as a guide to show him up and down stream."

"What's he looking for?"

"I don't rightly know, but he always seems quite pleased once we've returned."

"No doubt that's due to your company, Janey."

"Well the allure of my company must have worn off because before we left to come here tonight, he told Aunt Ruth and me that he was going to camp out along the stream for a few days."

"Alone?"

Jane nodded.

"Did he say why he wanted to stay out there?"

"Just that it would save time. I guess packing and unpacking his equipment everyday can be a chore."

Curtis scoffed.

"Something troubling you?" Jane asked.

"Doesn't it strike you as odd that a city-boy should be so at ease roughing it alone out here?"

"Not really," Jane confessed. "I imagine he's had to do this sort of thing on other jobs."

"Maybe. But that still doesn't explain why he wants to stay out there alone. The creek isn't that far from town and I don't believe that it's worth camping out just to spare himself fifteen minutes to set up his gear...."

"You sound as if you don't trust Mr. Mason," Jane said.

"I don't, to be honest with you. Something about that boy just isn't right. I can't put my finger on it, but I suspect he came to Copper Creek for some other purpose than to help us improve our town."

"I'll confess I was rather suspicious of his arrival at first too."

"And now?"

Jane shrugged. "I'm getting to know him better."

"Did you know he proposed the council scratch their plans for minor improvements and proposed a major renovation of the entire town? He wants to turn Copper Creek into a big city."

"No. I didn't. He did mention something about electric lights, but I assumed that was the council's idea."

Curtis shook his head. "Adding a few new buildings was all we had in mind."

"I wonder why he would suggest otherwise."

Curtis raised an eyebrow. "You're a bright girl, Janey. Surely you can think of a reason?"

"No. I'm afraid I can't."

"Don't let his looks blind you, Jane," Curtis said bluntly. "The answer is money. It can't be anything else."

"What do you mean, Mr. Webber?"

"That Thomas Mason intends to swindle us so he can make a fortune for himself. He's a confidence man...a charlatan, pick any name you like, but I for one won't be surprised when the economy of Copper Creek goes bust and we haven't got a single *improvement* to show for it."

"That can't be, Mr. Webber. I can't believe Uncle Michael would trust him if he really were a criminal or something."

"It's possible Michael doesn't know."

"And you do?"

"I've done some digging since he made his grandiose proposal to try and get to the bottom of things. So far, I've managed to uncover that he never earned a degree in architecture."

"Never earned...why that's not possible."

"I tell you it's a fact. His freshman year he enrolled in architectural design courses at Harvard and then dropped out nine months later. He never earned a degree."

Jane shook her head. "But all those other commissions, all the talk about his reputation..."

"Is just that, Janey. Talk."

"Are you sure you aren't just jumping to conclusions because you don't like Mr. Mason? Maybe he finished his education at another school."

"This isn't a question of prejudice, Janey. This young man is only the architect of a carefully laid scheme and, believe me, plotting is the only thing Mr. Thomas Mason is capable of."

"I don't know what to say. Have you mentioned this to anyone else?"

"Not yet, Janey. I'm waiting on a couple more telegrams from back east."

"What will they prove?"

"That Thomas Mason is a fraud who deserves to be run out of town on a rail."

Stunned by such damning accusations, Jane returned her attention to her plate and found suddenly she had lost her appetite. She hadn't realized it, but somehow along the way, she'd let her guard down and Thomas Mason had managed to work his way into her affections. Now that their association seemed to be in jeopardy, she found she desperately wanted to continue believing the things Uncle Michael had said about Thomas were true; that there was no dark secrets about him, no mysteries surrounding his presence.

Yet, Curtis Webber was not a man to lie. She had known him since her earliest days in Copper Creek and she had come to trust in his judgment. Her mind struggled to choose between her divided loyalties without success. There had to be an explanation that would satisfy the conflicting reports she had received about Thomas. Most likely it would have to come from Thomas, himself.

Jane fidgeted in her chair, wondering how she could ever dare to bring the subject up to him. Just then she heard the doors to the dining room slide open. She looked across the room and watched as another problem crossed the threshold. Henry Kohl had finally arrived.

❖ ❖ ❖ ❖ ❖

Everyone stared at the minister, in awe of his appearance and his audacity. Dressed in a simple grey suit, he wore no tie or collar or any outward sign of his vocation. His hair was brusquely combed and fell dashingly across his brow. He seemed quite calm and poised. His face was stern and much less mischievous than Jane remembered. She thought she could detect a hint of anxiety in his eyes, but she dismissed it as embarrassment over his tardiness.

"My apologies, Mr. Winston. Mrs. Winston," Henry said. "I know I am inexcusably late, but I hope I may still accept your hospitality for the evening."

Stunned by the minister's unexpected entrance, James hardly knew what to say, but as usual, Ginny came to his rescue. She stood and walked over to Reverend Kohl. "Of course," she said, taking his arm. "You are most welcome."

"Yes," James finally added. "Come and sit here." He gestured to the chair beside him. Henry walked around the table to take the proffered seat.

"Where is your sister, Mr. Kohl?" Ginny asked. "I understood she had come to Copper Creek to join you."

"Yes, ma'am. That's right. But she wasn't feeling well enough to come tonight."

"Oh, no! I hope it isn't anything serious," Ginny pursued.

Henry didn't answer at once. A troubled look seemed to come over him before he answered. "I think she is just overwrought by the strain of her journey. She should be fine in a couple of days."

"Yes. Rest should put her to rights," James agreed. "Copper Creek is such a peaceful place."

"For the present, I'll take your word for it," Henry replied.

"Do," Mayor Winston said. "And allow me to introduce you to our other guests."

James began with Ruth Randolph and circled the table adding a humorous remark or notable fact about each individual as he went until finally he came to Jane.

"Yes," Henry Kohl replied. "I am well acquainted with Miss Randolph. It is so nice to see you again."

"Thank you," Jane replied.

"My sister was of course devastated she couldn't come tonight, but she most especially regretted missing the opportunity to visit with you again."

"I had been looking forward to seeing her too," Jane replied.

"I will tell her you said so," Henry said. "But I hope you would do her an even greater kindness by coming for tea after services on Sunday. I know Olivia would love to have your company."

"Yes...of course," Jane replied. "Thank you."

"Good."

"I am surprised you intend to begin services so soon," the mayor interrupted.

"The church is ready for use isn't it?" Henry asked.

"Well, yes."

"Then I see no reason to delay any longer. It's well past time I set about doing God's work in Copper Creek. After all, that's why I'm here. Isn't it?"

"Why...yes," the mayor replied.

"Then I can count on you all to help spread the word among your neighbors to come for services on Sunday?"

"Certainly," Ginny said.

"I'll be sure to put a special notice in the paper tomorrow," Mr. Webber added.

"Fine."

"I trust, then, that you are suitably prepared to give your first sermon to the town," Ruth commented.

Henry paused and gave her an appraising look that made Jane uneasy.

"Mrs. Randolph, the blessing of my ordination at the hands of men considered to be pillars of the church would seem to confirm that."

Ruth offered a weak smile. "To be sure. I only hope Copper Creek is ready to hear what you'll have to say."

"Ready or not, Mrs. Randolph. I think it's time they heard it."

"Perhaps."

"I'm only sorry your husband isn't here to be among them," Henry added.

"Oh? Why the particular interest in Michael?"

"Based on our past acquaintance, I feel certain he'd want to be present."

Ruth raised one brow. "I wasn't aware you had met my husband."

"Weren't you?"

"No." Ruth affirmed.

Henry glanced at Jane before he added. "I was sure someone would have mentioned it to you."

A knot started to tighten in Jane's stomach. She had never told anyone about meeting him unexpectedly in the woods and now she was terrified her concealment would seem motivated by deceit or possibly something worse.

He wouldn't mention it, Jane thought, *it would only embarrass him too. But then he's the sort of man who probably wouldn't care.*

"Well," Henry went on. "As I said, it was long ago. No doubt, Michael has forgotten all about it."

"If you don't mind, I'd like to know how you met." Ruth persisted

"Yes," James added. "Do tell us. It might clear up the mystery."

"Mystery, Mr. Winston?"

"Michael had been behaving most peculiarly before your arrival. And when he mentioned your coming at the last town council meeting, he said very little before abruptly leaving the chambers. I gathered he was rather nervous about your coming."

Henry didn't speak, but something in his face led Jane to believe he was intrigued to hear her uncle had been so unsettled.

"He was rather withdrawn and distracted before he left town," Ruth confirmed.

"Downright disturbed, if you ask me," Sam Jenkins added.

"In any case, it wasn't like him," James concluded. "I was hoping since the change in him coincided with news of your arrival that you might be able to offer us some explanation, Mr. Kohl?"

Henry appeared pensive for a moment. "I cannot claim to know what passes between a man and his conscience."

"Of course not," Ruth replied. "But certainly, you can tell us something?"

"Such as, Mrs. Randolph?"

"Anything…how you met Michael? When? Where?"

"I never really knew him," he said. Seeing the confusion in their eyes, Henry hurried on. "At least, not as well as I thought…he was…that is he worked for my father, on our ranch."

"Then it was some time ago," James noted.

"Yes. I was only eleven or twelve."

"I never knew Michael had worked on a ranch," Ruth said.

"It wasn't for long and the things he did for us couldn't really be called work," Henry replied. "For that reason, I'm sure our little place in Texas has been the furthest thing from his mind during the intervening years. But still, he was with my family long enough to have had a profound effect on my life."

"Reunions are always such happy affairs, I find," Mr. Hibbert observed. "I can see now why you were distraught to find Michael gone. And I must say it is good of you to remember him so kindly all these years."

Henry smirked. "Indeed. I have never forgotten him."

"Don't look so down-hearted, Mr. Kohl. My husband won't be gone forever. I'm sure he will return in only a matter of weeks, once he has our daughter properly settled at school."

"So that's where he is?"

"Yes. I'll admit the trip was rather sudden. But you know how young girls are. Michael seemed determined to indulge Rachel in her sudden show of independence."

"Of course. However, I do hope I will have the pleasure of meeting your daughter some day."

"I'm sure you will. Confidentially, I think that once Rachel discovers what she's gotten herself into she will soon tire of the notion of school and long to come home to her friends and familiar surroundings. A mother can always tell. Not to boast, but I find I have always been more than perceptive about people, particularly those closest to me."

Henry met her defiant stare and smiled indulgently. "How fortunate for you," he said. All the while thinking to himself, *if she only knew....*

If Ruth Randolph could have seen the smile beaming on Rachel's face at that very moment, it would have deflated all confidence in her motherly intuition. The journey from Copper Creek to New Orleans had been longer and more arduous than Rachel had expected. But since stepping on the paved streets of that shining city, she had been enchanted.

Her love affair only deepened upon their arrival at George Mason's residence. Far grander and more luxurious than anything she could have imagined, Rachel soon found herself at home there.

Servants were at her beck and call all day long and the signs of wealth adorned everything from the doorknobs to frescoed ceilings. Mr. Mason was just as charming as his son and appeared to Rachel an older, more distinguished version of Thomas. He was a widower, quick-witted and thoughtful, with a dazzling circle of friends.

Every night they had shared the company of artists, politicians, scientists, or inventors at the dinner table and last night George Mason had entertained some members of the European aristocracy.

Rachel was dazzled by this rich, new world, and the more she learned of it the more she longed to be a part of it. She wondered how she had ever endured the past seventeen years in Copper Creek. But her reflections about home were pleasantly diverted by parties, concerts, lectures, or in tonight's case, a ball.

Mr. Mason's good friends, the Richardsons, were giving a ball in honor of their daughter's birthday. Louise Richardson was a tall, stately girl with classic features and the elegance to match her careful upbringing. She excelled in watercolors, dancing and flirtation, all of which enshrined her in Rachel's eyes as the perfect mentor for this new chapter in her life.

That evening, Rachel's senses tingled with excitement as she entered the Richardson's town house. An amber glow flooded every room, spilling down from crystal lamps and chandeliers over rich, well-bred faces and bowers of fragrant blossoms. The delicate scent of roses and gardenias mingled with exotic perfumes, imported tobacco, and expensive alcohol creating a heady atmosphere. Music wafted out from the ballroom, smothering the laughter and conversation of the guests who chattered on oblivious to the melody of the orchestra and the rhythm of the city around them.

Rachel barely had time to take it all in before she heard Louise call her name. She spun around to greet her new friend.

"Rachel Randolph, don't you look sweet in that dress!"

"Louise! Is it really all right?"

Rachel held out her skirt.

"It's absolutely heaven! Where ever did you get it?"

Rachel tried not to blush. She was afraid to admit her mother had made it because Louise was so accustomed to store bought gowns from French designers.

"I can't remember now," she said.

"No matter," Louis simpered. "The important thing is that every man here has his eyes on you."

Rachel looked around embarrassed and pleased at the same time.

"Nonsense. It's your birthday, Louise. I'm sure the only reason any one might be looking at me is because I'm with you."

Louise closed her fan and shook her head. "Lord, you country girls are too modest. C'mon, now. There are a lot of people I want you to meet."

"Who?"

"People."

"From your school?" Rachel persisted.

"Gracious, no."

"But you promised me you'd help me to pick a school and that your…"

"I declare, you have a one-track mind. Why waste your time with school? I know a way you can be a whole lot better off without ever cracking a book."

"How?"

"Richard Thorpe."

"What's Richard Thorpe?

"Not what, silly. Who. Richard Thorpe is a man."

"Yes, I see that now. But what makes him so much better than school?"

"He's rich. He's single. And he's only twenty-seven."

"So. What's that got to do with me?"

"Honestly, Rachel! I don't know how you expect to do well in any school at all if you're this dense. Don't you see...you could be rich too if you were to become Mrs. Thorpe."

"Me! Why me?"

"Why not you? I've got plenty of money thanks to daddy and although Richard is a charming brute, he just isn't my type."

"Thank you, Louise but..."

"Don't say no until you've met him."

"What difference will that make? He probably won't even like me."

"Pardon me, ladies."

Rachel turned to identify the cultured voice that had interrupted her objections and was stunned to see a young man with thick, blond hair and dark, penetrating eyes standing beside her. He smiled at her, revealing two devastating dimples and perfect white teeth. He was the most extraordinarily overpowering picture of masculinity Rachel had ever seen.

"Ah, Richard. We were just talking about you," Louise confessed. "Rachel, may I introduce Mr. Richard Thorpe. Richard, this is my new friend, Miss Rachel Randolph."

Richard took Rachel's hand and kissed it lightly. "Miss Randolph. I will be devastated if you haven't saved a space for me on your dance card...."

"More brandy, Michael?"

"No, thank you, George."

Michael Randolph took the last sip from his glass and set it down on the table beside him. He settled back in the comfortable leather chair opposite his friend and let the fire crackling in the library hearth soothe his aching feet.

George finished refilling his glass and resumed his seat beside Michael. Rain had begun tapping at the windows and off in the distance the grandfather clock chimed the early morning hour.

"Two," George counted. "It seems these balls last later all the time. But it was worth it though. I think Rachel thoroughly enjoyed herself."

"Yes," Michael replied. "New Orleans seems to agree with her."

"And why not? She was the belle of the ball."

"Thanks to you and your friends. I can't tell you how grateful I am to you for allowing Rachel and me to stay with you on such short notice."

George Mason waived his hand to dismiss his friend's unnecessary gratitude.

"It's no more than you've done for Thomas."

"It's only right. You helped me become a success and I'll never forget it."

George nodded and swallowed another mouthful of brandy.

"Now that you mention it," George said, setting down his glass. "Why did you leave Copper Creek? I thought you understood our arrangement?"

"I did but, there were…complications," Michael replied.

"What sort of complications?"

"A few days before I left Copper Creek I received word that Henry Kohl was appointed to take over as the new pastor of our church in town."

"Yes, Thomas wrote to me about him," George replied.

"When?"

"He enclosed the letter in the parcel you brought."

"I see. Then you should understand why I was in such a hurry to leave."

"Frankly, no."

"What else could I do? I couldn't risk facing him again."

"Were you even sure it was the same Henry Kohl?"

"I couldn't take the risk."

"That's fine....You were too scared to wait and see for yourself, so you just ran away like a scared rabbit."

"I suppose I did. But I didn't have any choice."

"You chose to jeopardize everything we've worked for!"

"No. We'll just continue on elsewhere."

"Elsewhere! You fool! You cowardly, miserable fool!" George hurled his glass into the fireplace. "Damn it, Michael! I'm not going to give up a fortune just because you haven't got a spine."

"That isn't fair, George. You weren't the one being hunted like an animal all those years."

"You were hardly in real danger. Henry Kohl was just a boy."

"A boy with a gun and he wasn't working alone."

"That may be. But apparently he's turned over a new leaf."

"I don't believe he's really a reverend, anymore than I can believe he'll ever forget what I did to his family. Which is why you have to call off the whole deal and wire Thomas to come home."

"Oh, just as simple as that?"

"Why not?"

"Because I don't give up as easily as you!"

"There isn't anything else we can do. Henry Kohl knows too much about me. He'd blow the whole thing up in our faces."

"Not necessarily."

"George! You don't know Henry Kohl like I do. He's relentless. He'd stop at nothing to ruin me and if he gets wind of what we're up to…"

"So what if he does? We can handle him."

"How?"

"I have ways, Michael. Or have you forgotten the resources at my disposal?"

"He'd cut down anyone you'd send at him."

"Violence may be the obvious solution, but not necessarily the most effective. I was thinking of a subtler means of controlling him…specifically information."

"You mean blackmail don't you?"

"If you prefer," George replied, rising from his chair. "But whatever you call it, it's often more reliable than the deadliest weapon. And since you've seen fit to hide here like a coward, we'll have to trust Thomas to try to sound out Mr. Kohl's intentions. Should they be opposed to our aims, we may be able to use our previous experience with him to our advantage."

"Think whatever you want about me. I still say it would be safer to cut our losses. I mean what is there in Copper Creek that could possibly be worth our necks now?"

George turned to retrieve something from his desk drawer. He pulled out the package Thomas had sent along with Michael from Copper Creek.

"This," George replied, shoving the opened parcel at Michael.

Michael pushed aside the brown paper and peered inside the box. He saw a small vial filled with several smooth, shiny rocks.

"The first test sample?" Michael said.

George nodded.

"He found it? The copper is really there?"

"Thomas tested it himself and he assures me in his letter it would be a rich haul."

"How big? I mean how much copper does he figure is there?"

"He can't be exactly sure, but he is certain the ore runs at least the length of the ridge beside the creek," George replied.

"A deposit that big could mean a fortune!"

"It means a big mining operation. And once we get it out of the ground..."

"We'd be hard pressed to meet the growing demand for copper," Michael finished.

"Thanks to the new interest in electric lights, copper wiring is headed for a boom that would make your head spin. We'd be making money faster than we could get the copper out of the ground and you're ready to throw a set-up like that away."

"I didn't think Thomas would ever really find any copper."

"You mean you thought my claim to have found it all those years ago was an exaggeration."

"It's just I never expected to run into that kind of luck."

"Well, now that you have, don't be a fool and walk away from it," George insisted. "We've bided our time long enough for the right conditions to cash in so we wouldn't tip our hand. This sample is proof the waiting is over. With Thomas' skills, your influence and my resources, we can't lose."

"But Henry Kohl..."

"Forget about him. I tell you he won't interfere."

Michael turned to stare into the fire, while fear and greed battled inside of him.

"George."

"Yes?"

"You've never failed me before. Tell Thomas to go ahead."

George bobbed his head with satisfaction. "I knew you'd see reason."

Chapter Seven

"Bad news?"

Thomas crumpled the telegram in his hand and tried to plaster on a smile. He expected to be alone in the parlor until the store closed, so he was surprised to see Jane standing behind him.

"No," he replied. "My father's just checking up on me."

"Did he mention anything about Uncle Michael or Rachel?"

"Not specifically. But I can ask about them when I write him, if you like."

"Thank you, but I'm sure we'll get a letter from them soon."

Jane walked over to sit in her chair and Thomas frowned at her playfully. "You are all together too gloomy today, Miss Randolph. What's worrying you?"

Jane shrugged.

"It's got to be something."

Jane shook her head. "It's nothing really."

"Jane, you are obviously troubled," he observed, sitting in the chair beside her. "C'mon, tell me all about it."

Jane looked sullenly at her lap for a moment. "I don't want to upset you," Jane began. "But last night I heard some disturbing things."

"About me?"

Jane nodded.

"I'm flattered."

Jane made a face. "You don't even know what I heard."

"No, but it's always flattering to be the subject of conversation."

"Not always," Jane warned.

"Then I take it you heard something unfavorable?"

"Puzzling," Jane replied.

"All the better. Perhaps the intrigue will give me an added allure."

"Can't you ever be serious?"

Thomas composed his features. "Very well then, out with it. Name the crime of which I am accused."

Jane found it curious Thomas would choose to use those words when criminal intent was exactly the charge Mr. Webber had brought against him.

"Where did you go to school?" Jane ventured.

"Why does it matter?"

"I'd like to know," she persisted.

"I started at Harvard and finished at Oxford."

"Oxford? In England."

"Where else. I never could seem to fit in at Harvard so I made the transfer a few months into my first year and I never looked back."

"Then Oxford is where you earned your degree?" Jane tried to clarify.

"Certainly," Thomas said smiling. "Why the interest in my alma matter?"

Jane eyed him warily and finally confessed. "Mr. Webber was of the opinion you never had one because he couldn't find any record of your graduation. But I guess he didn't think to check any European schools."

Thomas couldn't repress a smile. "Then he doesn't believe I am really an architect?"

Jane shook her head.

"What does he think I am?"

"A confidence man."

Thomas burst out laughing. "That's rich. I knew he didn't like me, but I never thought he'd take his distaste that far. I suppose you were inclined to believe him?"

"I didn't know what to believe."

"And now?"

"I feel quite foolish."

"Would it help if I said I forgive you?"

"Very little."

"Then we must do something else to cheer you up." He paused a moment. "I think I know just what will do the trick." He reached inside his breast pocket and pulled out a small present wrapped in brown paper.

"What's this?" Jane asked.

"It's for you," Thomas said, handing her the bundle. "Open it."

Jane took it from his hand and, trembling a bit, she pulled on the string.

"Thomas," she gasped, pulling out a gorgeous scarlet colored ribbon.

"I hope you like it," Thomas said, as she fondled the length of satin. "I thought you could do with a little color in your lovely hair besides that black ribbon you're so fond of."

His minor criticism made Jane self-conscious and her hand darted up to the black ribbon around her braid.

"I...I've never worn anything else," she confessed. "It belonged to my mother. After she...died, I found it in the bottom of a carved box she kept her baubles in. Not that she ever had many. The few pieces of jewelry she owned she gave to my father to sell so they could meet the mortgage payments on the farm. She had a hand-painted pendant she used to wear with this ribbon. The pendant was sold, but she kept the ribbon. I put it on the day of her funeral and I've worn it every day since to keep her with me."

"You must have loved her very much," Thomas said.

"I still do."

"I wish I'd known before…"

Jane reached out for his hand. "I'd still like to keep it for special occasions."

"If you wish."

"I don't know if scarlet suits me, but it is very beautiful, Thomas. I'll always treasure your gift."

Thomas covered her hand with his and squeezed. His eyes focused intently on her face. Unable to bear his arduous scrutiny, she looked down at her lap and slowly drew her hand away. Just then, Reverend Kohl appeared in the doorway and saw their tender exchange. Seized with a sudden fit of irritation, Henry knocked brusquely on the open door. At the sound, Jane's eyes flew to his face and Thomas stood.

"Forgive me for intruding," Henry said. "But Mrs. Randolph was expecting me and I was told by your housekeeper to wait for her up here in the parlor."

"Of course. Please come in, Reverend, and have a seat."

"Thank you," Henry said.

"Reverend, may I present our guest, Mr. Thomas Mason."

"Reverend," Thomas added, holding out his hand.

"I understand you're the architect everyone's been talking about," Henry replied shaking Thomas' hand.

"So Jane's just been telling me," Thomas answered, moving to sit at the other end of the couch from him. "But I must disclaim at least half of the rumors you've heard about me."

"I'm not one to indulge in idle gossip, Mr. Mason."

"No. Of course not, Reverend. But I fear you aren't immune to being the subject of it either."

"I expect not," Henry replied. "But I am new around here, much like you. And that naturally stirs up curiosity."

"And are you inclined to satisfy that curiosity?" Thomas asked.

"What is it you'd like to know, Mr. Mason?"

"Anything you'd care to share. Other than the fact you are ordained and have a sister, there is precious little in circulation."

Jane could sense that the reverend was becoming annoyed with Thomas' impudence, but was masterfully controlling his frustration. However, she figured she'd better intervene.

"Speaking of your sister," Jane said. "How is Olivia this morning?"

"Much recovered. Thank you, Miss Randolph."

"I am looking forward to seeing her on Sunday."

"As is Olivia. In fact, she asked me to remind you about your visit when she learned I was calling on your aunt."

"I won't forget."

All conversation ceased then, leaving the ticking of the mantle clock to fill the silence in the room.

"I don't know what's keeping Aunt Ruth," Jane finally offered. "She usually doesn't keep guests waiting. I hope your business with her isn't pressing?"

"No," Henry assured her. "I'm here at her invitation. I expect she has some more *advice* to share before I give my first sermon."

"Nervous about your first time out?" Thomas asked.

"Not really," Henry answered. "This won't be the first time I've preached, Mr. Mason."

"Yes, but if you don't do it right, Mrs. Randolph could see to it it's the last time you do. At least in Copper Creek."

"Thomas, I think that's a bit harsh. I grant you Aunt Ruth can be difficult at times, but she isn't as spiteful as you make her sound."

"My apologies."

The quiet that ensued next was painfully awkward until Jane suggested she ought to go look for her aunt.

"Allow me to go," Thomas offered, rising to his feet. "I seem to feel the reverend would prefer it that way. Reverend."

"Glad to have met you, Mr. Mason."

"Likewise."

Thomas backed out of the room making a sarcastic face for Jane's benefit before leaving her alone with Henry.

"I hope you won't think I'm overstepping, Miss Randolph," Henry began. "But I hardly think it polite for Mr. Mason to speak so rudely about your aunt when he is a guest in her house."

"I know and I agree with you, Reverend. But Thomas doesn't seem to follow conventional rules of behavior."

"I noticed that when I arrived."

Worried he might have misinterpreted her exchange with Thomas, Jane looked at Henry with a curious expression.

"Did you? I…"

"I didn't mean to spy, but I couldn't help but notice he was quite forward when…forgive me, I shouldn't have said anything."

"No…please go on."

"It's just that I had the impression you were uncomfortable with his behavior and I wouldn't want you to feel…that is I wouldn't want him to take advantage of you."

"That's most kind of you, Reverend. But he didn't mean me any harm."

"I sincerely hope you're right, Miss Randolph."

The gentleness in his voice was mirrored by the tenderness of his eyes. Jane had never before seen such vulnerability in those mocking, playful eyes. It touched something deep in her core. But before she could fully appreciate its implications, Ruth bustled in through the door full of apologies for her delay.

"I'm so sorry to have kept you waiting, Reverend."

"Think nothing of it, Mrs. Randolph. It was worth the wait to have the chance to enjoy your niece's company." He looked at Jane again with that same intensity she'd seen in his eyes down by the creek. But this time it didn't frighten her; it stirred hope inside of her for something she never thought she'd have and never knew she wanted until now.

Henry's new church sat just on the edge of town. The recent repairs had rendered it sound once more, but it had always been a pretty little building, nestled among a grove of locust trees. The entryway was trimmed with wild morning glory and ivy and the steeple above boasted its own small bell tower. On Sunday morning, the tones resonating from that peak were a welcome sound, as they once again called the faithful to worship in the humble edifice.

Inside, the church was flooded with tremulous, early morning rays streaming through three unadorned panes on either side of the church. A wood pulpit, finely carved with the image of a cross, stood alone at the far end of the room. It was flanked on either side by an American flag and two, identical, hand-sewn banners. Every seat on the hewn benches opposite the pulpit was taken.

A low murmur of conversation from the expectant congregation permeated the sanctuary until the first notes of a favored hymn resounded from an upright piano. Henry Kohl emerged from the side door. His new flock rose in reverent recognition of his arrival. He lowered his bible to the pulpit and cast his eyes out across the gathering. He lingered on each face, considering the spirit of God that resided behind it, and reminded himself of his vow to shepherd each of them to a heavenly reward. His gaze finally came to rest on Jane Randolph.

Jane looked lovelier than he remembered. She was wearing a straw bonnet trimmed with yellow ribbons and white daisies, which Henry found most becoming. Her hair was swept up under her chapeau, except for the few tendrils that lay softly across her brow. Her eyes were still as bright and appealing as they had been the night he first saw her.

Jane couldn't help but notice Henry's fixed attention upon her. The longer he watched her, the more she wondered what he must be thinking. Finally, the music stopped and Henry was forced to return his attention to the duty at hand.

The congregation resumed their seats and he stood silently before them for several seconds. Finally, he broke the peace with the bold pronouncement of one word...*revenge.*

"Revenge," he said again. "It is far too easy for the human heart to desire this one province which belongs solely to God. The evils committed in this world. The anger. The hatred. The pain. All seek an outlet for retribution, repayment. Slights committed against us must not go unnoticed, or unanswered. The unjust and the wicked must be punished, we think. But this is faulty thinking. What's more, it is dangerous for any one of us to desire, seek, or demand revenge upon those who injure us. Apart from all considerations of human laws, we must never permit the poison of revenge to deny us the peace and freedom that only comes with forgiveness."

Henry paused. He looked to Olivia, who was sitting before him in the first pew. She offered a gentle, encouraging smile and he went on.

"I know enacting this teaching is a constant struggle. In my own experience, I know too well how easy and even satisfying it can be to hold on to revenge and all the bitter emotion that goes with it. But good people of Copper Creek, I am also proof that salvation from revenge and any other evil is not beyond our grasp.

I have experienced the goodness that comes with forgiveness and I want you all to know that I am here to help each one of you to have that same experience. "

"I'm sure many of you have questions about me; about how I plan to run this church and minister to you. I can answer them all with one word...forgiveness. That is my philosophy. I teach it and I practice it. Nothing we do or believe cannot be changed or healed by forgiveness. So, when you come here for services or you come to me privately, there will be no questions asked. I hold no judgment against anyone. I welcome everyone into this church. Nothing is more important to me than the peace and salvation of a person's soul."

Henry looked out across the congregation, pausing to allow his words to sink in to their minds.

"So, from today forward," he continued, "no one in Copper Creek will have to fight temptation alone. We will walk together in fellowship; trusting one another, helping one another and when we falter, forgiving one another."

"In closing, I encourage you all to put aside your judgments of others, your preconceived notions and reach out in the true spirit of forgiveness to love your neighbor. It just might be the most profound experience you ever have."

"Now in conclusion, I'd like you to turn to the book of Matthew."

Everyone turned to the appointed verses in chapter six as Henry read aloud about forgiveness of thy neighbor. When he had finished, he charged them all to take the words of the Lord to heart.

Another hymn began and Henry left the way he had come in. When the song ended, the citizens of Copper Creek filed out of their pews, animatedly discussing the brief and radical presentation of their new minister.

"Ready to go, Jane?" Thomas asked, as Jane closed her hymnal.

Before Jane could reply, Olivia Kohl came up the aisle to join them.

"Miss Randolph," she called. "I hope you'll forgive my intrusion, but I was so eager to see you again. I was also curious to hear how you think Henry's first sermon went."

"He comported himself quite well," Jane replied. "And I do think he gave the congregation a lot to think about."

"Indeed," Thomas agreed. "I take it you are the reverend's sister?"

"Olivia Kohl. And you?"

"Thomas Mason. I'm a guest of the Randolphs."

"Oh?"

"Yes, Mr. Mason is working with the town council to make improvements on our town," Jane added.

"I do recall hearing some of the other townsfolk talking about changes to the town when I arrived this morning. From the way they spoke, I assumed an apocalypse was about to descend upon Copper Creek."

"Hardly, Miss Kohl. I am merely here to bring progress and prosperity."

"Well, I wish you luck, Mr. Mason. Change and those who bring it are often unwelcome, particularly in a close knit community."

"That's what I've been trying to tell him," Jane added.

"I do appreciate your concerns, ladies, but I assure you I am up to the challenge."

"Where do you plan to begin?" Olivia asked.

"I have already begun, Miss Kohl. Right now I'm engaged in surveying the area. But before that I, like your brother, was subject to the advice of Mrs. Randolph."

Olivia's face suddenly grew sullen at the mention of Ruth.

"My aunt does tend to be outspoken," Jane added. "But she means well."

"I'm sure," Olivia mumbled.

"I would like you to meet her?" Jane asked, looking around. "She just went off to speak with one of our neighbors but...There she is."

"I'm sorry," Olivia said abruptly when she an older woman, she presumed was Ruth, coming toward them. "But I can't keep Henry waiting any longer. Until this afternoon." She turned then and hurried away.

"Goodbye," Jane called after her.

"Was that Miss Kohl?" Ruth asked, when she reached Jane.

"Yes."

"She seemed in something of a hurry."

"She did act rather oddly," Thomas noted.

"I'm sure she just has a lot to do today with her brother's first service and all," Jane replied. "No doubt she has a lot of people to meet."

"Yes, well she didn't seem very keen on meeting your aunt," Thomas pointed out.

"No," Ruth agreed. "I wonder if it was a mistake to let you accept that invitation."

"Why?" Jane asked. "Olivia is just new around here. I'm sure any idiosyncrasy in her character is just due to the fact she's worried about fitting in."

"Perhaps, but how do you account for her brother's eccentricities?"

"I'm not supposed to try," Jane said. "Or weren't you listening to the sermon?"

Ruth grimaced and Thomas smiled.

Henry Kohl was waiting outside to greet his parishioner's as they filed out of the church. After a quick word and a handshake or two, he suddenly found himself face to face with Ruth Randolph again.

"Your sermon was quite heartfelt, Mr. Kohl," she said.

"I'm glad you approve, Mrs. Randolph"

"I did not say that. Still, it was an acceptable effort for your first attempt. Perhaps next time though you can offer a little more substance and a little less sentiment?"

"I'll do my best," Henry replied.

"That's all I ask, Reverend," Ruth finished, as she stepped aside allowing Jane to assume his attention.

"Miss Randolph," Henry said.

"Mr. Kohl."

Henry took Jane's hand and he lingered longer than he intended before releasing it. Startled by the sound of Thomas' voice, Henry turned abruptly to address him.

"My compliments, Reverend," Thomas was saying.

"Mr. Mason," Henry acknowledged. "I'm glad you could make it to the service."

"I wouldn't have missed it. Tell me, do you really believe everything you were spouting from the pulpit?"

"I wouldn't have said it, if I didn't," Henry answered firmly.

Thomas nodded. "I confess I was intrigued by your vague reference to past personal experience with revenge. I rather hoped you'd fill in some of the details for us."

"Thomas," Jane chided, embarrassed by his intrusive questioning.

"It's quite all right, Miss Randolph. Your friend's interest is only natural."

"There, Jane, you see."

"I'm only too happy to share my experience, if it will help to lighten someone else's burden," Henry added. "However in your case, Mr. Mason, I feel any elaboration on my part would only serve as entertainment and not enlightenment."

"I am sorry, Reverend," Jane said.

"Don't apologize for me, Jane," Thomas snapped.

"No," Henry agreed. "It's always best to take responsibility for oneself. Mr. Mason is the one who should apologize. Isn't that what you meant, Mr. Mason?"

The tension between Thomas and Henry became uncomfortably palpable. Uncertain how to halt the unspoken challenge being exchanged between the two men, Jane simply took hold of Thomas' arm to lead him away. But Thomas held his ground. Smiling in his usual carefree manner, he said,

"You are quite right, Reverend. My apologies. I suppose I am too eager to get to know people all at once. It has been a lifelong failing."

"Think nothing of it, Mr. Mason."

Afraid their truce might only be momentary, Jane tugged on Thomas' arm and said, "Well, we'd better not keep Aunt Ruth waiting. You know how much she hates cold chicken."

"Good day, Reverend Kohl," she added, leading Thomas away.

"Good day, Miss Randolph," Henry replied, wondering why she was so anxious to protect Thomas Mason and worried that he already knew the reason. He watched them stroll away, arm in arm, until more well-wishers required him to ignore their progress.

Jane, Ruth, and Thomas joined the Hibberts and three of their cousins for a picnic lunch following the services. Most of the other townsfolk out picnicking were spiritedly discussing the new pastor

and his sermon. But Jane refused to join in any of the gossip and instead concentrated on her aunt's delicious fried chicken. At around half past one, Jane excused herself from the company and started on her way to the Kohls.

Since the afternoon was so mild, she decided to walk rather than ride and set such a steady pace she came in sight of the Kohl's home sooner than she expected. She decided to stop and gather some wildflowers as a gift for Olivia before venturing up to the door. When Olivia answered her knock some minutes later, she was glad she had made the bouquet.

Olivia's face was beaming as she took in the beauty of the blossoms Jane presented her. "How kind of you, Jane!"

"I thought they might make a nice house warming gift," Jane replied. "I'm sure you haven't had much time to do more than unpack since you arrived."

"That's quite true. Henry rather embellished his letters about the readiness of the place. But I'm sure with his skills, it will be a fine cabin in no time."

"It's quite nice already with such lovely things." Jane reached out to touch a rocking chair beside the hearth. "Family heirloom?"

Olivia smiled. "In a way. Henry made it. He made all the furniture. And these too." She turned to the table behind her and picked up an intricately carved box and a stunning wood vase."

"They're beautiful."

"Henry has always had such a way with wood," Olivia replied, replacing the items on the table. "Such sensitivity in his hands...you know."

"I had a notion," Jane confessed, remembering how she had admired his hands as he had crossed the stream that first night.

"Well, I expect you're tired from your walk. Please sit down while I fetch the tea from the kitchen."

"Shouldn't we wait for your brother?"

"No. He won't be coming."

"Oh?"

"He intended to be here, but he was asked to pay a visit to a Mrs. Burns."

Olivia returned a moment later with a tray laden with two cups, an old teapot and a small plate with a few sweets.

"I believe the poor lady is quite ill and her family was afraid she might not be with us much longer," Olivia added, as she took hold of the steaming teapot.

"I'm sorry to hear it." Jane accepted the cup Olivia offered. "But I'm sure it will be a comfort to her to have your brother there."

"I do hope so."

The ladies sipped their tea and then Olivia ventured to ask, "Have you lived in Copper Creek long?"

"Since I was ten or eleven," Jane replied. "I came to live here with my aunt and uncle after my parents died."

"What a tragedy to lose one's parents so young."

"We had a farm, though I don't remember much about it now. I suppose it's just as well. My father wore himself to the bone caring for the place and he contracted a fever. My mother worried so about him that she took sick looking after him and in the end the fever took them both."

"We had a ranch of our own, Henry and father and I. Unfortunately, we were forced to give it up."

"What happened?"

A haunted, far-off look came into Olivia's face for a moment.

"What happens to so many people...a lack of money."

"Your father had to sell it?"

"No. By that time our father was...he was gone. The land was repossessed by the bank and Henry and I had to move in with our father's sister and her husband in Ohio."

"I'm sorry."

Olivia forced a smile. "It was long ago. And you see how well off we are now. Henry has made a fine home for us."

"Indeed."

Olivia took another sip of her tea and then asked, "So how do you think Henry's sermon was received today? I'm afraid I couldn't really tell...people want to be kind and so..."

"They don't tell the truth?" Jane finished.

Olivia nodded.

"I don't think you have anything to worry about."

"Really?"

"I imagine there were a few detractors in the crowd," Jane answered, mentally noting her aunt's objections. "But that has to be expected. I'm sure, on the whole, everyone found his sermon quite refreshing. Personally, I think it was quite nice to hear something other than the usual fire and brimstone."

"I hope you're right."

"Why should you doubt it?"

"Forgive me, it's just that I worry about Henry. He's had so many difficulties. So many burdens to bear since our father died that...well, what I mean is, he's tried his hand at several professions and he's never found any peace or satisfaction in any of them. It's only been in the last few years he came to the church and decided to become a minister. He loves it so, you see. But even during his formation, he often found himself at odds with his superiors over points of doctrine and the best ways to minster to the people."

"And you don't want to see his hopes and good intentions dashed by unkind words," Jane interpreted.

"Yes. This is Henry's first real assignment and he's been so eager to make a go of it. I'd hate it if we had to leave."

"I wouldn't worry. It might take some folks a little time to get used to him, but Copper Creek is a progressive place."

Olivia smiled. "At least it will be if Mr. Mason has his way, eh?"

Jane nodded.

"The way I see it, if this town is willing to endure the alterations Thomas Mason has in store, then they'll be more than ready to embrace you're brother's somewhat radical ideas about religion too."

"You really think so?"

"Certainly. What better fit can a progressive town have than a progressive pastor?"

"I suppose you're right."

"Don't worry about it for another instant. Copper Creek is your home now, so get used to the idea."

Olivia smiled. "I knew we would be friends when we met at the stage office."

"In truth, Olivia, I'm glad to have a friend. Right now, I need one."

"What's troubling you couldn't possibly have anything to do with Mr. Mason, could it?"

Jane looked into Olivia's eyes, surprised at the older woman's shrewdness. Olivia's face softened into a gentle smile.

"Am I that obvious?" Jane asked.

"No. But it only makes sense. A man who's that handsome would cause any young woman heartache."

"He is handsome," Jane agreed, setting her cup down on the tray. "And he knows it too."

"If you are suggesting Mr. Mason is a little vain and cocksure, I never would have guessed."

"I'm afraid he was rather rude to your brother this morning."

"Maybe he's jealous."

"Why? I mean the reverend certainly hasn't given him any cause to be jealous. Has he?"

"You tell me?" Olivia said, arching one brow as she sipped from her cup.

"I scarcely know your brother!" Jane insisted. "For anyone to have the idea that he...that we... it's ludicrous."

"I suppose you're right," Olivia replied. "I guess in that case, we'd best start from the beginning if we hope to decode Mr. Mason's behavior. Tell me about him."

"All about him?"

"Everything. From the day he first arrived in town," Olivia confirmed.

"I think that will call for another pot of tea," Jane replied.

Chapter Eight

Henry Kohl's mind was unusually agitated as he made his way home. Even the muffled clip-clop of his mare's hooves against the rocky path could not penetrate his introspection. He was too preoccupied by the distressing nature of his visit this afternoon to let any other thought or observation intrude.

Rosemary Burns had been the first parishioner in Copper Creek to require his spiritual guidance and he felt as if he had failed her. He'd had no advice or knowledge to offer which might ease the old lady's present pain and it appeared no authority to match the faith that so clearly sustained her through a lifetime of hardship. Mrs. Burn's belief in a loving God and his mercy shamed Henry.

He felt like a fraud, as he sat beside her bed in the guise of a theological authority. In truth, he knew so little about God and even less about the kind of unwavering trust and devotion Rosemary Burns had practiced since childhood. She had spoken to Henry simply and honestly about her life, her trials and God's presence in the midst of it all. Her words called into sharp relief the years Henry had led a life void of faith.

It was only recently that Henry found peace with God. Sufficient time had distanced him from old wounds, leaving room for hope to grow again. Dissatisfaction with himself and his former way of life, combined with devotion for his sister, had been the remaining ingredients for change. He had become a preacher for Olivia's sake and he was sure the only reason he succeeded was due to her prayers.

Since his ordination, Henry had become comfortable with a life in the church, even grateful for it, because it had freed him from the bitterness of the past. However, this liberation was not all-encompassing. To his perpetual agony, Olivia was still suffering and it seemed there was little he could do for her. Just as there had been little he could do for Rosemary Burns.

Henry's thoughts continued to drift between memories and meditation, pausing abruptly here and there to pray. Before he realized it, he'd reached home and was startled by the sound of laughter coming from an open window. Surprised and equally delighted to hear such glee emanating from his house, his mood lightened as he dismounted. He paused on the porch to look at his watch and wondered who could be keeping his sister company so late. Remembering Jane Randolph had been expected for tea, he could not believe she would still be at the house. But as he came through the door, he found Olivia and Jane comfortably ensconced in front of the fireplace chattering away.

Olivia's face was brighter and more animated than he had seen it in months. Henry caught himself smiling. He hated to barge in when his sister was obviously having such a good time, but before he could make a decision one way or the other, Olivia looked up and saw him standing by the door.

"Henry! How wonderful you could make it after all!"

Still smiling, Henry hung up his hat on the peg beside the door and strode into the room. He grasped Olivia's outstretched hand and kissed her on the temple.

"I'm afraid tea time was over long ago," he said.

"Oh?"

"It's after six o'clock," Henry pointed out.

Olivia looked up at the clock on the mantle. "Goodness. We never realized."

"So I gathered." Henry smiled down at his sister and squeezed her hand before looking at Jane. "Miss Randolph, I am so glad you were able to spend the afternoon with Olivia."

"It was a pleasure," Jane said.

"And I must apologize for my absence this afternoon but I…"

"There's no need. Olivia explained everything. I hope you were able to help Mrs. Burns. She is such a kind lady."

"She is quite remarkable," Henry agreed.

"Yes, dear, but how is she?" Olivia pressed.

Henry shook his head. "The doctor doesn't seem to have much hope and from what I observed, she seems to be in considerable pain. But even so, she hasn't let it dampen her spirits. I promised I would call again tomorrow."

"I'll remember to say a prayer for her tonight," Olivia replied.

"I think that's the best any of us can do for her now."

Jane inclined her head and cast her eyes down to her lap.

"I seem to have put a damper on everyone's high spirits," Henry observed.

"No," Olivia reassured him. "Come. Sit with us and have some tea." She reached out for the pot and realized, as she lifted it, that it was empty. "Oh!"

"Never mind," Henry replied.

"It won't take a minute to boil some more water. Jane, wouldn't you like another cup?"

"No thank you, Olivia. I really should get home. Aunt Ruth will be getting worried."

"Yes. Yes, I suppose so."

"Next time you must have tea with Aunt Ruth and me at the store," Jane told Olivia.

Olivia became quite solemn again at the suggestion of meeting Ruth. "If you like," she answered vaguely.

"You are most welcome too," Jane added, looking to Henry.

"Thank you. But in the meantime, you must let me take you home."

"I wouldn't want to trouble you. It's not far to the store."

"At least let me fetch your horse for you."

"She didn't bring one," Olivia replied. "She walked."

Henry furrowed his brow and looked at Jane who nodded to affirm what Olivia had said.

"It's such a pleasant evening," Jane pursued. "The exercise will do me good."

"No doubt," Henry replied. "But my conscience will feel much better if you let me walk with you to ensure you don't run into any trouble."

Jane opened her mouth to refuse his company and then she paused when she saw how distressed Olivia seemed to be.

"Please," Olivia said. "It's the least we can do."

Jane would have preferred to leave alone. After the scene Thomas made that afternoon and the unsettling feeling she had in Henry Kohl's presence, his company was the last she wanted to share at that moment. Yet, she couldn't think of any way to excuse herself graciously from his offer.

Jane nodded. "Thank you."

Relived that Jane had accepted Henry's escort, Olivia smiled. She hugged Jane, while Henry went to the door to retrieve his hat. Jane collected her shawl and wrapped it around her shoulders. She bid Olivia a final good bye and headed through the door.

"I'll be back as soon as I can," Henry assured his sister.

"Don't be in such a rush," Olivia teased. "Take your time. Supper can wait."

Henry offered a wry smile and then turned to follow Jane.

Olivia watched them from the porch. Once they had gone, she put her hands behind her back and then, looking up to the heavens, she crossed her fingers tightly.

"Miss Randolph."

Henry was surprised to discover he was falling behind and called out to slow Jane's feverous progress down the lane. He quickened his pace, regaining his place beside her with a few strides.

"You seem to be in a hurry," Henry continued.

Jane glanced over at him. "I'm sorry. I didn't mean to…"

"No. I find it refreshing to meet a young lady that enjoys a brisk walk."

"I'm afraid I'm not unique in that respect. Most of the women in Copper Creek work hard from sunrise to sundown and they don't have time to mosey."

"So I'm discovering. My visit with Mrs. Burns today was quite eye-opening."

"It was good you could be with her. Mrs. Burns has always held a lot of store in her faith. I'm sure it was a comfort to her to have a preacher at her sick bed."

"I hope so."

"Why should you doubt it?"

Henry shrugged and reached out to snap a leaf from a tree branch hanging low beside the path.

"Mind you, I don't have any misgivings about Mrs. Burn's sincerity."

"Then you question your own usefulness?" Jane interpreted.

For a moment, Henry was astounded at how quickly Jane had articulated his dilemma. He hadn't intended to tell her of his uncertainties and yet she had guessed his secret. He nodded.

"But why should you?" Jane went on. "I admit I don't know you very well. But apart from your propensity for startling women when they least expect it and offering advice when it isn't solicited, I think you are a credit to your vocation."

"What makes you say that?"

"Well…judging by your first sermon, it seems obvious you care about people and genuinely want to help them. That alone is key to succeeding in your chosen profession. On the other hand, you aren't afraid to speak out and correct someone when you see them *going astray*."

"I suppose you are referring to my encounter with Mr. Mason."

Jane nodded. "I thought you handled the situation quite well."

Henry reached out to rest his hand on her arm. The pressure slowed her steps and she turned to look at him.

"I was afraid you might think I was too sharp with your friend."

Jane shook her head. "On the contrary, you were quite generous with him, considering how rude he was to you. In fact, it would probably do Mr. Mason good if more people talked to him the way you did."

"I'm glad you think so. I mean…it's always reassuring to a pastor to know he has done his job. However, I wonder if you will tell me something I'd really rather know."

"What is that?"

"Your honest opinion of me…personally."

Jane blushed, embarrassed by the suddenness and directness of his request. "Why should my opinion matter more than anyone else's?"

"Because I think your good opinion is something worth having. And if I haven't earned it yet, I'd like to know."

"Reverend Kohl…I don't know what to say."

"I realize it's an awkward request and, really, I have no right asking it when I have treated you so shabbily."

"Shabbily?"

"When we first met. I wasn't exactly forthcoming about my identity and, as I recall, I acted quite improperly."

"Yes, well…I think you more than made up for that by keeping our meeting a secret from Aunt Ruth."

"I was surprised you hadn't told her about me."

"I didn't dare."

"You don't think she would have approved of encountering a strange man in the woods, just by chance?"

"Definitely not."

"Why doesn't that surprise me?"

Jane cracked a smile. It made Henry smile too.

"I am glad you and Olivia had such a pleasant time this afternoon," Henry said. "It does me good to see her so happy."

"You are very close to your sister?"

"Is that so unusual?"

"Not unusual. But rare."

"Do you have any siblings?"

"No. My cousin, Rachel and I grew up together but…we never seemed to share the kind of bond you and Olivia have. I envy you that."

"Well, don't think for a moment the credit for it goes to me. Olivia is an extraordinary woman. Everything good in our lives is due to her."

"I can believe that. She isn't like anyone I've ever known," Jane confessed. "I enjoyed spending time with her. I've been rather lonely lately since Rachel left and it was good to have the company of…a friend."

"I'm sure."

Jane lifted her eyes to meet Henry's. In the dusk, she could feel the intensity of his gaze more than she could observe it. It was then she fully recognized Henry Kohl was more than he allowed people to see. He was a mixture of shadow and light. His goodness was obvious, but so too was his pain. Something troubled him deep in his soul. It was an injury that cast a cloud over his sister as well. Jane felt both of the Kohls were wary of the world, a trait that had no doubt been learned through repeated trials. Their trust had been broken and so too had their lives, no matter how bravely they tried to hide it.

A gentle breeze tugged at Jane's hair and distracted her from her introspection.

"Perhaps we had better continue on," Jane proposed. "It's getting quite late."

"Yes," Henry agreed. "Yes. We don't want your aunt to worry."

Jane felt a pang of conscience at the disappointment in Henry's voice. It stirred some regret of her own, as she suddenly discovered a craving for Henry Kohl's company. His intellect intrigued her. His attitudes challenged her. His gentleness made her yearn to belong to his world and Olivia's. She had to admit the combination was exhilarating and unexpected.

They walked on, allowing the hum of evening to fill the silence between them. Now more at ease in Henry's company, Jane kept her pace in check. She was debating what she might say to him when a bird sang out softly in the distance.

"A whippoorwill. I haven't heard one of them in years," Henry said.

"Have you studied birds?" Jane asked.

"No. I just remember the whippoorwill because it reminds me of home."

"Olivia told me you had a ranch once."

"Yes. In Texas. It was our father's pride and joy and no two children where ever in a happier home. I still remember evenings on the ranch. I'd stay out on the porch after I'd finished my chores and listen to the whippoorwills and the tree toads." Henry paused to shrug. "My mother always told us the night music was God's lullaby to soothe his children to sleep. So, whenever I heard it, it gave me a sense God was nearby. I took especially great comfort in that after my mother died. I was still just a little tyke when it happened but…it made me feel like she was nearby too. It still does."

Jane was touched. Such a story was obviously personal and she wished there were some way she could assure him she could be trusted with this confidence. But by this time they were coming to the center of town. Henry walked with her to the store and paused out in the street as Jane stepped up on the porch.

"Thank you for bringing me home," Jane said.

"You're most welcome."

Jane nodded as he tapped the brim of his hat. He turned to go, but Jane stopped him.

"Mr. Kohl," she called. "Since you asked, it is my opinion that anyone would be fortunate to count you a friend. I hope that's how you'll consider me from now on."

Stunned by her surprising confession, Henry could only stare at her as she smiled at him and then slipped behind the door of Randolph's General Mercantile. Upstairs, the curtains to the parlor window fell against the glass as Thomas Mason turned away from the window and scowled.

"Henry? Is that you?"

Olivia set down the wooden spoon in her hand. She bunched up the front of her apron and wiped her sticky fingers in its folds. As she did, she walked around the partition that separated the kitchen from their living quarters and came in full view of the doorway just in time to see her brother hang up his hat.

"Did you and Jane have a pleasant walk?" Olivia asked.

Still a bit dazed, Henry did not answer immediately.

"Henry?"

"Yes…It's quite a pleasant evening."

Moving closer to her brother, Olivia scowled a bit. "Are you all right, dear? You seem out of sorts." She reached out to brush his tussled bangs aside.

"Do I?"

"Yes."

Troubled by the familiar gleam of anxiety in his sister's eyes, he clasped her hand. "Don't fret about me, Livy. There is nothing seriously wrong."

"Only slightly wrong," Olivia interpreted.

Henry smiled. "Today has been a humbling day, sister mine. Your little brother was faced with the realization he's not as all-knowing as he thought."

"Oh. Is that all."

"All! Why, Livy, you know for a man like me the certainty of knowing I'm always in the right is my only consolation in life."

"Henry! I won't have you saying such dreadful things about yourself."

"It's the truth."

"The truth is God is the only being that is all-knowing and you never thought anything else. What are you really brooding about?"

Henry grimaced and stepped aside to sit in his chair.

"Did something happen with Jane?" Olivia pressed.

"Stop hoping," Henry scolded.

"That's no answer Henry Kohl."

"Well, if you must know, she considers me a credit to my profession."

"And?"

"And she feels anyone would be lucky to call me a friend."

Olivia could not repress a grin. "Why, I call that very encouraging."

"You can stop scheming, my girl. Where I'm concerned, marriage is the furthest thing from Miss Randolph's mind."

"Why must you always think so meanly of yourself? You are very handsome. You're thoughtful, talented, compassionate, reliable..."

"And dead inside like all the Kohls."

Olivia turned away, hurt by her brother's scornful words. Henry stood and moved up behind his sister. He placed his hands on her shoulders. "I'm sorry, Livy. I didn't mean to release my venom on you. I just don't want you to get your hopes up over an attachment between me and Miss Randolph. I confess, I like her. But even if there were a chance we both favored each other, you know as well as I do that it would never work."

"Because of Michael," she said.

Henry bowed his head in acknowledgment, ashamed to have reminded Olivia of her personal tragedy.

"Why should what Michael Randolph did to me rob you of your happiness?"

"Olivia, what he did ripped our lives apart. God may require I forgive him for it, but I'll never forget it."

"I still don't see what that has to do with Jane."

"She's his niece, isn't she?"

"So?"

"So...Even if Jane could overlook our family feud and I could bury my reservations about trusting anyone with the name Randolph, I'm sure Michael would never give me his permission to court her."

"You're just making excuses."

"I'm being realistic. Jane Randolph and I are worlds apart."

"Stop being so proud and stubborn! Pride is a sin, Henry. Not to mention a heavy burden. I know. I've carried it all these years."

"Livy, please. Don't."

Olivia shook her head. "I see now I was selfish. We should have talked about this years ago. But I was too ashamed of myself. Too full of pride to lay my mistakes open to scrutiny. All this time, I've been struggling with my own loss, my own disillusionment and pain that I never saw how it was hurting you."

"Nonsense."

"Henry, I'm sorry."

"You have nothing to ask my forgiveness for. I'm certain I wouldn't be standing here now if it weren't for you. Your strength and courage helped me to give up a life of hate."

"I'm not that persuasive."

"It's true. Your faith in me is the only reason I made it to ordination. Our new beginning here has been the fruit of your efforts, not mine. I'm only sorry my first assignment had to be in the hometown of the man who started all our trouble."

"You had no way of knowing that when you accepted the appointment," Olivia reassured him. "And perhaps that was God's doing. Maybe it's his way of telling us it's time we both laid the past to rest once and for all."

"Perhaps. But how?"

"By loving our enemy."

"It will take a supernatural power to make me love Michael Randolph."

"Then why not start with a lesser evil so to speak."

"What do you mean?"

"Start with another Randolph."

"Jane?"

"Jane," Olivia confirmed.

Henry sighed. "How do you always manage to bend me to your purpose?"

"I don't bend you to anything, Henry. I just help you to start looking in the right direction."

Henry scoffed and Olivia offered a weak smile.

"Is dinner ready? I fear all this enlightenment has given me quite an appetite."

Chapter Nine

"This is just awful!" In disgust, Ruth crumpled the letter she was holding.

"What is it?" Jane asked from her rocking chair. "What does Uncle Michael say?"

The sunlight filling the cheery parlor was dimmed by the storm brewing on Ruth Randolph's face.

"Very little," Ruth replied bitterly. "Only that he and Rachel will be delayed another two weeks in New Orleans."

"Has Rachel picked a school?"

"He doesn't say. All he talks about are balls and parties and concerts."

"It sounds as if they are having a splendid time," Jane observed.

"Yes. At our expense! Doesn't he realize this store doesn't run itself? It will be time to take inventory soon and order in enough supplies for the winter."

"I'm sure Uncle Michael will be home in time for that."

"I'm not. That man is such a nincompoop! I'm certain he's been too busy enjoying the pleasures of George Mason's house to even think of us. And there is no doubt in my mind he hasn't once come out of his perfumed cloud of cigars and aged brandy to serve as a proper chaperone for Rachel. No doubt she's running wild with all the wrong sorts!"

"Aunt Ruth, calm yourself. I'm sure that both Uncle Michael and Rachel are just taking their time to be sure they choose the right school. If anything, their thoroughness should be a comfort to you rather than an irritation."

"It would be if I knew that was the reason for the delay. But why doesn't Michael say as much? As far as I can gather from the few letters he's written me, they haven't even looked at one school."

"Then why not write him and ask directly what progress they've made?"

Ruth considered the suggestion for a moment and felt a bit irked that she had not arrived at such a simple solution herself. "Yes, I suppose that does make sense, Jane. I'll go to my room and begin drafting a letter this minute."

Ruth gathered her skirts and steamed towards the doorway. But as the cogs of her mental processes spun, she halted, realizing she'd misplaced George Mason's address. She'd mislaid Michael's previous two missives and just now she had destroyed the envelope from his latest note in a fit of temper.

"Oh, bother."

"Aunt?"

"I no longer have the correct address to post a letter to Michael."

"I'm sure Thomas can help you."

"Indeed. Only too delighted," Thomas Mason chimed in. He had just arrived from his room down the hall and was very pleased to find his hostess was in need of him.

"What can I do for you, Mrs. Randolph?"

"I am intent on writing to my husband and I would appreciate it if you would give me the address to your father's house in New Orleans."

"Of course. In fact, I just began a letter myself. If you'd like, I can enclose your letter with my own to save you the price of postage."

"Why thank you, Thomas. That is most considerate."

"My pleasure."

"You sure you don't mind?"

"Not at all. It's been some time since I've had news of home and I was becoming rather anxious myself. Usually my father is a better correspondent."

"There seems to be an epidemic in New Orleans. Perhaps they've run out of ink," Ruth posited.

"More likely a shortage of paper," Thomas teased.

"Whatever the problem, let's hope it is remedied by the time our letters arrive so they can respond."

"Let's hope," Thomas affirmed. "And in the meantime, if anything should come for me from my father, you will let me know?"

"Of course…I wouldn't….Oh. Where is my head?" Ruth rummaged in the pocket of her apron. She felt around for the sealed bit of parchment that had arrived from George Mason. "I picked this up for you when I collected my husband's letter, but I was so distracted by his news or rather lack of news, that I completely forgot about it."

"That's all right, Mrs. Randolph."

Thomas took the letter from Ruth's hand and studied the handwriting on the envelope.

"It's from father all right."

"If you'll excuse me…," Ruth said, "I want to get my thoughts down before I forget them all." She skirted around Thomas and headed down the hall to the privacy of her bedroom.

"Do you think that's possible?" Thomas said teasingly to Jane.

She smiled as Thomas tore into his letter and began reading intently, while slowly wandering farther into the parlor. He looked up from the page to see Jane studying him.

"I'm sorry. I suppose I should have waited," he said, folding up the letter.

"No. Please finish your letter."

"It can keep," he replied, putting it away in his vest pocket. "How was your tea at the Kohl's yesterday?"

"Very nice," Jane said. "Olivia Kohl is a lovely woman."

"Yes, but it must have been a trial to endure an afternoon with that brother of hers."

"Why?"

"Parsons usually make poor conversation, preferring to preach and scold and instruct. Besides, this one strikes me as an insufferable prig."

"Just because he dared to disagree with you?"

"I take exception to that, Jane. Have you forgotten that his remarks to me were equally cutting? Don't I have a right to defend myself?"

"Not when you started the quarrel in the first place."

"It was not my intention to quarrel. I was merely being inquisitive and his reaction was overly sensitive. It makes one wonder if the *good* reverend isn't hiding something."

"That's absurd."

"On the contrary, Jane. I've encountered more than one man of the cloth whose professed calling was no more than a cover up for some crime or other disreputable episode."

"Well, I'm sure that isn't the case with Reverend Kohl. I'll grant you I suspect there was some tragedy in the Kohls past, but I hardly think…"

"Ah ha! You see. You just admitted you feel the same as I do."

Jane parted her lips to protest, but pressed them firmly together and sighed.

"It's not the same thing at all," she grumbled. "And I don't see why you are so anxious to see the worst in Reverend Kohl."

"Why are you so determined to defend him?"

Jane looked away from Thomas.

"Could it be you're allowing your feelings to blind you, Jane?"

"I don't know what you're talking about."

"Come now, I saw the way you parted from him when he walked you home last night."

"You..." Jane's temper flashed in her eyes as she shot out of her chair. "You should be ashamed of yourself for spying, Thomas Mason!"

"I was merely taking in the view."

"I didn't do anything wrong. We just said goodnight."

"And yet, I'm beginning to wonder if Rachel wasn't right about your proclivities when it comes to men."

"How dare you!"

"I dare because, behind that demur façade, you are a decided flirt. I'll admit you had me fooled at first. I was even amused by the challenge of how to overcome your virtuous objections, but not anymore. When your attentions can waffle so readily between conquests, it spoils the game."

"I ought to slap your face for making such crude remarks about me. I could even point out that if anyone's behavior should be held up to scrutiny, it's yours! Sneaking around the countryside, smirking and flirting with every woman you see, and lying to everyone's face."

"Lying!"

"Yes. I can see, now, the way you twist words, as well as people, to suit your will. In fact, I have no doubt everything Mr. Webber told me about you is the truth. You're a fraud and a cheat and everything you've said about yourself has been pure fabrication; made up for your own selfish purposes."

"I wouldn't share that opinion with anyone, Jane. Or you might be sorry."

"I'm only sorry that Uncle Michael ever invited you into this house!"

Jane glared at him and Thomas sternly met her gaze, with his arms crossed. The next moment he sighed and let his arms drop to his sides.

"What are we fighting about?" he said gently. "I don't know what got into me; why I said those things... Aw, Jane, I never meant to hurt you." He reached out to take hold of her arms, but Jane pushed his hands way.

"It's a little late for that, Thomas."

"Won't you forgive me?" he asked, bewildered.

"I think you'd better go now," Jane replied.

Thomas ground his jaw and his posture turned rigid once more.

"If that's the way you want it, Jane. But don't forget I warned you."

Without another word, he brushed past her and stormed out of the parlor, slamming the door behind him.

❖ ❖ ❖ ❖ ❖

Jane fell back against the cushions in her chair and tried to rein in her fury. As the minutes passed, she had little success and tried pacing to wear out her ire. Finally, she paused beside the window.

Down in the street, she saw many familiar faces. The customary comings and goings she observed made her wonder if Mr. Webber and she weren't wrong to keep their doubts about Thomas quiet. Her neighbors had a right to know what sort of man had been charged with shaping the future of their community. And this quarrel with Thomas had revealed the self-serving and secretive aspects to his character, of which she had not been aware previously.

She began to debate the points of reality and inference in her judgment, when she spotted Thomas coming out of the store and onto the street below. He was carrying bulging saddlebags, a rifle and a bedroll. He headed straight for his horse, stowed his gear and mounted. His face looked like a thundercloud and he roused his mare forward with almost cruel force. Disturbed by his unplanned departure, Jane hurried out of her room to find her aunt.

Ruth was still busily penning a reprimand to Michael when Jane knocked at her door and entered.

"Aunt Ruth. Did Thomas say where he was going?"

"Going, dear?"

"I just saw him ride off."

"No. I'm afraid he didn't say a word to me. Perhaps it's just another of his surveying outings."

"Yes…I suppose so."

"Jane, I've finished my letter. Would you be a lamb and take it into Thomas' room. I'm feeling rather fatigued."

Jane visibly balked at the suggestion, but Ruth pressed the letter into her hand.

"You said yourself he's gone. Just leave it on his desk. I'm sure he'll see it. Then he can enclose it with his letter, as he promised."

Unable to reply, Jane found herself bundled out into the hallway. In her present mood, visiting Thomas' room was the last thing she wanted to do. But as Ruth had reminded her, the room would be empty. This provided her a rare opportunity to get to the bottom of her quandary once and for all.

Jane hesitated outside the door to Thomas' room, still reluctant to do anything so daring as invade a man's bedroom to spy. Hadn't she just admonished Thomas for the same crime? Yet, the stinging memory of his reply served to crumble the last of her reserve. She firmly grasped the knob and pushed her way inside.

At first, the room appeared like a typical bachelor's quarters, with clothes, books and papers strewn about everywhere. Jane followed the narrow path uncluttered by debris from the door to his desk. She wondered how safe it would be to leave her aunt's letter amid the assortment of blueprints, telegrams and sketches littering the surface. Not wanting to disturb too much, she moved a few of the pages aside. Beneath them, she found a thick reference volume. She placed the book towards the back of the desk and then propped up Ruth's letter in front of it. As she drew back from the desk, she noticed the letter Thomas had just received and casually discarded on the desktop. It was lying open beside the book and, to her surprise, her name popped out at her a few lines down the page...

> *...Jane Randolph may still be the key to succeeding in our plans. Despite the news you wired regarding Henry Kohl, Michael insists on remaining in New Orleans. His cowardice is becoming more of a liability every day, which is something I shall remedy soon. He has been very foolish in coming to me now when we need him to keep the other council members distracted, while you do your work. However, the rich ore sample you sent has gone a long way in restoring his enthusiasm for our plans.*

> *Since his influence and interests in Copper Creek have fallen to Jane in his absence, it is more vital than ever you continue to have a hold over the girl so she will be willing to sway any remaining detractors to our side.*

> *I do sympathize with you in having to lavish so much attention on a plain spinster, but her situation should only make it easier for you to take advantage of her emotions. And remember son, when this is all over, you'll have more than enough compensation for your efforts.*

> *I'm relying on you to keep me informed of any*
> *new developments in Copper Creek. I will join you*
> *soon. Till then, I am*
>
> > Your Father,
> > G. P. Mason

Jane read and re-read the letter, heedless of etiquette or decorum. The more she read it, the more enraged she became. Not only was her hometown primed to fall victim to a nefarious scheme, its perpetrators intended to manipulate her into doing their dirty work.

"Well," Jane said to herself, "this *spinster* may have a few surprises in store for them."

She set George Mason's letter aside and pulled out the chair tucked under Thomas' desk. If the Masons wanted her opinion to sway the rest of the town, then she would happily oblige. Jane searched for a blank sheet of paper in one of the drawers and then seized Thomas' pen. A thick, black blob dripped from the nib onto the page. It soaked into the parchment like a raindrop into a parched bit of ground. The sight of it sent the words gushing forth....

> *Dear Editor,*
>
> > *I take my pen in hand to inform you and,*
> > *indeed, all of my fellow citizens, of a great peril.*
> > *Since our daily activities require so much of our*
> > *attention and our natures are more inclined to*
> > *welcome a stranger than to suspect him of*
> > *treachery, it is not surprising many in Copper*
> > *Creek are unaware of our present dilemma.*
> > *Namely, we have entrusted the future of our town*
> > *and our lives to a man who cannot be trusted.*
> >
> > *He is not a politician or businessman or in*
> > *fact any member of our town. He is an outsider*
> > *whose very nature makes him the architect of a*

*plan to destroy all that is good about our home.
The attitudes and practices so recently
demonstrated by this individual leave no doubt of
his unsuitability to propose, lead, or benefit from
any alterations to our town and its people. To put
it bluntly, this man is a liar and a fraud.*

*In short, I urge you all to be vigilant against
change and the false promises that accompany it.
Grow and better yourselves by all means, but not
at the urging of a man whose cardinal interest is
his welfare rather than yours.*

*Help save Copper Creek by banishing this
fiend who masquerades as a friend.*

Amazed at how quickly the page had been filled, Jane paused
to take a second sheet from the drawer to finish her letter.

*This man would savage our landscape, abuse
our resources, and bankrupt our prosperity for his
own profit. Stand with me in exposing Thomas
Mason for the charlatan he truly is and together
we can save our way of life.*

With her final line, Jane felt relieved. She blotted the page
then folded it, finally reaching for George Mason's letter to add
proof to her own. She tucked the two letters into her pocket and
hurried out of Thomas' room making her way straight for the
newspaper office.

"I just don't know what to do."

"For starters you're going to stop panicking and start listening
to me." The confidence in Louise's voice settled Rachel's nerves.

"Of course," Rachel replied. "Only it seems Mr. Thorpe's
intentions are becoming quite serious."

"And what's wrong with that?"

Rachel made a face and Louise giggled. "You are a ninny."

"I am not," Rachel asserted.

"Then don't over-think this. Honestly, Rachel! Do you want to be a child the rest of your life?"

"Simply because I am wary about a man I only met a few weeks ago, doesn't make me a child."

"Well, your flighty attitude over his invitation to dine doesn't make you a woman."

"I get the impression my father doesn't like him. I know he would never give his permission for me to go."

"Then don't ask him."

"Louise, I couldn't do that. What if he found out?"

"Should that happen, I promise you, it won't make any difference. By then it won't be your father you'll have to answer to, but your husband."

Rachel blushed. "How can you be so sure?"

"Trust me. I can tell when a man is ready to pop the question. He has the most defeated air about him."

"And Mr. Thorpe,"

"Is positively pathetic."

"I guess you've known him for a long time?"

"Since we were children."

Rachel nodded feebly.

"You might look a little more excited," Louise admonished.

"I am. I mean, I will."

"Where did he ask you to meet him?"

"Outside the flower market…in the park."

"Have you decided what to wear?"

Rachel hesitated. Then, bracing her shoulders, replied, "I still am not convinced I should go."

"Rachel. You like it here in New Orleans, don't you?"

"Yes."

"And do you have any doubts that Mr. Thorpe is respectable?"

"No.

"Do you enjoy his company?"

"Yes, of course. But…"

"And do you have any reason to ever go back to Missouri?"

"I suppose not."

"Then what's left to decide? You admit you want to stay here, that you could be happy with Richard, so what could possibly be holding you back?"

"Well, when you put it that way. I guess you're right."

"I know I am. Now, do yourself a favor and just leave the thinking to me. You go to the flower market tomorrow and I promise you, you'll be thanking me for the rest of your life."

The following afternoon, Rachel set out on foot from George Mason's house wearing a chic ensemble of Louise Richardson's choosing. A flattering shade of blue in the cape and matching hat brought out the luster of Rachel's raven hair and sun-kissed complexion. Determined to put aside her fears, Rachel made her way down the street with Louise's instructions ringing in her ears.

The afternoon was unexpectedly mild and quite lovely. Whispers of spices and herbs were carried on the gentle breeze. The cosmopolitan atmosphere of the city delighted Rachel's eye wherever she looked. She turned down the street, leaving behind the temptations of shop windows and bustling traffic, for the green glory of the park. Late summer flowers were still in bloom and the birds chirped in the trees above. Couples strolled arm in arm down the paved pathways passing nannies with their perambulators and the occasional group of rowdy children chasing a ball, a kite, or a hoop.

When Rachel arrived at the flower market, she saw no sign of Richard Thorpe. She quickly subdued an initial twinge of panic at his nonappearance and resolved to be patient. He was probably just delayed. She turned to admire the blossoms for sale in abundance in a seller's cart. Their bright cheerful faces made her smile. The colors reminded her of the marigold's Jane and she had planted in the garden out back of the store. The seeds had been a special gift for Ruth's birthday. Jane and she had planned and worked for months to build the garden for her mother in time to see the first blooms on Ruth's special day.

A hollow feeling began to tug at Rachel's heart. The memory of Jane only reminded her of her angst at their parting. So much had happened during the interim. Rachel could no longer summon the resentment she had felt towards Jane that last day in Copper Creek. Such thoughts made her wonder how Jane was and what was happening at home. She could see now she had been petty. Perhaps Louise was right, it was time she stopped acting like a child in more ways than one. She decided to write to Jane as soon as she returned to the Masons.

"Miss Rachel."

Startled from her thoughts, Rachel turned around to see Richard Thorpe striding up behind her.

"I am so glad you came," he confessed, as he reached her. "I'm sorry I kept you waiting."

"I haven't been here very long," Rachel consoled him.

"It was good of you to wait."

"I must confess I was intrigued by your invitation, if not a little confounded."

"But why? Surely you must realize how greatly I treasure your company?"

"I do now, Mr. Thorpe."

He smiled warmly and Rachel felt an overwhelming warmth rush to her extremities.

"Would you care to walk, Mr. Thorpe? It is such a pleasant day."

"I should like to. But I'm afraid there is a question on my mind, which would keep me from enjoying any such endeavor. That is until I've received an answer from you."

"Oh?" A mixture of panic and excitement stirred inside her. "What question is that?"

"Not here, please. I was hoping you would accompany me in my carriage. I have something at home I should like you to see first."

He could see the debate going on behind Rachel's eyes. Determined to sway her to his purpose he added, "I know it seems an odd request, but I promise you there is no question of impropriety. As you see, I've brought an open carriage and we won't be alone once we reach my home. My mother is currently in residence. As is all my staff."

"Well…"

"Oh, please, Miss Rachel. It would mean so much to me to have you meet my mother."

At that word, she could hear Louise saying, *when a man wants you to meet his mother that's the best indication possible he's thinking of you as marriage material.* Encouraged by Louise's advice and Richard Thorpe's devastating looks, Rachel ceased her internal struggle.

"Thank you, Mr. Thorpe. I would love to meet your mother."

Richard smiled again and reached out to take Rachel's hand. He kissed it and looked into her eyes. "Splendid," he uttered.

With that, he led her toward the carriage and as he assisted her inside, he exchanged a sinister look with his driver. Understanding his silent orders, the driver roused his team and whisked his passengers away, just as the wind began to rise heralding a coming summer storm.

Chapter Ten

George Mason had long considered himself a patient man. His position and power afforded him the luxury of patience and, on more than one occasion, his practice of that virtue had not failed to attain his ultimate goal. But in the past few weeks, he found his reserves of patience waning. Diplomacy, subtlety, and secrecy were vital, if his scheme in Copper Creek was going to succeed. However, Michael Randolph's sudden show of weakness threatened to undermine their entire operation. And if there was one thing George Mason wouldn't tolerate, it was defeat.

George leaned back in the large leather chair in his study and swallowed the last draught of brandy in his glass. The alcohol burned a searing path of clarity in his thoughts. There was no room for loyalty and honor in this last stage of the game. Thomas' latest letter was the final confirmation. It was time to make his move. He folded his son's letter and concealed it in the top drawer of his desk. As he rose and went to the side table to pour another glass of brandy, there was a knock at the door.

"Come in." George set down his glass and turned to face the door.

"You sent for me, George?"

"Sit down, Michael." George turned his attention back to refilling his glass then resumed his seat behind the desk opposite Michael.

"You seem pale, Michael. Aren't you sleeping well?"

"No...I...I'm afraid I haven't."

"That's too bad. But perhaps that's just a sign you're homesick."

The intimation in George's tone made Michael uneasy.

"A man always sleeps best in his own bed. Isn't that true?" George pursued.

"I suppose," Michael replied.

"Then I think that's exactly what you should do."

"I don't understand."

"Then let me spell it out for you, Michael. It's time you went home to Copper Creek."

Michael stood. Panic spread through him lending a sickening pallor to his features.

"No, George. We agreed it would be best for me to stay here out of Kohl's reach."

"You agreed. I didn't."

"But if he were to see me again, it might spoil everything."

"I'm afraid your spinelessness has been far more detrimental to our plans than any revenge Henry Kohl might have planned. It's time you faced him like a man."

"No man could stand up to him. You know his reputation. And after what I did to his old man...his sister. He'd kill me. I know it. What good would I be to you dead?"

George sneered. "What good are you to me alive?"

"I thought we were friends, George."

"Your misconceptions aren't my responsibility. We had an agreement Michael. You haven't held up your end and until you do we can't make any more progress. You must return to Copper Creek and sway the rest of the town council to give Thomas a free hand."

"There's no guarantee they'll listen to me."

"Then there are the necessary papers that need to be drawn up."

"Thomas could handle that."

"Not to mention the records you promised to alter so we could legally take possession of the land without a loss in profit."

"Thomas…"

"My son has already done more than enough! If you expect to walk away with your share of the take, you'll have to do something to earn it."

"I have," Michael protested. "I set everything in motion and I convinced the council to hire Thomas. I encouraged them to trust in his recommendations."

"Then you proceeded to run like a scared rabbit just when negotiations were most delicate. Thomas says everyone in town thought your sudden departure was suspicious. They are all beginning to wonder whether or not you're in your right mind. If that kind of gossip starts to stick, we're dead. No one is going to listen to a lunatic, let alone trust him with their businesses."

"What else could I have done? If I'd stayed, Henry Kohl would have exposed me as a thief and a murderer."

"Both of which would have been unfounded allegations that your friends and neighbors would have dismissed out of loyalty, if nothing else. Instead, you had to give them legitimate proof of your instability by running off."

"Don't forget you were in on that business in Texas too. Half of that money went in your pocket. Do you really think Henry Kohl is going to forget that?"

"I will deal with Mr. Kohl should the need arise. In the meantime, I think that you had better remember who is in charge."

"I do, George. You never let me forget it."

"Good. Then I won't hear any more arguments about going back to Copper Creek. Since the vein of copper has taken and unexpected route, it's more vital than ever you return."

Michael scowled. "Unexpected?"

"Thomas informs me it runs right near the center of town. We'll need you to help us take possession of all the property along the route so we can mine the copper without any interference."

"But if that's the case, you'll have to do some blasting and the buildings…"

"Will have to be demolished," George finished.

"And the people?" Michael replied. "Where do you expect them to go?"

"What difference does it make? So long as they go," he paused to smirk. "Even if they don't, it won't matter much."

"My store is on Main Street," Michael reminded him.

"So?"

"So, I can't say I'm fond of the idea of seeing it destroyed. You know how hard I worked to build that place up, what I sacrificed…"

"What *are* you complaining about? With your take from the mine, you can build ten stores anywhere you please."

"It won't be the same. Damn it, George! I sold my soul to get that store. We both know what I did to the Kohls to be able to build it and now…"

George sneered. "Stop sniveling about the past and act, like a man for once! The fact you've made so many *compromises* to get this far is exactly why you can't turn back now."

"But where does it end, George? How many more people have to suffer?"

"Enough! I have no intention of altering my plans now and neither should you. Not when we are so close."

"No, George," Michael asserted.

"No what, Michael?"

"I won't allow you to take things any farther. I can't. I owe it to my friends and neighbors."

"You were perfectly willing to over look their interests when it didn't inconvenience you."

"Then I was wrong," Michael asserted. "I've let you force me into making one bad decision after another, starting with the Kohls. But you've crossed the line now."

"Have I?" George said with deadly calm.

"Oh, I know what you could do to me and I haven't forgotten what I owe you. But I've had enough. I'm tired of ignoring my conscience to play by your rules. I won't take a suicide trip back to Copper Creek or ruin a lot of good people's lives just so you can line your pocket with more money. You can consider this an end to our partnership. I'm getting out, George. Right now!"

George closed his eyes and clenched his jaw. Slowly, he rose to his feet and walked past Michael towards the bell pull by the fireplace.

"I had hoped it wouldn't come to this," George began. He pulled the cord then crossed back to face Michael. "But I suspected you were going to be difficult."

"There is nothing you can do to me, George. I've made up my mind. Rachel and I are leaving. And we aren't going back to Copper Creek. I'm going to send for Ruth and Jane and we'll start over again somewhere else. Away from Kohl and away from you."

George smirked. "You are so fatally unimaginative, Michael. I haven't the least intention of laying a finger on you. However, you may find yourself persuaded to do as I say after all."

Michael eyed him warily.

A knock sounded against the study door and a lady entered.

"Michael, I hope you remember Miss Louise Richardson."

"Yes."

"She and Rachel have been spending a great deal of time together since your arrival. Haven't you, my dear?"

"Yes, quite a lot," Louise replied.

"Well, Louise. It seems Mr. Randolph does not wish to cooperate with me any longer. Would you be so kind as to tell him why he ought to change his mind?"

"George. What is this? What game are you playing with this girl?"

"This is no game, Michael. For if you had been kind enough to let Miss Richardson explain, you'd have learned that your daughter has been kidnapped."

Michael's eyes flew to Louise's face for confirmation.

"That is true, isn't it, my sweet?" George asked.

"Quite," Louise confirmed. "Rachel left here on foot several hours ago and was met by my fiancé."

"A wonderful chap. In a selfish, brutal sort of way," George added.

"He is holding her in a safe place until he receives word from, Mr. Mason," Louise finished.

"No…," Michael uttered. "Even you wouldn't be low enough to involve Rachel in this."

"Again you misjudge me. I am not opposed to using any means in my power to achieve my purpose."

George paused and looking to Louise asked, "Do you have it?"

She nodded and demurely extracted a locket from her reticule. She handed it to Mr. Mason who held it up and let it dangle from his fingers. Smiling, he handed it to Michael.

"It's time you learned. I always get what I want."

Michael closed his fingers around the locket and felt his heart sink in recognition. Ruth and he had given that locket to Rachel on her thirteenth birthday. The forget-me-not Rachel had pressed from her crown of flowers was still inside.

"Thank you very much, Miss Richardson," George said. "And as promised for your help." He withdrew a fat envelope from his breast pocket and handed it to Louise.

"I hope you and Mr. Thorpe will be very happy," George finished.

"I'm sure we can be now," Louise replied. "Thanks to this." She put away the money in her reticule, then offered a polite curtsy before exiting the study.

Michael sat with his head in his hands, Rachel's locket draped between his splayed fingers.

"Now, cheer up, Michael," George teased. "Your stubbornness has helped that young couple get a start in life. Their parents didn't consent to the match, you know. So there wouldn't have been any dowry for her or any inheritance for him. But now they can be wed in spite of narrow minds and it's all thanks to you."

He slapped Michael on the back and that jolted him from his depression. Michael shot up on his feet and struck George across the face.

"Bastard!" he shouted.

Surprised by Michael's sudden show of temper, George reeled a bit from the blow. Righting himself, he straightened his dinner jacket and scowled. "Now, if you're little show of temper is over, you might be interested in hearing how to get your daughter back alive."

Every nerve in Michael's body was aching to strike again, but he restrained himself and reclaimed his seat.

"Good," George said. "Now, let's talk about our trip to Copper Creek."

"Mr. Webber, I have to speak with you immediately!"

Jane's abrupt entrance into the office of the Copper Creek Gazette was hardly noticed. Under the familiar strain of a printing deadline, Curtis Webber was frantically directing his two assistants on how to set the type for the latest edition, while simultaneously editing two stories and trying to select the best letters for the advice column.

"No, Danny! Paragraph. Paragraph here damn it!"

"Mr. Webber," Jane tried again.

"Wes, get that tripe off the front page. Marcus Graves isn't getting any more free advertising!"

"Mr. Webber!"

"What! Huh? Oh, Jane. Whatever are you doing here?"

"I have to talk with you."

"Well, can it wait? As you can see, I'm rather pressed for time just now."

"I've found something that I think is very important," Jane insisted.

"Uh, huh."

"It's about Thomas Mason."

"Uh huh…this one goes on page three, Wes."

"Mr. Webber are you listening to me!"

"And be sure to leave room for the world news column."

"I have the proof you've been looking for," Jane persisted.

"Proof? What proof, Janey?"

"That Thomas Mason is a thief."

"He is? I mean, of course he is. But what's convinced you?"

"I'm ashamed to go into the particulars, so let's just say I found this letter."

Jane handed him the damming missive she had found in Thomas' room and waited while he read the contents.

All concern for his deadline vanished as Mr. Webber finished the letter. His face was animated with concern and fury.

"The filthy son of a …"

"Mr. Webber!'

"Well, there's no doubt anymore. This proves Mr. Mason and his father are involved in something fishy. The only problem is the letter doesn't explicitly say what."

"No. But still, it should be enough to justify warning our neighbors and to that end I've penned a letter to the editor that should get things rolling."

She handed him the letter she wrote and he eagerly took it from her.

Curtis shook his head. "No. No, Janey," he said finishing the letter and handing it back to her. "It's a good letter, but I can't print this."

"Why not?"

"Without proof I'd just be opening myself up to a libel suit."

"Surely Mr. Mason's letter…"

"It's not enough, Janey. It's not specific enough, like I said."

"Then why don't you write something? Don't name any names of course, but print up a big front page exposé and rouse Mr. Mason into some kind of enraged reaction to trap himself."

"No. I'd just be creating the same problem. Besides, a cool character like Mason wouldn't jump at that sort of bait." He paused a moment to consider what might be best and then he added. "But that doesn't mean we couldn't get the right kind of bait."

"How?"

"We need to stake this Mason fella out. Watch him. Follow him wherever he goes and find out what he's up to. Then we can catch him in the act so to speak."

"I'm afraid that will be difficult."

"I know. He's a slippery character."

"I didn't mean that. I meant he's left town."

"Left town! When? Where'd he go?"

"He left from the store about a half hour ago. I saw him from the window. He headed down the main road then turned west out of town."

"Confound it, Janey! Why didn't you say so earlier? C'mon!"

Mr. Webber grabbed her by the arm and forcefully led her to the door.

"Where are we going?" Jane asked, as he put on his coat and finished fastening his gun belt.

"We're going hunting," he replied. "For a rat."

"Wes, Danny," he called to the boys. "I expect you to mind things while Miss Jane and I are gone. I probably won't be back till late, so you'll have to finish putting the paper to bed."

"Alone?" Wes squeaked.

"There's nothing to it," Curtis assured him. "I've marked all the articles for placement and you both know how to set the type and run the press."

"But, Mr. Webber, we've never printed a page without so much as you okaying it first," Danny reminded him.

"Danny, I'm going to tell you something my mentor, old Gregory Kincade, once told me; *There's a first time for everything.* Now get to work! I'll expect to see the paper ready for circulation by the time I get back."

"Yes, sir," both boys replied. They returned to the frenzy of activity they had been conducting when Jane arrived and neither noticed the smile of pride beaming from Curtis Webber's face at their industriousness, as he led Jane out to the street.

"Mr. Webber," Jane said, as they walked along. "Do you really think it is a good idea to go out after Thomas alone?"

"We don't have time to wait for anyone else. He may have already made an escape. Now stop with all the questions and go get your horse, girl! We have to ride."

Uncertainty paralyzed Jane.

"What are you waiting for? Go on! Or has Mr. Mason succeeded in his efforts to rob you of your wits with his charms?"

Jane bristled at the harsh reminder of how close Thomas came to doing exactly that. It infuriated her to think how easily she had allowed him to dupe her. But fate had given her the chance to turn the tables on him now and she wasn't going to let the opportunity pass.

"I'll meet you at the edge of town," Jane replied.

"Good girl."

Curtis mounted his dapple-gray mare, turned its head, and, with the lightest touch, roused his horse into a canter. He rode until he reached the edge of town and paused to wait for Jane. Within minutes, he spotted her coming on her palomino. In an instant, both were off at a gallop for the wide prairie, which was enveloped in the amber embrace of the western sky.

"Hey, Wes," Danny said picking up a single sheet of paper from the floor. "What's this?" He handed the page to his peer.

"Looks like a letter to the editor," Wes said, scanning the first few lines, unaware the rest of Jane's missive was still lost on the floor among the discarded proofs of tomorrow's paper. "How'd it get on the floor?"

"I don't know? I just found it lying there."

"You think Mr. Webber could have dropped it on his way out?"

"Could be. What do you think we oughta do with it?"

"Dunno'. Mr. Webber didn't leave any instructions about it.

"Read it out loud," Danny said. "Then maybe we can decide."

"Dear Editor," Wes began. "*I take my pen in hand to inform you, and indeed, all of my fellow citizens of a great peril.*"

"What's that?" Danny interrupted.

"What's what?" Wes snapped.

"Great peril…what's it mean?"

"Trouble," Wes explained. "Don't you know anything?"

"I know plenty," Danny insisted. "I been to school ya know."

"Aw, shut-up about school and just let me finish reading!"

"I'm not stopping you."

Wes made a face and then went on. "This here says, *we have entrusted the future of our town and our lives to a man who cannot be trusted.*"

"Go on. Go on."

"Says this here fella i*s an outsider whose very nature makes him the architect of a plan to destroy all that is good about our home.*"

"Who? Who is this fella?"

"The letter doesn't say."

"That sure sounds serious," Danny decided.

"And important."

"Perhaps we'd better put it in the paper," Danny suggested. "We still have some room on page five."

Wes shook his head. "I think something like this oughta be on the front page."

"Won't Mr. Curtis be mad? He already marked out all the space for the front page."

"That was before he knew about this," Wes pointed out. "Besides, now that I think on it, it seems more'n likely he left this behind for us intentional like."

"How's that?"

"Don't you see, stupid? This is a test. A test of our ability to sniff out a big story."

"Go on!"

"Think about it, Danny. He left us in charge, didn't he?"

"Yeah."

"Well then, that's just what we should do…take charge! Prove we have the guts to make the tough decisions and print the hard hitting news, just like Mr. Webber."

"Wow. You really think so?"

" 'course. You wait and see, Danny. When Mr. Webber sees what we've done, he'll be so proud of us he won't have words."

"That's not likely for Mr. Webber."

Wes snorted. "That's the truth. Now take this letter and get busy. We've got a lot of rearranging to do."

Olivia awoke after a fitful night. Her dreams had taunted her, reminding her of old injuries and fears long past. The few hours of sleep she had managed to wrest from her troubled thoughts were not enough to help her escape the fear she might be succumbing to illness once again. She turned her attention to the bright morning sunshine spilling through her bedroom window. Cheered by its inherent warmth, she shoved the covers aside with some feeble hope all would be well and rose to begin her long day of chores.

As she made her way into the kitchen, she was relieved to find Henry had already gone. He had hastily scribbled a note reminding her of his visit to Mrs. Burns and asked her not to prepare any lunch for him. She worried her brother might be avoiding her because she had pressed him too hard about courting Jane. Yet, with the way she felt this morning, it was just as well she was alone. Henry always could tell when she was out of sorts and it would only add to his worries to know she was feeling depressed.

She wanted so much for Copper Creek to be the new beginning she and her brother had hoped for. At first, it seemed ghosts from the past would continue to rob them of a future. When they learned Michael and his family were settled in Copper Creek, Olivia dreaded meeting any of them. However, Jane's impromptu introduction at the stage office had sparked the hope things might not be as bad as she feared. Now, since their afternoon together, Olivia found she didn't require Christian duty or anything else to make her like Jane. She was genuinely fond of the girl for herself alone. More than that, Olivia had no doubt that Jane Randolph was a godsend. All she needed to do now was make Henry realize it too.

By the time she finished her breakfast, Olivia's spirits were much improved. Certain that Henry wouldn't take the time to eat properly if he stayed out on calls all day, she decided to make him some sandwiches. She packed them in a small basket and then prepared to go to town. She had some shopping to do anyway and hoped that once she was finished, she would be able to find her brother and convince him to eat a little something. She also hoped to call on Jane.

Her journey into Copper Creek was quite pleasant, as the gentle morning atmosphere helped to soothe her nerves. When she arrived in town, she was met by the usual hubbub of activity. There were still a good number of faces she did not recognize and to her regret even more names she had yet to memorize. But as she proceeded down the street, she greeted passersby in hopes that a show of friendliness might help to solidify relations with her new neighbors.

However, with each encounter, she noticed a decided lack of warmth. People seemed to be eyeing her with suspicion. Even though no one had been rude enough to ignore her completely, Olivia had the feeling there was something terribly wrong. She tried to shake off the notion as she prepared to enter the post office. Just outside the door, she passed a stand with the latest issue of the Copper Creek Gazette. Too distracted by her business, Olivia failed to notice a letter to the editor printed prominently on the front page entitled:

The End of Copper Creek?

Don't be deceived by the stranger in our midst

"Absolutely shocking. That's what it is."

"How can Mr. Curtis justify printing such a thing?"

"By presenting it as just what it is, my dear…an opinion."

James Winston had accompanied his wife to Randolph's General Mercantile to make certain she remembered to buy his favorite tobacco. Of late, she had been conveniently forgetting to purchase his blend and he wasn't about to go another day without his evening smoke. However, he might have been willing to make the sacrifice, if he had known he would have to endure such irrational gossip.

"I don't care what you call it, James," Ruth Randolph replied. "Obviously someone has the real facts about our new pastor and he was just trying to do his civic duty."

"But submitting a mysterious note to the gazette?" James retorted.

"I think it's a perfectly sensible thing to do," Ginny Winston said. "He might have been afraid Mr. Kohl would retaliate somehow, perhaps even violently, if his identity were known. After all, James, we do know so little about him and you have to admit his behavior has been rather odd."

"Not to mention reclusive," Ruth added. "That sort is always up to something."

"Ladies, please. You've taken up an idea and run wild with it. There is absolutely no proof Mr. Kohl is untrustworthy in any way."

"Perhaps not. But a woman can sense these things," Ginny replied.

"Then do a dull male the favor of explaining how you even came to the conclusion the letter is about Henry Kohl."

"Who else could it be?" Ruth said. "He and his sister are the only new people in town."

"So that automatically makes them criminals?"

"Not Olivia Kohl, dear," Ginny explained. "The letter only speaks of a *he*."

"Although, I'm sure she must be in it with him," Ruth observed. "She's so meek and submissive; those kinds of women are always being imposed upon by men. Not to mention how slavishly devoted she seems to be to her brother."

"Since when did modesty and loyalty become vices?" James demanded.

"You just don't understand," Ginny replied.

"Neither do you. As my wife, you have a responsibility to treat everyone in this town with the respect that is due to them. What's more, I expect you to set an example and behave like the good Christian woman you are."

"James…"

He raised his hand to stay her protest. "You will not persist in this witch hunt. Nor will you help to spread malicious gossip. Do you hear me, Ginny?"

Exasperated by her husband's scolding, in Randolph's of all places, Ginny was not inclined to give him the satisfaction of agreeing to his demands.

"Ginny!"

She tried to stare him down, but she knew her husband's temperament too well to delay submitting any longer.

"All right, James."

"Good. Now, I'll just take my tobacco, Mrs. Randolph, and be on my way."

Ruth finished tying up the bundle of tobacco she had been preparing before they started discussing the reverend and handed it to him. Just then the bell rang as another customer entered the shop. Ruth looked up and saw it was Olivia Kohl. She walked straight to the counter.

"Why, Miss Kohl!" the mayor exclaimed. "It's so nice to see you."

"Good morning, Mr. Winston," Olivia replied.

"I hope you and your brother are settling in nicely," James pursued.

"Oh, just fine."

"I'm glad to hear it. Well, you must have business to take care of so I'll leave you to your shopping."

Olivia nodded and stepped aside to make room for him to leave. Touching the brim of his hat, James thanked Ruth for the tobacco then leaned in to give his wife a peck on the cheek.

"Ginny, I'll see you at home."

Ginny knew that undertone in his voice was a reminder to treat Olivia Kohl kindly and she resented the inference she needed to be told how to behave. She smiled demurely, then watched in silence while her husband left.

"What can I do for you, Miss Kohl?" Ruth asked.

"I was hoping I might speak to Jane."

Ruth raised an eyebrow.

"I brought a few odds and ends for her quilting project," Olivia explained.

"I'm sorry, but my niece isn't here. If you'll leave them with me, I'll see she gets them when she comes home."

"Oh." Olivia set the bag down on the counter and tried not to show her disappointment.

"Was there something else?" Ruth asked.

"I need some black thread to mend my brother's shirt. I was hoping you'd have a spool that would match."

"Of course. You can help yourself from the selection over there." Ruth pointed to a display towards the back of the store.

Olivia forced a smile. "Thank you."

"Not at all."

Ginny waited until Olivia had moved off before she whispered to Ruth, "I hope you aren't thinking of allowing Jane to continue associating with the Kohls now that this letter has been published. It could ruin her reputation."

"I doubt I'll have much to say about it. Jane is peculiarly independent and willful."

"Still you must try to persuade her to avoid such unsavory company."

"Of course, I'll do what I can, but I won't be surprised if the Kohl's scandal only enhances Jane's desire to befriend them."

"You have my sympathies. Still, let us hope Jane will choose to act sensibly once she's been acquainted with the facts of the letter."

"Pardon me...what letter is this?" Ginny and Ruth turned to see Olivia standing behind them.

Ginny audibly gasped. "Oh, Miss Kohl...I never intended..."

Olivia had found the thread and had returned to the counter to inquire after the price. Her astonishment at what she overheard was her only excuse for eavesdropping.

"Please," Olivia said. "If there is a letter concerning my brother, I want to know what it says."

"Haven't you already seen the newspaper?" Ruth asked.

Olivia shook her head. Ruth exchanged a glance with Ginny and then took out her copy of the Gazette from under the counter. She handed it to Olivia, who set down the spool of thread to take the paper from her.

"The letter to the editor on the front page," Ruth explained.

Olivia began to read. By the time she was finished she was shaking.

"Who wrote such a thing?" she demanded.

"The letter is anonymous," Ginny explained.

"I can see that," Olivia replied. "But why would you think it's about my brother?"

"Everyone assumed the author was referring to your brother," Ruth answered, "since he's the only stranger to come to Copper Creek recently and...."

"And hold any influence over the town," Ginny finished.

Olivia's eyes were shining with tears. "And you would believe such lies? Without proof...without reason...."

Shame engulfed Ginny and Ruth. They could not find the courage to look at Olivia.

"Yes..." Olivia muttered. "You must...You must all believe it. That explains why everyone's been acting so...."

The newspaper fell from Olivia's hands. Lost in a trance, she turned quietly and left the store without another word.

"I'm afraid James will be very cross with me," Ginny said. "That poor girl."

"She had to find out sooner or later," Ruth replied.

"But not like that. Oh, James was right. I am horrible. Why couldn't I hold my tongue?"

"I suppose we were too harsh."

"I can't let her go like this. I'm going after her."

Stirred by regret and the need to make reparation, Ginny rushed out the door leaving Ruth alone to stew in her growing discontent. For weeks now, she had become dissatisfied with every aspect of her life; the tedious mundane tasks of minding the store; the interminable absence of her husband; the sudden way Rachel had rejected and abandoned her; the weariness and deterioration of her own body; and now this latest demonstration of the meanness of her own character.

She looked down at her careworn hands and wondered what had happened to that girl so full of dreams she used to see in the mirror. She had the crushing sensation that all her joys were over. No one had any further need of her and so her life was to be cast aside where it would wither and die in obscurity. Startled by such pitiful, self-indulgent thoughts, she straightened her spine and cast her woes down deep where they must stay. Olivia Kohl's misfortune was a tragedy, but Ruth would not allow it or her part in it to undo her. She must not. Still, she hoped that Ginny Winston would be able to set things right.

Deciding it would be best to get back to work, Ruth began to tidy up the counter and that's when her gaze fell on the parcel Olivia Kohl had left for Jane.

Jane, Ruth mused. *Where can that girl be?*

Chapter Eleven

"To tell the truth, Mr. Webber we've doubled backed so much I'm not certain where we are."

"I know. That devil has given us the slip sure enough. Let's dismount and stretch our legs a bit."

Jane nodded, grateful for the chance to rest. They led their horses over to a copse of trees and tied the reins to a low-hanging branch.

"Maybe we should think about heading back to town to stay," Jane suggested. "It was naive to think we could pick up Thomas' trail again this morning after we stopped last night."

Curtis grimaced. "Yeah, I guess so. I'm sorry, Janey."

"Don't be, Mr. Webber. It was a good idea. If we had been able to catch up with Thomas before dark yesterday, I'm sure we would have found something to incriminate him."

"Maybe. What irks me though is how a dude like him could find his way around here like a native."

"Apparently, Thomas Mason has more experience than we give him credit for. Perhaps, it's time we turned this problem over to a higher authority."

"I told you, Sheriff Simms won't lift a finger until he's got concrete proof of a crime and need I remind you we haven't found a thing?" Curtis replied.

"No, that is frustratingly obvious."

The defeat in Jane's voice touched Mr. Webber. "There now," he said encouragingly. "Don't look so downhearted. Just because we haven't been lucky so far doesn't mean our luck can't change."

Jane just sighed.

"Let's circle around and try looking a little farther south before we head back."

"I don't think it'll do any good," Jane replied, shaking her head.

"Don't be a defeatist, Janey. We can't give up yet."

"Why not? My aching backside is certainly willing."

"Well, I can't speak for you, but personally my pride and reputation as a newspaper man is on the line. Shoot, what kind of reporter would I be if I admit I can't find a slippery jasper in my own backyard?"

Curtis shivered at the proposition and it made Jane smile.

"Besides," he added, "it would be sweet revenge if you were to bring him in to the law after the way he tried to use you."

"I'm not concerned with revenge," Jane admonished him. "I just don't want him to succeed in ruining our town."

Curtis Webber gave her a skeptical look. "Rationalize all you need to, Janey. The reasons don't really matter. So long as you can hang in there. What do you say?"

Jane's first inclination was to put an end to her discomfort and head home, but the combination of her hurt pride and the imploring expression on Curtis Webber's face was enough to alter her decision.

"All right," she said. "Let's go. I guess with my stubbornness I can hold out a bit longer."

"There's the spirit."

They headed back to their horses to mount up when they heard the sound of a wagon rattling up the hill to their right.

Jane opened her mouth to speak, but Curtis held out his hand in warning. He motioned her to step back behind the cover of a nearby bush. Hidden from view, they listened as the wagon rolled closer.

"How much further is it?" One of the riders asked.

"About another four miles," his companion answered.

"Ever work for this Mason fellow before?"

"No. You?"

"Nah, but I'm beginning to wonder if it's such a good idea."

"Why? The money's plenty good."

"Don't I know it. That's the only reason I'm still here."

"It's easy enough work."

"So far. But when I hire out my gun, I like to know what I'm risking my neck for."

"Hell, I don't care what it is so long as he keeps comin' across with those fat bills."

"You said it. Where do you figure Mason gets all his dough from anyway? Gambling, extortion or inheritance?"

"Probably all three!"

Both men laughed and the sound of their sinister mirth faded away as the wagon moved further down the road. Jane and Mr. Webber waited until they were out of sight before they came out of their hiding place.

"Hurry up," Curtis said, as he raced to his horse.

"You don't mean to follow those men!" Jane cried, as she ran after him.

"You bet I do." He pulled himself up on his horse's back. "It's the only lead we've had and I'm not going to let it slip away. C'mon, Janey," he added. "We've got a wagon to catch!" Mr. Webber spurred his horse forward and was off like a shot.

Jane grumbled under her breath before scrambling up into her saddle. She turned her horse's head to follow him. Reason told her it would be better to go to town for help and, as if sensing her hesitancy, her horse circled towards town. Finally, deciding she couldn't let Curtis Webber face two gunmen alone, she righted her course and headed out after the intrepid newspaper man.

Within minutes, Jane caught sight of Mr. Webber and the wagon. She followed as closely as she dared until the wagon turned off after about three miles. Curtis had stopped to keep the gunmen from becoming suspicious. As he waited, Jane caught up to him.

"'Bout time you caught up," Curtis said.

"I'm sorry. I've never chased *after* criminals before and I wasn't in a hurry to die."

"Who said anything about dying? This is spying?"

"They are far too similar for my liking."

"Now, there's no reason to fret, Janey. Facing danger just takes practice. In time you won't even give it a second thought."

"If you say so, Mr. Webber. But I still don't like it."

Curtis patted her hand reassuringly before looking around once more. Then he said, "I think those fellas have gotten far enough ahead. We'll just ride up to the turn off and follow the wagon tracks on foot. That way it should be easier to stay undercover."

"I'm not sure that's such a good idea."

"Why not?"

"We might get caught."

"So?"

"So! Those men don't seem to have any scruples about killing."

"Janey, you worry too much. Who's going to shoot an old man and a pretty girl out for a stroll?"

"Do you honestly think anyone is going to believe that?"

Curtis shrugged. "It's always worked before."

Jane gave him a puzzled look, but before she could quiz him further, he rode ahead. Jane followed and when they reached the turn off, they dismounted and concealed their horses alongside an old fence near the road.

"Say," Curtis whispered, "wasn't this the old Garrety homestead?"

"Yes, I think you're right," Jane replied. "What would they be doing here. No one's lived on the place for years."

"Which is precisely why it makes an excellent hideout," Curtis noted. "C'mon."

"Listen," Jane said, reaching out to put a hand on Mr. Webber's arm. "I can hear riffles from the creek running nearby."

"Garrety used the water for his still," Curtis replied.

Jane scowled at him.

"Don't look at me like that. I didn't make the moonshine."

"But the fact you know about it suggests you helped consume it."

"So I took a nip on occasion. I was just being sociable. Besides, we have more pressing matters at the moment than my vices."

"You're right and I feel like such a fool."

"Don't fret about it, Janey. I know ladies are inclined to frown on drinking."

"I'm not upset about that," Jane snapped. "I mean I should have guessed Thomas might be here. That first time I showed him the creek, we passed by this place. He asked about the house and I told him it was abandoned. I never gave it a second thought. Do you think he's here?"

"I couldn't hazard a guess," Curtis replied. "Let's see if we can find out."

They crept closer to the house, keeping to the protection of the underbrush, until they reached a small clearing. They could hear voices and the sound of horses. A small campsite, consisting of a couple of tents, had been set up. The two men who'd passed them were busily loading sacks and equipment into the wagon they had been riding. More crates stood stacked outside the tent closest to Jane and Mr. Webber.

"Looks like they're packing up to leave," Curtis whispered.

Jane nodded.

"But I don't see that Mason rat anywhere."

Jane strained her eyes to scan the campsite for Thomas. Finally, she spotted him as he emerged from the far tent. A dirty looking drifter followed him out.

"The deal is final, Mr. Garrety," Thomas was saying. "You made your mark and all this property is legally mine."

"But I told ya. I didn't know what I was doing. I was drunk."

"Drunk or not, we have an agreement for which you have been handsomely paid and I expect you to honor it."

"Well, I won't. I'll go to the sheriff. I'll tell him everything! Even if he throws me in the pokey for moon shining, I'll stop you before I'll let you take Garrety land!"

"Consider what you are saying, Mr. Garrety. You are treading on dangerous ground."

"You can't threaten me. I've spilled my blood and sweat to keep this land and you got no right to tell me what to do with it."

"I'll see to it you spill the rest if you don't fall in line. Now I won't tell you again."

Thomas stalked away to join his hired hands.

"You foul, stinkin' coyote!" Garrety drew out a knife from inside his sleeve. He raised his arm to hurl the blade, but before it could reach its mark, he crumpled and fell to the ground in a cloud of dust. The echo of gunshot faded as Thomas Mason holstered his weapon and callously turned away from Garrety's corpse to resume his business.

"Barnes. Foster. What took you so long to get here?"

Barnes and Foster stood gaping at the dead man.

"I asked you a question," Thomas snapped.

"We had to wait in town on the wagon, Mr. Mason," Barnes replied.

"The wheel needed fixin'," Foster explained.

Thomas eyed them. "You mean a keg of beer needed guzzling, don't you, Mr. Foster?"

"What makes you think that," Barnes interjected.

Thomas sneered at him, then grabbed Foster by the throat. He yanked the bandanna from his neck and then pushed him to the ground.

"It's still damp. And if that's not enough, smell it, you filthy liar," Thomas demanded, tossing the soiled bit of cloth to Barnes. "I haven't paid you men a fortune to let you get sloppy now. I won't tolerate deceit or drunkenness from either of you. Do I make myself clear?"

"Yes, Mr. Mason."

"Good. Now, get the rest of that stuff in the wagon. I want to be out of here as soon as possible. And be careful with that assaying equipment. There are dangerous chemicals in some of those crates, so don't jostle them around."

"Yes, sir."

Satisfied his orders would be obeyed, Thomas headed back to the tent he had come from. When he reached Garrety's body, he nudged it with the toe of his boot. "And clean this mess up," he called over his shoulder, before going back inside the tent. Barnes and Foster set to work. As they lifted Garrety's limp corpse, Jane recoiled in horror against the support of a large tree behind her.

"Janey, I think I've seen proof enough, even for Sheriff Simms," Curtis said. "How about you?"

Unable to speak, Jane nodded her head. Mr. Webber helped her get to her feet and together they crept off, picking up speed as they distanced themselves from camp.

"God knows what he's about, Mr. Kohl. You just have to trust him."

Mrs. Burns' words kept rattling around inside Henry's head. He knew she was right. But it didn't make the application of her lesson any easier. Some part of him still couldn't supplant the resentment he felt toward God for making Copper Creek his first appointment. Didn't God think Livy and he had suffered enough? Why did he have to hurl Michael Randolph back into their path? But even more confusing, why did God permit him to have such strong feelings for Jane?

He turned his mount toward Copper Creek to pay a call on the mayor. As he rode, his mind pondered the questions. Could the things Olivia said be true? Could he really love Jane Randolph? More importantly, would she ever think of him in that way? The notion was disquieting. Not only because of what it might do to him, but how it would impact Olivia. She depended on him. Henry dreaded what would happen to her without the protection and companionship they had shared since tragedy ripped their family apart.

He could never cast Olivia out of his house or deny her the comfort of running it. Should he marry, he feared no wife would ever be willing to tolerate such an arrangement. He cringed at his own arrogance. He wasn't as self-sacrificing as that. Olivia couldn't be blamed for the fact he never married. He had never wanted to for the simple reason no woman had ever meant enough to him to create such a dramatic upheaval in his life. At least, not until now.

He couldn't deny he felt drawn to Jane. He had ever since he stumbled upon her by the creek. His fascination for her had only grown with each meeting. But to admit he loved her; to pursue a romance, would be an irrational gamble. There was too great a divide for him to cross to pursue a future with Jane Randolph.

There were too many variables; too much uncertainty. To seize a life with her would cost him his present sense of security. And that was too high a price. He had struggled for so long to put Michael Randolph behind him. He couldn't entangle himself with any Randolph ever again. No matter how strongly Olivia felt otherwise.

Satisfied he had reached the only reasonable conclusion to his dilemma, he resolved to put Jane out of his mind. However, Henry became so distracted that before he knew it, he had arrived at the Winston's door. Suddenly aware of the rumbling in his stomach, he regretted his decision to skip lunch. With any luck, his visit shouldn't take long and then he could still make it home in time to join Livy for a bite to eat. He climbed the Winston's front steps and knocked purposefully.

"Why, Mr. Kohl," James Winston pronounced upon opening his door. "What brings you here?"

"There's something important I want to discuss with you. If you aren't too busy…"

James felt a twinge of dread, expecting to hear about Henry's displeasure with the newspaper's front-page story. Nevertheless, he smiled and stepped aside to welcome the reverend.

"Please, come in," James said, congenially.

Taking off his hat, Henry crossed the threshold and followed the mayor into a neatly appointed room toward the front of the house.

"Won't you have a seat, Reverend Kohl?" the mayor offered, settling himself in a comfortable wing-back chair.

"Thank you," Henry replied. "I'm not quite sure how to begin."

"Then perhaps I can help you," James interrupted. "You need have no concern that I or anyone else with any sense will believe that nonsense printed in the Gazette this morning."

Henry furrowed his brow. "I don't understand."

"The letter to the editor. Haven't you read it?"

Henry shook his head. "Should I?"

"Yes. I mean no…I mean. I thought you had come to see me because you were upset about the gossip flying around town about you."

"Mr. Winston, I take very little interest in gossip. I came to ask you how you felt the town received my first sermon."

"I see."

"But it appears I made more of an impression than I realized, if the paper is printing wild stories about me."

"It hasn't."

"But you said…"

"What I mean is someone wrote an anonymous letter to Curtis Webber warning of some imminent peril to our town from a stranger, who has recently moved here and managed to acquire a deal of influence."

"And the good people of Copper Creek assume this villain is me since I am the newest resident to fit that mold."

"Unfortunately, yes. It seems the author did not have the courage to name the accused and so you have been singled out."

Henry fell silent. His mind was working frantically to process the disheartening news. *Who could have penned such a damning letter and why? What good would it do anyone to malign me?*

Then the answer came like a bolt of lightning. *Michael Randolph.* He was the only one who could possibly want to see Henry dismissed from his post. So he must have left town for the sole purpose of sending that letter to rouse his neighbors into expelling Henry from Copper Creek permanently.

James could see the tension building in the reverend's face as he contemplated the news. "I'm sorry," he said. "I thought you knew or I never would have brought it up."

"It's all right, Mr. Winston."

"I really don't think you have anything to worry about. As I said, the letter isn't specific and these things blow over soon enough."

"Do they? I hardly think so."

"Reverend Kohl…you aren't suggesting there is some truth to this?"

"Mr. Winston, the only truth I know is that I came to Copper Creek to minister to the people here without guile, malice, or the intention of gaining anything for myself, other than the privilege of doing God's work. After what you've told me today, it seems I have quite a bit of work to do."

Henry rose and James stood too.

"Now, if you'll excuse me," Henry said, replacing his hat.

"James! James I…." Ginny Winston burst into the room where James and Henry were standing. "Mr. Kohl, I didn't realize you were here. But perhaps it's for the best."

"Ginny, what's the matter?" her husband demanded.

"I know you're going to be terribly cross with me, James. But there is nothing you can say to me that I haven't already said to myself."

"What are you talking about?"

"Olivia Kohl."

"What about my sister," Henry interjected.

"I'm ashamed to admit it to you, but she overheard Ruth Randolph and me talking about that awful letter and she was frightfully upset."

"Ginny! How could you?" James scolded.

"I don't know. The nasty words slipped out before I realized it."

"What's happened to Olivia?" Henry pressed.

"She seemed dazed and just wandered out of the store in a sort of trance," Ginny explained. "When I realized how horrible I'd been, I ran after her to try and apologize. But I couldn't find her. She just disappeared."

Henry had heard enough. He strode past Mrs. Winston and headed straight for the door.

"There aren't words to say how awful I feel about this, Mr. Kohl," Ginny called after him. She followed him outside onto the porch and as he mounted his horse she added, "I do hope you can find her."

Henry looked over to her and said solemnly, "So do I, Mrs. Winston."

Without another word, he spurred his mare forward, desperately hoping he would find Olivia safe at home. If he didn't, he feared no power in heaven or on earth could keep him from abandoning his vocation and finally exacting his revenge on Michael Randolph.

Henry rode straight for his cabin at break-neck speed. When he reached home, he bolted off his horse and barged through the door, calling to his sister. No reply came. His pulse began to race as his eyes feverishly searched every room. He hurried out back and called for Olivia again, but she still did not answer. Determined not to give up, he went back into the house and searched her room. Nothing seemed to be missing other than the shawl she kept on the back of the door.

Genuine fear began to settle into his breast. He remembered all too well the last time Olivia had fallen into a trance and gone missing. It was nearly twenty years ago. The search lasted four days until finally, on the evening of the fifth day, they found her in a ravine. She was dehydrated, malnourished, disoriented, and lame. The doctor said if Henry had arrived a few hours later, Olivia would have died. It had been a long recovery for her. It took several months to heal her broken bones and rebuild her strength and years to put back the shattered pieces of her mind. Michael Randolph had been the cause then and Henry would be damned if he'd allow that coward's malicious actions to harm his sister again.

Not wanting to waste another second, Henry started filling a sack with some food. Then he went into his room and extracted a smooth case from the top of his bureau. He hesitated to even touch the lid, but the thought of Livy out there in agony urged him to throw the case open. Inside was his Colt .45. He took out the holster from the drawer and strapped it on. Then he loaded the pistol and slid it into its rightful place on his hip. The old sensation of power seemed to swell from his side and it made his hand ache with a familiar itch.

He had not worn his gun since the day he left for divinity school. He promised Livy that day he would never use it again. But he did not know what he might encounter during his search and he was prepared to kill, if he must, to protect Livy from either man or beast. Without a second thought, he swiftly left his bedroom and set out to find her.

Once he was outside, he grabbed a canteen and filled it at the pump. Then, stashing it with his other gear on the saddle, he rode out. With every mile, his anxiety and rage grew. He pressed on westward, hoping to find something; a sign, some tracks, or a passerby who'd seen Olivia.

The sun was beginning to climb to its zenith and the hunger he had felt on the porch at the Winston's threatened to burn a hole in his stomach. Sweat began streaming from his brow and, at one moment, he was sure some of the droplets on his face were tears. He wiped them away and pressed on.

The futility of wandering aimlessly began to nibble away at him until at last he saw two riders approaching. He hoped against hope they would have seen his sister and so he called out to them.

They continued riding closer, but showed no signs of slowing down. He called to them again.

"Please," he shouted. "I need your help."

At last, were close enough for him to discern one of the riders was an older man and the other a young woman.

"Reverend Kohl," the woman called back in answer to his plea.

Henry clenched his jaw in recognition of that voice. *Of all people*, he thought, *it has to be a Randolph!*

"What's wrong," Jane Randolph pursued, as she rode up to meet him.

Henry glared at her, so blinded by his hatred for Michael that he pushed all memory of their tenuous friendship from his thoughts. Terrified by the murderous look marring Henry Kohl's kind face, Jane asked again, "What's happened?"

"My sister has gone missing," he replied in measured tones. "Have either of you seen her pass this way?"

" 'fraid not, Reverend," Curtis said.

Henry looked at Jane, but she shook her head, dashing his feeble hope.

"How long has she been gone?" Jane inquired.

"I'm not sure. Mrs. Winston was the last one to see her and that was around nine o'clock."

"You don't think she was kidnapped?"

"No. She was upset by...No," he said, not wanting to go into details. "But I don't doubt she's in trouble."

"Look, we'd be glad to help you," Curtis interrupted. "Only, Janey and I have to get to the sheriff's office on the double."

"We came upon some gunmen a few miles back," Jane explained. "They are in collusion with Thomas Mason to perpetrate some kind of trouble for the town." Jane paused. "A man…Mr. Garrety, was killed by Thomas Mason. We're on our way to report the murder to the sheriff."

Henry's eyes grew wide at Jane's news. *What if Olivia unwittingly wandered into their path?* He closed his eyes to push that thought away. Realizing Mr. Webber was addressing him, Henry shook off his fatalistic thoughts.

"From what we overheard, they plan on skipping town and getting rid of all the evidence. So we've got to hurry if we're going to stop them."

"Yes. Well, I won't keep you," Henry replied.

"Good luck to you," Curtis added. "We'll keep our eyes peeled on the way back in."

"Thank you."

"C'mon, Janey."

"You go ahead, Mr. Webber. It doesn't take two of us to deliver the message. I'll stay here and help Reverend Kohl."

Henry appeared thunderstruck by Jane's offer.

"Have it your way," Mr. Webber replied. "I'll try to organize a search party for Miss Kohl, once I've got this hash with Mason settled."

"That won't be necessary, Mr. Webber," Henry said.

Curtis paid him no heed and galloped onward to town.

Alone with Jane now, Henry gave her a hard appraising look.

"Why did you stay?"

"Why did you tell Mr. Webber not to bring any help?"

"I have my reasons," Henry replied more sharply than he intended.

"So do I," Jane replied. "Chief among them is the fact Olivia is my friend."

"I'm sorry."

"Don't be. Olivia told me how difficult it has been for both of you since your parents died."

"Did she?"

"She also told me that you haven't been able to trust much of anyone."

"It seems my sister has been very talkative."

"I want you to know you can trust me," Jane asserted.

Struck by such a candid remark, Henry was moved by the openness and sincerity he saw in Jane's face. Those wide, sparkling eyes of hers still dazzled him. They spoke volumes about the goodness and innocence of her soul. Part of him had always yearned to hold a place of reverence and trust in the heart of such a woman and he felt himself weakening towards her gesture of friendship.

Just then his horse fidgeted. The movement was enough to shake him out of his daydream and bring him back to reality. The very idea of trusting a Randolph would be insane. His father had trusted Michael Randolph and it cost him his life. Olivia had trusted the same Randolph and it cost her well-being. Now Jane Randolph wanted his trust and, if he gave it to her, he might lose everything he held dear. He couldn't take the risk.

"I'll keep that in mind," he finally told her. He tightened his grip on the reins and nudged his pinto forward at a canter.

Undeterred, Jane followed close after him.

"Where are we going?"

"After Olivia," Henry replied.

"I know. But if we keep heading this way we'll run into those gunmen."

"We'll have to take that chance."

"Why? What makes you so certain Olivia came this way?"

"You ask a lot of questions, Miss Randolph."

"Then perhaps you could do me the courtesy of answering one of them."

"I didn't ask you to come along," Henry barked. "If you don't like this trail then follow one of your own. Or better yet, go back to town and keep that old fool from frightening Livy with an armed posse."

"As far as I can see, you're the only fool...trying to find Olivia on your own!"

Henry pulled back sharply on his reins and rounded on Jane.

"Look, I don't need any advice. I know what's best for Olivia and in the condition she's in, a lot of strange men, racing around the woods with guns, *isn't* going to help her. It will only make things worse."

"Worse? How?"

Henry clenched his teeth. "I don't have time to explain."

Jane reached out and grabbed his right arm.

"I'm not going anywhere, Henry Kohl. So if you want to get out of here, you'd better explain."

Her touch jolted him out of his tantrum and made him realize fear and hunger were making him irrational. He reined in his temper and said in a more moderate tone, "She had a nasty shock in town after she overheard some vicious gossip about me. It seems it stemmed from an article printed in this morning's paper. Based on what Mrs. Winston told me, I'm afraid the news triggered one of her spells."

"What kind of spells?"

"I don't know exactly what the doctors call it, but they're a kind of defense mechanism. Her mind shuts down to block out the stress and anxiety of a trauma."

"And this has happened to Olivia before?"

"Once."

"Well, if it only happened once, how can you be so sure it's happened again? Maybe she isn't lost at all. Maybe she just wanted to be alone."

"And maybe you are just making excuses to waste my time."

"I don't make a habit of being frivolous, Mr. Kohl. Especially, when someone I care about is in danger. I'm merely trying to point out there might be some reasonable explanation for Olivia's disappearance that would help point us in the right direction."

"I don't need to speculate on any other explanations. I know what's happened."

"How!"

"Because this is exactly how Livy reacted before. She's been wounded by the town's foolishness and she's run away to try and escape the pain. But I'm afraid she's too devastated to be out here alone."

"Then what you're suggesting is she's been traumatized so much that she isn't in her right mind?"

"Yes. She wouldn't recognize a search party as help. They would only frighten her and drive her deeper into hiding or…"

"Worse," Jane finished.

"Now do you understand?"

"Not as much as I'd like to."

"I can't tell you any more, Miss Randolph."

"Why not?"

"Because I don't think you really want to know the truth."

"I just told you. I do."

"Even if it concerns someone close to you? Someone who you depend upon?"

"I want to help Olivia," Jane insisted. "Tell me."

"You won't believe me."

"Don't presume to read my mind, Mr. Kohl. I might surprise you."

Henry smirked. "All right, then. I suppose Olivia told you some of our story…why it meant so much to us to have a fresh start here in Copper Creek."

Jane nodded. "She told me a bit, yes."

"But I don't imagine she told you the reason why we needed a fresh start."

"She said you lost your father's ranch."

"That's right. We lost it because of your uncle, Michael Randolph."

Jane's eyes widened in surprise.

"More than twenty years ago he came to our ranch and stole everything we had for his own selfish pleasure," Henry continued. "He broke every promise he made to us. But it was to Livy that he promised the most. They had barely been married a month when he went on a cattle buying trip with our father and murdered him out on the trail for the money he was carrying. Fifteen hundred dollars. That was all the savings we had. But he took it and ran. Without it, we lost the ranch and had to go live with our father's brother in Ohio. Livy was just sixteen then and pregnant with his child."

Jane looked pale and Henry worried that he had gone too far.

"Please. Don't stop," Jane uttered.

"Are you sure?"

"Please." Jane reiterated. "What happened to Olivia's baby?"

"He died, stillborn…a few weeks after we settled into our relatives' house. That was the final indignation. That last loss, compounded with all the others, caused Olivia to slip away from me. Her mind shut down and one morning when I went to her room to check on her, she was gone. We searched for her for days and when I finally found her, she was so badly hurt…"

Jane saw he couldn't bear to go on. She reached out for his hand.

"Her health was never good after that," Henry finished. "Even the journey here was too much for her. She had a bout of dizziness the night of the Winston's party. I was afraid to leave her alone, but she insisted I go without her."

"Then that's why you were late?"

"Yes. I've tried my best to take care of her all these years. But there is still one thing I haven't been able to do for Livy…"

"Take your revenge on the man who caused your family so much suffering," Jane finished.

Henry nodded. "I searched for him for years after he abandoned her. I dedicated myself to learning how to handle weapons; how to kill, so that I could make him pay. But I never caught up with him."

"Until now."

Henry bowed his head. "I'm a different man now. At least I thought I was. I convinced myself I'd put it all behind me when I pledged myself to the church."

"But you haven't?"

"I wanted to. I tried to for Olivia's sake, as much as mine. But now that he's raised his hand against us again with that cruel letter…"

"Letter?"

"This morning the Gazette printed an anonymous letter to the editor. It implied a new stranger in Copper Creek, with authority over the lives of its citizens, was a threat to the town's future. Everyone assumes the letter is about me and I'm sure Michael is the one who wrote it. Both Livy and I are a threat to his reputation. He can't afford to have us around and so he's trying to get rid of us with slander."

Jane grew tense. A sense of dread began to spread through her.

"Do you have a copy of the letter with you?"

"No. I haven't even seen it. But Livy did and that's why she's run off. She must be convinced our chances of starting over are ruined."

Jane felt terror grip her throat. Obviously, a horrible mistake had been made and she was afraid to contemplate it was her letter about Thomas, which had caused it. Just how it got into print, she couldn't guess. Even so, she realized she must not let Henry go on believing her uncle was at fault.

"Reverend Kohl," she began. "I can understand how you feel about my uncle now, but you can't blame him for writing that letter."

"I can blame him and I do."

"But you see I…"

"It is admirable of you to want to defend your uncle," Henry interrupted." I suppose it's only natural. But to persist in shielding him at the cost of your own integrity is not only futile, but wrong."

"I'm not shielding anyone. I'm trying to explain to you that I think I'm the one who wrote that letter."

"You?"

"Yes."

"Why would you do such a thing?"

"I was trying to help the town. I found what I thought was proof Thomas Mason and his father intended to use me to help them take over the town. So I decided to write a letter to the editor to expose their scheme and stop it before things could go any farther. But when I brought it to Mr. Webber he refused to publish it. I can't understand how it got into print. And I certainly don't understand why everyone assumed the letter was about you. I distinctly named the perpetrator as Thomas Mason. "

"Apparently not."

"Please you must believe me. I've told you the truth."

Henry shook his head. "I'm sure you'd say anything to defend your uncle now. But at this moment, it really doesn't matter who wrote the damn thing. All I care about it getting Livy home and I prefer to do that on my own. Now, stay out of my way."

Henry righted his horse and with one swift kick he rode away.

Jane called after him, but to no avail. Angry and confused, she turned and rode off in the opposite direction. Gradually, the horrible realization of what she had done began to sink in. Rather than avenging her hurt pride and saving the town, her scribbling had somehow managed to endanger the life of her only real friend and destroy the trust of a man she had come to respect greatly. Overcome with emotion, she crumpled over in her saddle. She covered her mouth to muffle the sobs wracking her body. Furious with herself for breaking down, Jane dismounted and wiped her eyes. She realized it probably would be best to go home, but in her present mood, she wanted to be alone. The only place she could think to go was her favorite spot by the creek. Tired of riding, she walked on, leading her horse behind her. As she walked, the warm stillness of the day closed in around her. She was spurred on by the sound of water gurgling over the rocks in the creek bed. She was very close now.

The first thing she planned to do was take a long, cool drink of water and then thoroughly wash her face and hands. A weak breeze tried to stir in the treetops as Jane emerged from the woods. The creek was clearly in sight. Its ripples winked in the bright sunshine. Comforted by the familiar sight, she began to rush forward when she noticed someone sitting on the large rock embedded along the bank. It was a woman. She turned her face at the sound of Jane's footsteps.

"Olivia?" Jane said.

Olivia Kohl smiled weakly at Jane, though it did not hide the fact her eyes were red and swollen with tears.

Chapter Twelve

Concerned by Olivia's appearance and mindful of Henry's warning, Jane cautiously moved closer to her friend.

"Olivia, are you all right?" Jane asked.

Olivia shrugged and turned away. Jane knelt down beside her on the rock and reached out to touch her arm.

"Won't you come home now?" Jane pursued. "Your brother is terribly worried."

"Is he?" Olivia replied, still unwilling to look at Jane.

"I passed him on the road a while back. He thinks you're lost and he's been out looking for you. I offered to help him search, but... he told me he preferred to find you on his own. He seemed to feel it would be better that way."

"I suppose, then, he told you about the last time I went *missing*?"

"Yes."

"Everything?"

"Enough."

"Even about my...husband?"

"Yes. He told me about you and Uncle Michael."

Olivia nodded. "I hope you'll forgive Henry. He isn't always the most tactful of men and I'm sure having news like that blurted out unexpectedly must have been distressing for you, Jane."

"It was a surprise," Jane admitted.

"I'm sorry that I didn't tell you about it myself," Olivia shrugged. "But we'd barely begun to get acquainted and sharing something like that isn't usually the best way to make a friend."

"I don't blame you for wanting to protect your privacy."

"Don't you? I can't help feeling like I've deceived you."

"Why?"

"You've been so kind, so trusting. You shared personal things about your own life with me, not realizing I was your uncle's wife."

"I suppose I should have guessed something was wrong when you were less than eager to meet Aunt Ruth."

"I can't fault her for what Michael did to me. But I can't help resenting her for taking my place. Even if she doesn't know she did."

"You should tell her," Jane ventured.

"I couldn't do that," Olivia answered. "I'm not selfish enough to destroy her life too."

"It isn't a matter of selfishness. Uncle Michael has broken the law."

"No one knows that but us and I prefer to keep it that way. Things are already bad enough with this nasty gossip about Henry. Letting people know I'm married to a bigamist would only add fuel to the fire."

"I know how anxious you are to make a new start here in Copper Creek," Jane said. "But are you really getting a fresh start if you persist in shielding Uncle Michael?"

"It's all I can do, Jane," Olivia insisted. "Henry's worked so hard to overcome his hate for Michael and make himself a new man in the church. And he's done that. But he won't be allowed to succeed, if he continues to be saddled by damming accusations like that viscous letter in the Gazette."

Jane felt a painful twinge of guilt. She wished now she had never written that letter. She knew she had to admit the truth. But, somehow, confessing to Olivia was even harder than telling Henry. Jane swallowed hard and prepared to begin some form of explanation when Olivia spoke first.

"Henry was so young when tragedy hit our family," she mused, gazing out over the peaceful stream. "It made him feel helpless. He's got it fixed in his mind that he didn't do enough to protect me and our father. When really, I think by dwelling on us, it's made it easier for him to ignore his own pain. He's kept on ignoring that pain by worrying about me."

"He loves you."

"Yes. And I love him. But tell me, Jane. How would you go about keeping a man you love from destroying himself?"

"I'm not sure there would be anything I could do except...go on loving him."

"I'm afraid that isn't enough," Olivia replied. "Not anymore. I guess I was naïve to think we'd ever get our chance, especially in Michael's town."

"Did you know Uncle Michael was here?"

Olivia nodded. "Reverend Porter told us. Before we were due to leave, he had lunch with us at our uncle's house. That's when he casually mentioned his friendship with Michael Randolph. He told us what a pillar of the community Michael was and how much he could help Henry in his work. Henry's face changed as the reverend spoke...the lightheartedness I had seen blossoming inside of him since his ordination seemed to vanish. Afterword, he dismissed my concerns about meeting Michael again after all this time. Still, I was afraid when he said he wanted to come to Copper Creek alone, ahead of me."

"You didn't think he would really pursue any kind of violence?"

"I wasn't sure and that doubt ate away at me. You see, I'm older than Michael. I've always felt I should be the one looking out for him. But I've had few opportunities with the way my health has been."

"He doesn't seem to mind."

"But I do."

"Why?"

"He was robbed of his youth because of my burdens."

"From what he told me, they weren't all yours. Both of you lost a home and a father."

"Because of my mistake. I'm the one who brought Michael into our family. I'm the one who was foolish enough to trust him because he had a handsome face and a fine way with words."

"You can't blame yourself."

"I do. I should have heeded my instincts about so many things."

"Don't torture yourself about things that are out of your control now."

"I can't help harboring regret. But not for my sake...for Henry's. I can't help feeling sorry he's never had a chance at love."

"You can't be certain of that. Besides you talk like his life was over and done with."

"He'll never be free as long as I'm around to remind him of the past."

"Olivia, what are you saying?"

"That its time Henry and I parted ways."

"You can't leave. That wouldn't solve anything."

"It would force Henry to get on with his life. To stop being so preoccupied with my happiness and well-being and start pursuing his own."

"He would never be able to accept leaving you on your own."

"That may be. But what else can I do? What woman would ever want to come into his life, let alone his house, as long as I'm there monopolizing all his attention?"

Jane paused, as she struggled to think of an answer that would appease Olivia's worries, and was stunned by the almost instant reply that came to her mind. As if by telepathy, Olivia knew Jane's response and asked, "Would you?"

"Me?" Jane said, her cheeks flushed with embarrassment.

"Yes," Olivia pursued. "Would you be able to love Henry knowing how devoted he is to me and his church?"

"I can't imagine any woman could object," Jane offered. "If she truly loved him. You and the church are part of who he is and I've always believed that when you love someone…you love all of them."

Olivia's gaze softened and she reached out to take Jane's hand.

"Henry would be very lucky to have your love," Olivia replied. "Very lucky."

Jane's face went red and she bolted to her feet. "Don't you think we should go?"

"Not until you've told me one thing."

"But Henry is looking for you."

"I don't doubt it, but he can wait. Jane, do you think you could you love my brother?"

"Olivia, this is ridiculous."

"I think it very probable that Henry is in love with you."

"He has a strange way of showing it," Jane replied, recalling how sharply he had spoken to her.

"He's inexperienced in love, much like you. But I genuinely believe you could make each other very happy."

"Olivia…"

"Jane…Please. Think about it?"

Jane was ready to dismiss the whole topic, but as she turned to look at her friend, something in Olivia's face calmed the fears swirling in her mind. Jane nodded. "I will…If you promise to stay in Copper Creek."

"That's blackmail."

"That's my offer," Jane replied.

Olivia smiled. "I'll stay."

"Good."

"Shall we find my errant brother, then, and set him straight?"

"I'm afraid that will take a lot of doing."

"I've got time," Olivia replied. "Now."

It had been over an hour since Henry left Jane back on the road to town and his disposition had not improved. Jane was right. He shouldn't have wandered on aimlessly. But he didn't know what else to do. Defeated by his own stubbornness, Henry decided to stop and rest. He took out some of the provisions he had packed and ate a late lunch. He was somewhat mellowed by the food and the cessation of his biting hunger left his mind free to wonder about Jane.

He regretted the way he'd treated her and he worried if he'd over-stepped by revealing the truth about her uncle. Olivia and he agreed before they came to Copper Creek that they weren't going to talk about the past anymore. Olivia's marriage and baby were her secrets to keep and he shouldn't have used them like weapons to frighten Jane away. He would have to tell Olivia what he had done and ask for her forgiveness. Provided he could even find her. With that reminder, he quickly put away his left over rations and mounted up. He rode on until he came to a small stream and paused to let his horse take a drink. While he waited, he looked out across the landscape.

Dotted with trees and covered in grasses, the land was wide and golden in the afternoon sun. A narrow dirt road cut a swath through the vegetation where Henry noticed a cloud of dust rising in the air. He watched it until a coach emerged around the bend. It bore none of the familiar signs of a stagecoach and it seemed too large and grand to belong to a local farmer or rancher. The powerful team pulled the coach onward until it came to a large rock formation. Then, for no apparent reason, the driver pulled back on the reins and steered the coach off the road and into the grass.

Puzzled, Henry thought there might be something wrong with the coach or the horses and he debated whether to offer his help. But no one seemed to have disembarked to inspect the conveyance. Rather, both coach and passengers seemed to be waiting for something. Nothing happened for several minutes. Henry finally nudged his horse forward to get a better look. Still shielded behind some brush, he squinted to try to see inside the coach, but he could discern very little. However, he could hear a man's voice saying,

"Damn it! I've done everything you've asked. How much longer is this going to take?"

"Don't vent your spleen at me. Must I remind you again what will happen if you fail to cooperate?"

"No, George" the first voice replied. "But can't you at least look to see if he's coming?"

There was a long pause and then the door of the coach opened. A well-dressed man in his fifties stepped down. Shielding his eyes from the sunlight, he looked up at the driver.

"Any sign of them, John?" he asked.

"Not yet, sir."

"It shouldn't be long."

The gentleman walked back to the coach and pulled open the door.

"Might as well stretch your legs while we're waiting," he said to the man inside. "But remember, Michael. No tricks or Rachel will pay."

Henry's ears perked up at the sound of that name. The next instant another man descended from the coach; a man that Henry would know anywhere. It was Michael Randolph.

He was older of course, with less hair and more stomach. He had grown a mustache and he wore an expensive suit, but none of that could disguise his trademark bearing. Sweat was beading on Michael's brow and he drew out his handkerchief to wipe it away.

Henry watched him, unable to believe that, after all this time, he was just feet away from the man he'd spent a lifetime hating. An eerie calmness fell over Henry. His thoughts became incomprehensible, as he fixed his attention on Michael.

Still hot and flustered, Michael wandered around to the back of the coach. This was Henry's chance. As Michael drew out a small flask to cool his throat, Henry raced out from his hiding place and knocked him to the ground. Dazed, Michael shook his head and gazed up into the blinding sunlight. He raised one hand to shield his eyes and, as he did, the silhouette of a man came into focus.

Panic gripped Michael's chest as he was seized by the lapels of his coat and forced back up on his feet.

"Henry," Michael babbled. "Please, don't…"

"I'm touched you even remembered my name," Henry replied.

"Of course…of course I remember."

"Then you should understand this…"

Henry pulled his fist back and hurled another punch. Michael tumbled back into the dust and Henry quickly closed in on him. But just as he reached out to strike at Michael again, his arms were pinned back by George Mason's coachman, John. Henry struggled against the coachman's restraint until Michael's traveling companion intervened to help the driver hold him back.

"I don't know who you think you are," George Mason said.

"My name is Henry Kohl."

George smirked, delighted to see the terror in Michael's bruised face.

"So you're Henry Kohl," George said.

"You know me?" Henry replied.

"In a way."

"George, please," Michael interrupted.

"So this boy is the ominous fiend that set you running to my door?"

Henry strained against the driver.

"This skinny, bible thumper," George continued.

"George, you don't understand," Michael replied.

"Evidentially not. Because I just don't see what *man* would ever be frightened…by the likes of this." He stood toe to toe with Henry and stared into his eyes. "Well, boy? Should I be scared of you?"

Henry gritted his teeth and refused to reply. George grinned and the next moment belted Henry in the gut. He doubled over in pain and the coachman let him fall to the dirt.

"You didn't have to do that," Michael protested.

"Oh, yes. I did. Because now that boy will respect me. Won't you, boy?"

Henry glared at George and Michael.

"Is that contempt I see, Reverend? George clicked his tongue. "What ever happened to *forgive thy neighbor*?"

"With you, I'm willing to make an exception," Henry replied.

"I'm glad to hear it. I never did put any store in mercy."

George snapped his fingers. "Tie him up," he told John.

The coachman nodded. He turned to lead Henry to the coach, but the action forced him to loosen his grip just enough for Henry to free one arm and reach for his gun.

Henry prepared to spin around and take aim at Michael and George, but John quickly knocked it from his hand. It tumbled down across a slight incline and stopped just inches from George Mason's feet. George bent down to pick up the weapon, as Henry was dragged back to the coach. The driver bound his hands with a piece of cord and then shoved him inside. Henry landed with a hard thud on the floor. When he looked around, he saw he was lying at the feet of a young lady. Her ankles were chained together and her eyes were large pools of sadness.

Outside, Michael pulled George aside. "What are you going to do with him?"

"Mr. Kohl is going to provide us with a little insurance, if things should get rocky."

"You can't drag him into this."

"But I haven't. Thanks to his quarrel with you, he's graciously volunteered."

"You know what I mean, George."

"I hope I mistake you, Michael. Because, if I thought for one moment that you were suddenly growing a conscience, I'd have to do something about it."

"All right, George. Just don't hurt him."

"That's quite a reversal of attitude, Michael. For a man who's been such a thorn in your side, you should be anxious to be rid of him."

"I'm not a murderer and I don't intend to start now, even with him..."

"You always were too soft, Michael. Hence, your current dilemma."

"I don't care. Just promise me you won't kill him."

Still holding Henry's gun, George held it up and said, "That depends entirely on him."

The sound of a wagon approaching drew George's attention away. He smiled as his son came into view and he stuffed Henry's gun inside his belt.

"They're here," he said. He stepped around Michael to greet Thomas as he dismounted.

"Sorry for the delay, father," Thomas said.

"Did you run into trouble?"

"Nothing serious," Thomas replied.

"Good." George slapped his son on the shoulder. "The men can take the rest of the supplies on to the cabin. You ride into town with us."

"Us?" Thomas said.

"I decided it was time Mr. Randolph came home," George explained.

Thomas looked over his father's shoulder. "I see. His wife will be ecstatic."

They walked to the coach together. "You can help John transfer the prisoners to the wagon and then the boys can take them up to the cabin," George went on. "It won't do to ride into Copper Creek with them in tow."

George swung open the door and Thomas peered inside.

A wide smile spread across his face at the delight of what he saw. Henry Kohl was bound and laying at the feet of Rachel Randolph.

"Miss Rachel," Thomas said. "How nice to see you again. Though I must say, I'm surprised at the company you're keeping."

Rachel looked away from him in disgust.

"Now is that any way to greet an old *friend*?" he teased.

Thomas leaned in to grab Rachel and pull her closer. Repulsed by his touch, Rachel struggled against him. Rankled by Thomas' disrespect and Rachel's growing panic, Henry kicked out at Thomas repelling him backwards. Henry sat up and leapt from the coach landing on top of him. Rachel leaned forward and watched from the coach as they rolled in the dirt. Thomas eventually managed to push Henry away and once they were both on their feet, Henry clasped his hands together and struck Thomas across the face. Thomas answered with two punches before Henry knocked him to the ground with a leg sweep. This time, as they struggled to right themselves, George Mason closed in behind Henry and struck him soundly with the butt of his gun. Henry collapsed. Rachel shuddered at the sight of blood oozing from the back of his head.

"Get him into that wagon," George barked. Barnes and Foster rushed over from the wagon and dragged Henry away.

With his countenance decidedly sour, George Mason stalked over to the coach where he drew out a key from his vest pocket. He grabbed Rachel roughly by the wrist and bent down to unlock her shackles. Unfettered now, he pulled her down from the coach and led her over to the wagon.

"Maybe I'd better go along with the boys after all," Thomas said. "It appears Miss Rachel is going to be a handful." He leered at Rachel and his father slapped his face.

"Haven't you had enough for one day?" George growled. "Get inside."

George waited until his son moved along before dragging Rachel the rest of the way. He shoved her at Foster and then handed Barnes the cuffs and the key.

"Keep a close eye on her," he told them. "And don't lay a hand on her unless I say."

"Sure thing," Foster replied.

"We've already had enough detours with this operation. I can't afford anymore. Now get her locked up and get moving. John. Michael. We're going."

"Father!" Rachel shouted.

"George, you promised me Rachel would stay with us," Michael protested.

"Now what good would that do me? She'll stay with Foster and Barnes until our job is done."

"That isn't what I agreed to."

"You don't get a say in this anymore, Michael. Now get in that coach before I change my mind about anything else."

"Father!" Rachel cried again, as Foster pulled her into the wagon.

"It'll be all right," Michael called to her.

Tears blinded Rachel, as Barnes stirred up the horses and the wagon jolted forward. A sense of doom pressed down on Rachel's heart until her eyes fell on Henry. His head had nestled against her leg from the movement of the wagon. Carefully, Rachel reached out to wipe the blood from the kind stranger's face; a stranger who fought so gallantly on her behalf and paid so dearly for his chivalry. *Maybe*, she thought, *there was still some hope after all.*

Jane and Olivia had tarried beside the stream just long enough to eat some of the sandwiches Olivia had packed before coming into town. Olivia had insisted, seeing that Jane was done in from going without food. The nourishment had restored Jane's strength and resilience, but not her courage to confess the truth about the newspaper article. There were several moments when she felt she should tell Olivia that she was behind the letter. But Henry's reaction had been so angry, she didn't want to risk hurting Olivia without being sure the printed missive was hers. She intended to find a newspaper as soon as she got to town and read the article for herself. If, as she suspected, her letter had somehow made it into the paper, she intended to find out how before making amends.

When they'd finished with their repast, Jane and Olivia rode back to the spot where Henry and Jane had parted, hoping he might still be in the vicinity. When they didn't see a sign of him, they continued on for a mile or so in the direction Jane assumed he had taken. Olivia called out to her brother, but he did not answer.

"I'm afraid we aren't getting anywhere," Jane said.

"He has to be somewhere," Olivia replied.

"Well, it obviously isn't here. He must have been riding harder than I imagined. Unless…"

A sudden image of poor old Mr. Garrety laying at Thomas' feet stirred Jane's memory, only this time he had Henry's face.

"What?" Olivia said. "You don't think he's run into trouble?"

"I hope not," Jane confessed. "But I'm afraid it might be a possibility."

Fear darkened Olivia's countenance.

"Mr. Webber and I came across some gunmen early this morning. They were working for Thomas Mason."

"What about them?" Olivia asked.

"They helped Thomas Mason dispose of a body."

"A body? You don't mean they…"

"Thomas Mason murdered old Mr. Garrety."

Olivia gasped. "Henry!"

"I warned your brother about them," Jane assured her. "And Mr. Webber rode into town to get the sheriff and a posse. With any luck, they caught up to Thomas and his men by now."

"And if they didn't?"

"If they didn't…there's no reason to assume the worst. Henry probably decided to ride in another direction or maybe he even went home."

Olivia shook her head. "Not without me. You don't know how obstinate he can be. He won't give up looking until he finds me. Which means, I've got to find him."

At that moment, Jane felt positively wretched. She wanted to tell Olivia how sorry she was for creating this mess with her poison pen, but she realized that neither apologies nor confessions would improve the situation.

"It's getting late," Jane said. "It might be best if we rode into town and got some help. With more of us looking, we should be able to find him faster. And at the least, we can find out if Sheriff Simms has done anything about those killers."

"Then let's get started," Olivia replied.

Chapter Thirteen

The tiny bell above the door to Randolph's General Mercantile tinkled to announce the arrival of another customer. It was nearly four o'clock and Ruth's nerves were raw. She had been hoping to close the store early, but the sound of that infernal bell dashed all her hopes. Plastering on a fake smile, she stepped out from behind the shelf she had been dusting.

"Good afternoon," she began "How can I...."

She froze, shocked at the sight before her eyes.

"Ruth," the man said.

"Michael," she uttered.

He smiled weakly.

"Oh, Michael," she said again, running towards him. "I thought you'd never come home."

She rushed into his arms. So grateful to be in her husband's embrace, she failed to notice the aura of gloom that hung about him. Unable to speak, Michael tightened his hold on her and nestled his face in her graying curls. The scent of vanilla clung to her and stirred his memories of their happy past, now so horribly doomed by his own greed and stupidity. For weeks, his conscience had been plaguing him for deceiving her about so many things. Now, as he held her, his remorse was all the more acute. She deserved so much better. How could he ever tell her their Rachel was in danger because of him? A jumbled confession came rushing forward in his mind, straining to be released. But just as the words dared to come to his lips, the bell chimed again.

"Ah," a deep voice pronounced. "This must be Ruth."

Hearing the sound, Michael stepped back from his wife. Still keeping his arm around Ruth's waist, he turned to face the interloper.

"Allow me to introduce myself," the man continued. "I'm George Mason."

He extended his hand and Ruth took it. "How nice to finally meet you," she replied.

The bell rang a third time and Thomas walked in to stand beside his father.

"You see, Mrs. Randolph," he said. "I told you not to worry about your husband."

"Yes," she replied, beaming up at Michael. "But why didn't you wire me that you were coming home?"

"I didn't know myself," Michael replied.

George glared at him and Michael hastily added, "Until the last minute."

"Besides, we thought it would be a nice surprise," George said.

"It is that, Mr. Mason." Ruth rested her hand against Michael's chest.

"Now, where is this charming niece of yours I've heard so much about?" George asked. "From the things Thomas has written me, she sounds like quite a remarkable young woman."

"I'm afraid I don't know where Jane is at the present," Ruth replied.

"My dear lady, surely you must have some idea."

"Yes," Michael replied. "She can't have gone far."

"The last time I spoke with Jane was yesterday afternoon. She came bursting into my room to find out if I knew where Mr. Mason…I mean, Thomas was going."

"Oh?" George prompted her.

"She saw me leaving?" Thomas asked.

"Apparently she noticed your departure from the upstairs window. I told her I didn't know a thing about it. Although I heard her come in late last night, I didn't see her again until I looked out my window and saw her riding away early this morning."

All three of the men seemed disturbed, but it was Michael who asked, "Where was she going?"

"I have no idea."

"And doesn't that worry you?" George Mason asked.

"Of course it worries me," she said defensively. "But I don't know what I can do about it? For as long as I've known Jane, she has often taken it into her head to go off alone, despite my continual objections."

"Perhaps we should ask Sheriff Simms to help us locate her," Michael suggested, grasping for any excuse to get to the law.

George glared at him again and interjected, "I don't think that will be necessary. If, as your wife says, she has just gone off on one of her usual outings, it would be a waste of the sheriff's time to alarm him unnecessarily. "

"Mr. Mason is right," Ruth put in. "Besides, the sheriff has more pressing matters to attend to at present."

"What's happened?" Thomas asked.

"More like what hasn't happened," Ruth replied. "It all started with that letter to the editor in today's newspaper."

"That hardly sounds serious," George replied.

"Mysterious is more like it," Ruth answered. "Someone anonymously wrote to Mr. Webber about a stranger in town who is a threat to our homes."

Suddenly finding himself keenly interested, George encouraged Ruth to go on.

"Everyone in town was speculating who this stranger could be and the consensus determined it was our new pastor, Henry Kohl."

Somewhat relieved, George scoffed. "Quite a scandal for a small town. Still you can't take newspapers to heart, Mrs. Randolph. So much sensationalism."

"Usually, I'm inclined to agree with you," Ruth said. "But apparently the gossip generated by the story was too much for Mr. Kohl's sister and she disappeared."

"His sister," Michael commented nervously.

"That does sound worrisome," George added.

Ruth should have explained that in light of the nasty things Mrs. Winston and she had said, her reaction wouldn't have surprised anyone. But Ruth didn't like to draw attention to her failings. Instead, she went on to explain that Mrs. Winston had tried to find Miss Kohl and comfort her.

"In any case," Ruth finished, "the Winstons convinced Sheriff Simms to organize a posse to search for Miss Kohl after her brother rode off in a panic. Apparently, he went out looking for her on his own."

"Have they been able to find her?" Thomas asked.

"Not as far as I know. But what makes matters worse is Curtis Webber rode into town just as the men were preparing to ride out. He was in a fine lather about something and whatever he told the sheriff was enough to divert the posse."

"You don't know what was said?" George asked.

Ruth shook her head. "All I know is most of the men in town are out riding around the countryside with Sheriff Simms."

"It seems we've arrived just in time," George said.

"Yes. Though, I'm surprised you didn't run into anyone on the road," Ruth commented.

"It is curious. But perhaps we just passed them without realizing it," George offered.

"Perhaps," Ruth replied. "I suppose it's all for the best. If you had met the sheriff, he might have stopped you and tried to press you into his posse."

"I'm sure you're right," George replied. "That would have been a shame."

"I do wish you had told me you were going to meet your father and Michael before you left," Ruth said to Thomas.

Paralyzed by fear that his dealings with Garrety had been witnessed, Thomas failed to hear Ruth. His father discreetly jabbed him in the arm to bring him back to the conversation.

"What…"

"I said I'm sorry you didn't let me in on your secret, Thomas," Ruth repeated

"What secret. I don't have any secrets…."

Distressed by his abrupt reply, Ruth furrowed her brow and clung more tightly to Michael's arm. George grimaced and struggled to maintain his composure, as he took his son in hand.

"Mrs. Randolph means she would have liked you to tell her about our surprise arrival."

"Ah… of course."

"Yes. I could have prepared a special homecoming dinner," Ruth added. " But now…"

"Just seeing you and being home again is special enough," Michael said.

"I couldn't have said it better," George added. "Now if you'll excuse us, I'm sure the two of you would enjoy your reunion much more without us hanging around. Thomas and I will just take a turn around the town and do some catching-up."

"Thank you, Mr. Mason," Ruth said.

"Think nothing of it, dear lady. You two enjoy getting reacquainted and Michael…if you should need me, remember…I won't be far."

"I'll remember, George."

"Good."

George smirked and, with one more jangle, the bell sounded his exit with Thomas.

"Your friend seems most refined," Ruth commented.

"Yes, he does."

"I hope his accompanying you means he'll be taking Thomas home soon. I don't mean to complain of course. I know how important his work is to the town council and it has been pleasant to have a visitor for awhile. But it will be so nice to have our home back to ourselves again."

The sound of Ruth's chatter made him smile. He had forgotten how dear his wife's little idiosyncrasies were. But the menace of George Mason's threats had become ever present in his mind making him more aware of such things lately. He wished he had taken the time to appreciate his life earlier. Yet, wishing only made his regret greater and this precious moment bittersweet.

"I know what you mean, Ruth," he said softly. "But it will all be over soon."

"I forbid you to panic. It won't help the situation."

"But what if Webber can identify me as the one who shot Garrety? I told you he's been giving me a hard time since I arrived. He'll only be too glad to point the finger at me."

"He won't get that chance," George Mason decreed. "The next time he shows his face, I'll take care of him personally." He pushed aside his coat and drew out the pistol he had taken off Henry Kohl. "You just point him out to me, son. And I'll remove his burdens...permanently."

Thomas smirked.

"What about Jane?"

George put the gun away. "What about her?"

"Where do you think she is?" Thomas asked.

"You'd know better than I would, son. She's supposed to be your girl."

"It's not like I haven't tried with her."

"It's possible you had more of an effect on her than you realize."

"What do you mean?"

"Maybe she's missing because she went out looking for you."

"For me? Why would she...."

George winked and the corner of Thomas' mouth curved in a wicked grin. Both men laughed and the sound of their jocularity muffled the footsteps of someone moving up behind them. It was Jane. She had left her horse with Olivia at the edge of town and walked in alone. She convinced Olivia it would be prudent to split up, when actually her motive for caution had been to investigate the newspaper without Olivia's observation.

She didn't find anyone at the sheriff's office or at the newspaper office. However, she did find a newspaper in the stand outside Mr. Webber's door. One glance at the front page proved her suspicions were right. It was her letter. Disappointed and perplexed, she decided to go home. She expected Aunt Ruth would be able to give her an idea of what had been happening in town. However, when she arrived, she never expected to find Thomas Mason standing outside the front door bold as brass.

Unaware who Thomas' companion was, Jane ducked down behind the produce bins, determined not to let them see her. She held her breath as the two men took a few steps closer to her hiding place and continued with their conversation.

"We'll put her to the test when she shows her face," George said.

"Suppose she doesn't."

"With half the town out scouring the countryside, somebody's bound to come across her."

"That means they might find Barnes and Foster too," Thomas pointed out.

"They can handle themselves. Besides, they know what to do. Why else do you think we left them with two prisoners?"

"I don't mind dispensing with that pious preacher, but you wouldn't really kill Rachel Randolph?"

George arched one brow and glared at his son. "If I have to," he said.

Shocked by his own father's mercilessness, Thomas looked away.

"A man can't afford to be squeamish, son. Not if he's going to amount to anything."

"I understand, father."

"See that you do. Now, let's get a drink at the hotel and you can tell me about the final assaying results."

Jane crouched back as tightly as she could against the wall until she was sure Thomas and his father had passed. Her mind was spinning at what she'd overheard. Apparently, Olivia's worst fear had been realized. Henry Kohl had run into Thomas and his gunmen. But even more disturbing was the suggestion that Rachel was being held captive, as well. She couldn't fathom how such a thing could happen when Rachel was supposed to be hundreds of miles away.

Jane waited a few minutes. When she was sure the street was clear, she got back on her feet. She had been prepared to go inside and ask Ruth some questions, but as she progressed toward the door she got a glimpse of her aunt and uncle through the front window. They were wrapped in each other's arms and heading back to Michael's office. The sight gave Jane pause and she decided the best thing to do would be to make her way back to

Olivia. Although she was unsure what either of them could do to save their kin, she figured the best way to start was to stick together.

Olivia couldn't help feeling anxious. Every moment Jane was delayed in town was another moment lost and she feared it might be too late for her brother. From her lookout, the streets and surrounding shops seemed unusually quiet to Olivia. It made her worry Jane would not be able to find anyone to help them search for Henry. To her dismay, she discovered her premonition had been right when Jane returned alone. By the serious look on her face, Olivia could tell Jane did not have good news.

"Jane. Are you all right? What's happened?"

"I'm afraid things are worse than we expected."

"No. Not Henry. What…."

"I don't believe he has been harmed," Jane reassured her friend. "But I did find out he's been taken prisoner."

Olivia closed her eyes and audibly took a breath.

"That isn't all. My cousin, Rachel, is being held too."

"I don't understand."

"Neither do I. Rachel should be in New Orleans, well out of this mess."

"Then why do you suspect she's a hostage?"

"When I couldn't find anyone at the sheriff's office or the newspaper, I thought I'd go home. But when I got to the store, Thomas Mason was standing just outside the door talking to another man I haven't seen before."

"He had the audacity to stand in the center of town after killing a man?"

"I overheard their conversation. From what I could gather, the other man was his father. Rachel and Uncle Michael were supposed to be staying with him. So it's quite possible Thomas' father brought Rachel back here with him."

"But why? What do they want with prisoners?"

Jane shook her head. "I don't know. I heard them mention something about test results and this morning Thomas was crating up a lot of equipment."

"What sort of equipment?"

"Mr. Webber thought it was for assaying."

"What could he hope to find around here? Surely, not gold."

"Your guess is as good as mine. As far as I know, there is nothing of value out past Pin Oak road...just hills and sky."

"Did they say anything else?"

"Only that the sheriff was out with a posse and that the two men holding Henry and Rachel wouldn't hesitate to harm them if they ran into trouble."

"What are we going to do?"

"Wait, I suppose."

"For what?"

"Till the sheriff comes back. Then I can tell him what I overheard."

"But by then it could be too late to help Henry and Rachel."

"I know, but I don't see what else we can do. We don't have any idea where the Masons are keeping them."

Olivia sighed and paused a moment to think.

"We could follow them," she suggested.

"Where? Back inside the store?" Jane shook her head.

"They'll have to join up with those gunmen sooner or later to carry out whatever it is they're plotting," Olivia pointed out.

"Yeah. But even if they do go out to some hideout, it might still be too late."

"It's the only chance we've got."

"I guess. But suppose we can follow them without being seen and we do find Henry and Rachel. Then what?"

"We help them escape."

"How?" Jane pressed. "We don't know what we'll find."

"No. We don't," Olivia agreed. "But does that mean we shouldn't try?"

Olivia seemed determined to save her brother no matter the cost. Jane still wasn't convinced spying and stealth were their best options.

"We can't be hasty about this. If we're caught, we might all be killed."

"Jane. Please. I can't just sit around and wait for Henry to die. I have to help him."

"We're going to help him," Jane assured her.

"Then you agree we should tail the Masons?"

"Only as a last resort. I have an idea...." Jane paused a moment as a plan began to take shape in her mind. "I might be able to get them to *tell* me exactly where to go."

"Jane, that's ridiculous. They'd never give themselves away like that."

"Not directly, I agree. But they'll talk and I'll be there to listen."

"You're just fooling yourself. Why, if they did tell you anything then they'd have to..." Suddenly realizing what Jane was proposing, Olivia interrupted her own argument. "Oh, Jane. No," she urged.

"If we're going to spy I think the direct approach is the best," Jane replied. "I'll be able to gather a lot more information if I go home and introduce myself to Thomas' father."

"I can't let you."

"Don't worry, Olivia. This will work. I already learned a lot by eavesdropping. I'll have plenty more opportunities in close quarters at the store."

"But that's just it, Jane. They wouldn't dare be so careless when they know someone in the house might overhear them."

"I think it's worth the risk. Besides, if I'm in the house, I'll be in a better position to keep an eye on their movements. The instant they ride out, I'll know about it. But until then, I may catch a lucky break."

Olivia folded her hands and gazed apprehensively at her friend. Touched by this show of concern, Jane reached out to clasp Olivia's hands.

"I want to do this, Olivia. I have to."

"Why? Why must you be so reckless?"

Wrenched by the pain in Olivia's eyes, Jane knew the moment had come. If things went wrong with her plan, she couldn't leave Olivia without telling her the truth.

"Because it's my fault you and Henry are in this mess. Olivia...I wrote that letter to the editor."

Olivia looked as if Jane had struck her.

"It was all a mistake," Jane went on. "I wrote the letter after discovering some troubling facts about Thomas. I planned to use my letter to help Mr. Webber expose the truth about his credibility. But without proof to substantiate my claims, Mr. Webber said he couldn't print it. I don't know how the letter made it into the paper and I never expected anyone would assume it was about your brother. I'm so sorry."

It seemed like hours to Jane before Olivia finally spoke. When she did, Olivia's expression softened.

"The foolishness of others is no fault of yours, Jane Randolph. Henry is in trouble because he is far too hard-headed for his own good and because I'm overly sentimental. I should not have run off. I should have gone home and waited for Henry. Then I could have told him everything I told you instead."

"I should have torn up that stupid letter…or better still, never written it."

"Jane," Olivia chided. "It's always easy to assign blame. But when did that ever solve anything?"

"At least you understand now why I want to do this."

"I do. And I thank you. You are a true friend. I don't believe I've ever had one before."

Jane met Olivia's gaze and she was touched. "Neither have I," Jane confessed.

For a moment, they basked in the comfort and blessing of their friendship. Then Olivia wiped a tear from her eye and said, "Are you sure you'll be all right?"

"They don't have any reason to suspect me. Mr. Webber came into town alone to warn the sheriff. If anything, I think they'd be suspicious if I didn't show up."

"What do you want me to do?"

"I think you ought to stay around town, but lie low. You can keep your ears peeled for news about the posse. I'll try to sneak out tonight to tell you what progress I've made at the house. We can meet behind Mr. Webber's newspaper office around eleven."

"Okay. What if the sheriff should come back before then?"

"Go to see him and tell him our plans. Now I'd better scoot."

"Jane."

"Yeah?"

"Be careful."

Jane smiled. "You too."

Then, without a second look, Jane hurried back into town.

Chapter Fourteen

When Jane entered, she was surprised to find the store empty. She closed the door behind her and walked forward, pausing only to drape her shawl over the counter.

"Aunt Ruth? Auth Ruth."

There was no reply. In fact, the store seemed eerily quiet. She walked back to her uncle's office and found it unoccupied. Bewildered that her aunt and uncle were gone, Jane decided to have a look in the kitchen, hoping Sarah might still be around. Again, she found no signs of life. There weren't even any pots on the stove, which was unusual for this time of day. Panic began to gnaw at her composure, as she headed upstairs. She hurried to the parlor; sure she would find someone there. But as she burst into the room, she found she was quite alone.

Sick with dread, she massaged her brow, trying to think what to do next.

"So there you are."

Startled, Jane cried out and moved away from the source of the intrusive voice. She turned and her momentary distress was replaced with an intense fear. Thomas Mason smiled at her, as he strolled into the room and moved toward her. She tried to meet his gaze and appear unaffected by his presence, so as not to betray her true feelings.

"Everyone has been wondering where you've been," Thomas added.

"Have they?"

"Yes."

Jane tried to smile and nonchalantly took a seat.

"Well?" Thomas pressed.

"Well what?"

"Aren't you going to tell me where you've been?"

"Oh. Yes. Well I was... that is....Why do you care?"

"I was merely concerned."

"Concerned?"

"Yes. Is that so hard to believe? I *do* care about you Jane."

"That wasn't the impression you left me with the last time we spoke."

"I know. I behaved like a dog. I'm sorry, Jane. It's just that I was ashamed to admit I was jealous. I never meant to quarrel with you. I hope you can forgive me."

Jane's expression reflected her disbelief. Thomas took that moment as his opportunity to sit beside her. It required all of Jane's willpower to keep from recoiling, as he took hold of her hand.

"You've come to mean more to me than anyone," Thomas went on. "You understand what I mean, Jane."

Paralyzed, Jane didn't know how to respond. Her silence emboldened him to take hold of her waist. "I love you, Jane."

"Thomas!" Jane jumped to her feet, as he leaned in to kiss her. "I don't know what to say.... except this is unexpected."

"But not unpleasant, I hope."

"No...no. Of course not," she lied.

He moved up behind her and put his arms around her. Drawing her close against his body, he lowered his face to hers.

"Where did you go, Jane?" he whispered in her ear.

Jane's mind frantically searched for a plausible explanation, all the while becoming increasingly uncomfortable with his advances, as he gently kissed her temple.

"I...I went down to the creek," she said finally. "It's a favorite spot of mine and I always go there when I need to think. I suppose I just lost track of time."

He took a firm hold on her hips and turned her around to face him.

"What were you thinking about?" he pressed.

"You." Jane confessed, pulling away from him

"Just me?"

"I was worried when you left the house after we quarreled. I feared you weren't going to come back and I didn't know what to do," she explained, dodging behind a chair to keep her distance from him. "So I went off to think things out."

Thomas laughed.

"I'm glad you're amused," Jane said.

"Not amused, my sweet. Delighted."

"Tell me," Jane went on. "Where *did* you go?"

"It was meant to be a surprise."

"I confided in you. Won't you do the same?"

"I think I can answer that question, young lady."

Framed in the doorway, Jane saw George Mason standing beside her uncle.

"My son came out to meet our coach and bring your uncle home as a surprise," George continued.

"Father, this is Jane," Thomas said.

"So I surmised."

George led the way into the parlor and took Jane's hand. He kissed it and said, "I can't tell you how pleased I am to meet you at last, Miss Randolph."

"Mr. Mason."

George stepped aside so Jane could have a clear view of Michael. As he did, he looked at his son questioningly. Jane noticed Thomas nod at his father, who seemed pleased, and it made her wonder why. She had little time to contemplate their silent exchange before greeting her uncle.

"Uncle Michael," Jane said, embracing him.

He returned her sign of affection, but was unable to speak. His entire demeanor seemed defeated. She had trouble believing the pathetic figure before her could really be guilty of all the crimes Henry Kohl had charged him with. But now that she had met George Mason, she began to get an inkling of how he might have been forced into committing them. He seemed a very domineering and menacing sort of man.

"I hope she's given you some explanation for her disappearance," George said to Thomas. "Though with a face as sweet as that, I'm sure you could forgive her anything."

"We were just talking about that when you came in, father."

"Where is Aunt Ruth?" Jane asked.

"She went out with Sarah to gather some fresh herbs for dinner," Michael said.

"Yes, she wanted to prepare a special dish for your uncle's homecoming," George added.

"I see. And how was your trip?" Jane asked.

"A bit trying, as travel is wont to be," George piped up. "But I arranged for a private coach in St. Louis to bring us to Copper Creek, which removed the burden of public transportation."

"How nice. I trust Rachel is well."

"Couldn't be better," George said.

"Did she find a school she liked?"

"No," Michael started to say.

"That is not quite," George interrupted. "She's narrowed it down to a couple and plans to make a decision soon."

"Did she come home with you?" Jane ventured.

Michael opened his mouth to speak, but George jumped in again. "She preferred to remain in New Orleans with the Richardson's. They are great friends of mine and Rachel has become quite dependant on their oldest girl, Louise."

"In a pig's eye," Michael mumbled.

"What'd you say, Uncle Michael?"

George gave Michael a hard glare. "Nothing," he corrected himself. "I was just wondering when Ruth would be back."

"No need to worry," George said. "I'm sure she'll return soon. After all, it is nearly suppertime. Speaking of which, I'm sure Miss Jane would like to run off and freshen up."

Jane opened her mouth to say she could wait until Ruth and Sarah returned, but George Mason practically threw her out of the room.

"Now you needn't worry about us," he added. "We'll be more than happy to excuse you. I'm sure we can find *some way* to while away the time."

George looked pointedly at Michael. Then he closed the door behind Jane and waited a few moments to be sure she had gone. The next instant, he rounded on Michael.

"Any more attempts to cause trouble like that and I'll take it out of her hide."

"Damn it, George! If you hurt Jane, I'll kill you."

"Empty threats do not become you, Michael. Remember, I hold your life and the lives of your entire family in the hollow of my hand and if you get out of line once more...I'll start to squeeze."

"I won't let that happen."

"I'm glad you're willing to listen to reason."

"No! I mean I've had enough. I'm not going to let you manipulate me anymore."

"It's a little late for that."

"It's not too late to see you hang. Which is exactly what'll happen as soon as I see the sheriff."

George seized the lapels on Michael's jacket. "Take one step towards the law and I'll..."

"Father!" Thomas cried, as George raised his arm. "Not here. We couldn't explain it."

George released Michael, but murder was still evident in his eyes.

"I'm surprised you place so little value on your daughter's life. Or have you forgotten that if you cross me, she'll be the first to go?"

"You wouldn't dare, George. Not even you."

"Try me."

Michael turned away in disgust.

"Keep an eye on him," George told Thomas. "I'm going out."

"Where?"

"To collect on a little *insurance*."

Fortunately, Jane's bedroom was right next to the parlor. The moment George Mason hurried her out into the hall, she quickly assumed her listening post at the wall separating the two rooms. Her ears strained to make out every word, though the angry tone of conversation going on opposite her was crystal clear. She perked up at the announcement of George Mason's departure and carefully crept to her door. She waited for the sound of his footsteps to diminish, as he descended the stairs, before she peeked out.

Jane couldn't believe her luck. She had worried neither Thomas nor his father would risk going out at least until nightfall. Now, she had a good chance of finding Rachel and Henry in time. Mindful that she couldn't let Mr. Mason get out of her sight, she carefully crept out into the hallway. The stairwell was clear and she felt a rush of exhilaration until she heard the pounding rush of footsteps from inside the parlor. She froze as the door began to open and then it came to a sudden halt.

"Don't try it," Thomas growled from inside the parlor. Jane heard a click, as Thomas pulled back the hammer on his gun.

She drew a clear breath, relieved that he hadn't been talking to her. She was still safe.

"I will shoot you, old man," Thomas added.

"Not until I've gotten the mayor and the other businessmen on the council to sign over the town," Michael replied defiantly.

"I *can* shoot you without killing you. In fact, I think I will…"

The door had remained ajar, allowing Jane to see her uncle grab the gun in Thomas' hand. The two of them staggered about the room as they struggled for control of the weapon. They crashed into the folding screen poised in the far right corner. As it fell, the force of the screen pushed them back towards the door. Thomas' arm was outstretched when the gun exploded, shattering a vase. The sound roused Jane from her trance. She rushed into the room and took hold of a heavy flowerpot. Thomas had his back to her. He finally was able to wrench Michael away and leveled his pistol at him saying, "You've had this coming for a long time."

But before he could squeeze the trigger, he felt a mighty thwack against his skull. The gun dropped harmlessly from his hand and he fell in a heap beside it on the floor.

"J…Jane," Michael gasped.

"Are you all right?"

"Yes," he replied, somewhat out of breath. Jane helped him to get to his feet.

"Hurry now," Michael said. "Get that cord from around the drapes and we'll tie him up. We haven't a moment to waste."

Jane did as she was told. Together they lifted Thomas into a chair and secured him around the torso and ankles. While Jane tightened the final knot, she looked up and saw Michael staring at Thomas' limp figure.

"What's wrong, Uncle Michael?"

"I'm just glad you were here, Jane."

"So am I."

"I suppose I owe you an explanation."

"I understand more than you think," Jane said. "Now we'd better get going if we're going to rescue Rachel."

Michael's eyes widened in disbelief.

"You know?"

"I know the Masons are dangerous men. That they've taken Rachel hostage and used you to further whatever designs they have on the town."

"How?"

"That isn't important now. But I think I should tell you, Rachel isn't the only one Mason is holding."

Michael grimaced.

"He's got Henry Kohl too."

"Yes...I know," Michael confessed. "I was there when they took him."

"You've seen him? Is he hurt? Is he all right?"

"I'm afraid I couldn't say for sure. George beat him pretty badly. He was unconscious the last time I saw him."

"No."

"Worse...it was my fault he was taken." Ashamed to admit anymore, Michael paused.

"What do you mean?"

Michael turned away from her.

"Uncle Michael. Tell me."

He looked into Jane's eyes; so wide and tender. Since his pride had already taken such a beating, he realized the only way to set things right again was to start telling the truth.

"I knew Henry Kohl a long time ago."

"In Texas."

Michael gaped at her "Yes...how did you know?"

"He and his sister Olivia told me some of the story," Jane explained.

"Olivia...? Then she is here?"

"She came with her brother when he took over at the church."

"Is she well?"

"Well enough. She's waiting for me outside of town."

"Why?"

"We made plans to follow the Masons to their hideout and rescue her brother and Rachel. Speaking of which, we'd better hurry. Mr. Mason already has too much of a head start."

"You go, Jane...I...I couldn't face her."

"You have to come. We don't know where we're going."

"I can give you directions. You'll find it."

"Uncle Michael..."

"Besides somebody has to watch him," Michael added, indicating Thomas. "And I want to be here when Ruth gets back. I have a lot of explaining to do."

"We can lock Thomas in and leave Aunt Ruth a note," Jane protested.

"No, Jane. I shouldn't leave."

"You mean you're afraid to leave."

Indignant at her persistence, he glared at her.

"You know I'm right," Jane continued. "Don't you want to fix this mess?"

"Of course I do."

"Then the only way is to face up to your mistakes like a man. You've already taken the first step by changing your mind about George Mason."

"But that's different. Olivia was...you just don't understand."

"I know you abandoned her when she was carrying your child. Just one month after your wedding."

"Did you say Olivia was pregnant?"

"Yes. I…thought you knew."

Michael shook his head.

"It was a boy," Jane added.

"Was?"

"He died at birth."

Michael suddenly felt sick.

"You can't change the past," Jane offered softly. "But you have a chance now to help Olivia and her brother. Don't let it slip by. If you could save the only family she has left, I'm sure it would go a long way in making amends…to both of them."

Michael wiped the tears from his face.

"Do you really think she'd want to see me?" he asked.

"I don't know," Jane admitted. "But there's only one way to find out."

He thought for a moment and then nodded his head.

"Here's the key. You lock up while I write that note."

Jane nodded and a few minutes later, they both hurried downstairs to try to catch up with George Mason.

Olivia had been too anxious to stay in one place for long. She knew she couldn't risk jeopardizing Jane by going into the store. However, she found herself monitoring its premises every fifteen minutes. Part of her wished the sheriff would hurry and return. But part of her knew that if he did, he would take charge of rescuing her brother. In that instance, it was quite likely a shoot-out would ensue and Henry would be one of the first victims.

Her mind kept struggling with all sorts of gloomy scenarios and potential escape plans, when she saw a well-dressed, middle-aged gentleman come out of the store. He mounted a horse waiting at the post and rode off. She guessed that she had probably just seen George Mason, but she couldn't be sure. She waited, hoping that if Mr. Mason had left, Jane would soon emerge and signal to follow him. As the minutes slipped by, the mysterious man rode further and further out of view and there was no sign of Jane. Torn, Olivia finally decided to mount her own horse and try to follow the man she'd seen. She figured she could still return in time to meet Jane at eleven, if the trail turned cold. But if that man was George Mason, then she'd know where her brother was being held.

She had just situated herself in the saddle and reached for the reins when she felt a tug on her skirt.

"Olivia."

"Jane! Thank heavens. I just saw…"

Olivia's words fell away as her eyes focused on the man standing behind Jane. His hair was graying and his face was lined, but she would never forget those beguiling blue-grey eyes.

"Michael," Olivia uttered.

"Olivia," he replied. "I'm surprised you recognize me. It's been so long."

"Twenty-two years. But you haven't changed much."

"It's kind of you to say."

"Uncle Michael knows where George Mason is keeping Henry and Rachel," Jane interjected.

"Oh?"

Olivia and Michael seemed transfixed and just stared at one another for a few moments. It was Michael who finally broke the silence.

"Yes," he said. "I've been working with George Mason." He scoffed. "It seems I *am* still the same…a blind fool."

"Apparently, you weren't the only one," she replied.

Michael felt a rush of guilt at Olivia's subtle accusation.

"Olivia…I never knew…when I left I was…"

"I don't want to hear any excuses," Olivia interrupted.

"No," Michael insisted. "I want you to know...I haven't spent a day without regretting what I did to you and Henry."

"I've had regrets too, Michael. But the one I could never understand is why you had to kill my father."

"But I didn't."

Olivia looked away.

"It's true. We were riding out to Silver Springs when he just collapsed on the trail. His heart must have given out. He died a few hours later. So help me."

"But the money..." Olivia objected. "It was all gone. What else were we to think when..."

"I know. I shouldn't have taken it. But I was young and stupid. George Mason convinced me that taking the money was going to be my big break. It was the only way I'd ever be able to start a business of my own and I knew I'd never amount to anything without it. I wanted to get away from every poor and grubby thing I'd known all my life. So I took it. I wanted to at least take your father in for a proper burial, but George pointed out there'd be a lot of questions if we rode into a town with a body."

"So you left him on the trail."

Michael looked away in shame. "It was wrong. I admit it, but I was too blinded by greed and selfishness... I guess I always was. But...Aw...what good does it do me now? All I can say is... I'm sorry, Livy."

"So was I."

An awkward silence fell between them.

"Is it all right with you if Uncle Michael rides with us?" Jane asked finally.

Olivia lifted her head and looked at Jane. "Of course." Then she turned to Michael and added, "Thank you for offering to help Henry."

"Thank you for giving me the chance," Michael replied.

Olivia inclined her head and waited as Jane and Michael turned their mounts in the right direction.

"Follow me," Michael said.

"We're right behind you," Jane replied.

Chapter Fifteen

"Easy. You've taken quite a blow."

Henry groaned and reached up to probe his throbbing head.

"I bandaged your wound as best I could. They didn't have any proper supplies, so I had to use strips from my petticoat."

Henry's eyes began to clear and focused in on a lovely, female face.

"Where are we?" Henry asked.

"Some abandoned cabin. I'm not sure exactly where. They blindfolded me the last few miles. But before they did, we were heading southwest...away from town."

Henry grunted thoughtfully. "Did I hear right back there? Are you Rachel Randolph?"

"Yes. My father is..."

"I know," Henry interrupted. "Figures."

"What?"

"Forget it. We've got to start thinking of a way out of here."

"It's impossible. There are no windows in this room and one of the guards is always just outside the door."

"And the other one?"

Rachel shrugged.

"How long have we been here?" Henry asked.

"A few hours, I guess."

"I don't like it."

"Neither do I. But I don't see as we have much choice."

"How did you get into this mess anyway?"

"I trusted a man," Rachel replied

"Ah."

"I thought he wanted to marry me. But all he wanted was money."

"Somebody paid him to kidnap you?"

She nodded. "George Mason. I just can't understand it. I thought he was my father's friend."

"That alone is no endorsement of his character."

"What have you got against my father?"

"We don't have time to run through the list of grievances."

Henry tried to get to his feet and Rachel pulled him back down.

"Who are you?"

"My name is Henry Kohl."

"Kohl? Kohl. Why does that sound familiar?"

Henry stood while Rachel was distracted trying to determine where she'd heard his name. He walked carefully around the room looking for anything that might help in an escape. But he didn't find anything of use. The room seemed completely empty except for a few battered pieces of furniture.

"Do you live in Copper Creek?" Rachel questioned.

"Huh?"

"Do you live in Copper Creek?"

"For the moment, yes," he replied distractedly.

"I don't recall ever seeing you in the store before."

"No reason why you should. I only moved here a few weeks ago."

Rachel scrunched up her face, frustrated by her forgetfulness until suddenly the mist of confusion cleared. "Henry Kohl! Now I remember. You're the new reverend Jane wrote to me about."

"I'm flattered she took the time to mention me."

"She did more than that," Rachel replied.

"Oh?"

"She said you were the most inspiring, thought-provoking speaker she had ever heard and the most exasperating man she had ever met."

Henry smiled.

"I gather by your expression, my cousin sent an accurate account?"

"It's not my place to say."

"False modesty?"

Henry shook his head. "Earnest humility. It is a virtue I have been forced to practice more than I'd like to admit of late."

"And you. How did you get involved in all this?" Rachel asked.

"It isn't important."

"No. I want to know."

Henry thought for a moment and said. "I trusted a man."

"Did he want to marry you?" Rachel teased.

His lips curved in a slight smile. "He married my sister. Before their wedding, he was already so much a part of our family that when he and Livy married, I just assumed that meant he would be around forever. I looked up to him. I truly felt he was like a brother. But then one day he was... gone."

"But your sister. Didn't she go with him?"

Henry shook his head. "Left her. After he killed our father and took all the money we had."

"That's awful."

He looked away and began to pace again.

"But who? I mean how does that relate to..."

"My presence here?" Henry finished.

Rachel nodded.

"That man was riding on the coach today," he explained. "It was the first time in over twenty years I'd seen him. But when I did...something inside of me snapped. All I could think of was how much pain he'd caused and I wanted to hurt him. So I rushed out on the road and decked him."

"George Mason?"

Henry froze and looked away. He knew this would be a golden opportunity to hurt Michael Randolph. It would be so easy to utter his name and turn Rachel against her father. What better revenge could he ask for than to poison her obvious devotion to him? Yet, he couldn't do it. The mad passion of his rage had ebbed away in the disgraceful realization of what he had done. This *was* his new beginning and he couldn't overthrow everything he had learned and come to believe. He was a man of God now and it was time to forgive.

"Yeah," he said. "George Mason."

"I never thought anyone could be so ruthless or mercenary," Rachel replied. "At least not in real life."

"Evil is very real," Henry assured her. "And it has destroyed the lives and souls of far too many people."

"I guess you would know."

"I would know....For far too long, I've been one of them."

Rachel looked at him in awe. After a moment, she smiled and said, "You know. I think Jane was right. You are a rather remarkable fellow."

"I'm glad you think so, Miss Randolph."

"Rachel," she corrected him.

"Rachel," he repeated.

"So what are we going to do now?" she asked.

"Sit tight for the moment."

"And then?"

"We'll pray, Rachel. Pray we'll think of something."

"And if we don't?"

"Then we'll have to hope one of our guards will make a mistake."

Henry sat down beside her again.

"Don't worry. We'll get out of this." His voice implied more confidence than he really felt.

Though his reassurance comforted Rachel somewhat, all Henry could think about was Olivia. She was still out there alone and in trouble. The guilt eating away at him, because of that fact, was even more excruciating than the pain in his head. If he could have just ignored his need for revenge, he could have slipped past George Mason's coach and continued looking for his sister. Now, who was left to find her? At that thought, his burden lightened a bit. *Jane.* He remembered. *She knew.* With any luck, she would find Livy. That thought alone gave him solace to settle back and wait for whatever punishment he might have to face for his folly. He offered a silent prayer of gratitude for Jane Randolph and her stubborn devotion. *Perhaps*, he thought, *it wouldn't be so hard to love a Randolph after all.*

Outside the abandoned homestead, Foster set down his rifle against the sole column left standing on the porch and plopped down beside it.

Barnes stopped the rhythmic movement of his knife against the stone in his left hand to take note of his comrade's fatigue.

"Did ya finish unloading the wagon?" he asked.

"Over an hour ago. No thanks to you," Foster replied.

"Somebody had to keep an eye on the prisoners didn't they?"

"Remind me again why it had to be you."

Barnes grinned and hurled his knife at the post. It wedged itself dead center in the decaying wood just inches from Foster's ear.

"That reason enough," Barnes said.

Foster curled his lip, as Barnes rose from his chair to extract his blade from the splintered beam.

"What you been doin' then?" Barnes questioned.

"Investagatin'. I don't know 'bout you. But I'd like to know just exactly what Mr. Mason is up to."

"What difference does it make?"

"It might make a heap of difference, if we get tangled up with the law."

"You scared?"

"I'm smart. Which is why I'm still alive."

Barnes hooted with laughter. "Seems to me it ain't too smart to go poking your nose in Mr. Mason's business. He's libel to take offense at your snoopin'."

"I ain't afraid of him."

"What's going on here!"

Foster jumped to his feet.

"Mr. Mason!"

"Just takin' a little break," Barnes explained.

George Mason narrowed his eyes in disgust. He dismounted and led his horse the rest of the way round the house. As he lashed the reins to the old hitching post, he said, "I'm not paying you two to rest. Or to get curious." He looked pointedly at Foster, as he spoke the latter.

Foster swallowed hard. "Course not, sir."

"Where are they, then?"

"The prisoners are in there," Barnes replied, gesturing toward the house. "In the back bedroom."

"Why there?"

"Strategy," Foster explained. "There's no windows fur 'em to escape out of back there."

"I see. Quite astute...."

"Shoot, Mr. Mason. Twern't nothing."

"And tell me, Foster, what's to keep them coming through the door and climbing out another window in the house!" George demanded.

"The bedroom door is locked," Barnes intervened.

"Nevertheless, one of you should be inside to keep an eye on them. Heaven knows what they've gotten up to since you left them alone in there."

Without another word, George Mason stormed through the front door and marched back to the bedroom where his prisoners were being held. He paused to listen at the door before signaling Barnes to give him the key. Once the door was unlocked, he kicked it open with one swift movement and waited at the threshold. To his amazement, there was no attack. Rachel and Henry were sitting quietly on the opposite side of the room.

"Well," George said, as he walked in, "How refreshing. Docile prisoners."

Rachel and Henry just frowned at him.

"I trust you are both comfortable," George went on.

Neither of them replied.

"No matter."

"What do you want?" Henry demanded.

"I've come to appeal to Miss Rachel for help."

Rachel scoffed.

"You can hardly expect her to be cooperative," Henry pointed out.

"I think you underestimate her generosity," George replied. "Miss Rachel…"

"I won't help you," she said flatly.

"I hoped you'd have a more sensible attitude."

"Sensible? After you kidnapped me and abused my father!"

"Ah, well you see that's why I've come. It seems your father is being quite difficult and I'm afraid I'll have to take drastic measures, if you can't reason with him."

"I'm tired of your threats, Mr. Mason."

"Then perhaps you'll find it a refreshing change of pace should I carry them out," George replied.

He looked over his shoulder at Barnes and motioned him forward. "Take her."

Rachel's eyes widened in fear as Barnes rushed toward her and grabbed her arms. She struggled against him in vain. Within seconds, he had secured his arm around her waist and put his knife to her throat.

"No." Henry protested. "There's no reason to take your vengeance out on this girl."

George glanced in Henry's direction. "I hardly think you are in a position to chide me on the evils of vengeance, Reverend. When Michael tell me you are so fatally plagued with the same flaw."

"I was wrong," Henry admitted.

"I'm sorry you think so. Often vengeance is the only thing that keeps a man alive."

"That's no life."

"I'm afraid I don't have time to debate the point with you. Barnes…"

George's henchman increased the pressure of his knife against Rachel's skin

"No. No…please," Rachel cried. "I'll do whatever you ask."

George grinned. "Very wise. Now, Rachel, I want you to write a letter for me."

She nodded.

"Actually, I will compose the letter, but it must be in your handwriting."

"Fine."

"And then of course there is just one more thing I'll need. Just to make my argument convincing...."

"What?" she asked, holding back tears.

George moved closer to Rachel and his gaze fixed on her silky, dark tresses. He reached out to stroke her hair. "Have you ever seen anything so beautiful?"

Rachel tried to jerk her head away, but Barnes held her fast. George pulled out the pins holding her hair up and it fell around her shoulders.

"It seems a shame," George went on. "But then for a fortune such as this, some sacrifices have to be made."

He paused and looked Rachel directly in the eye. "I'm just sorry you'll have to be the one to make it."

Rachel began to tremble.

"Barnes," George said. "Cut it off."

"All of it, sir?"

"All of it," he confirmed.

Rachel cried out in terror as Barnes roughly gathered her hair at the nape of the neck.

"Stop it you swine!" Henry shouted. But before he could rush to Rachel's aid, Barnes sharp blade had severed her locks. He held the hank of hair in his left hand and gave it to George.

"Now, if you'll follow me, Miss Rachel," George purred. "We have a letter to draft to your father."

Tears flowed freely down Rachel's face. Horrified, she crumbled to the ground shuddering with sobs.

"Damn you, Mason." Henry said. "Damn you to hell."

George smirked. "I look forward to seeing you there, Mr. Kohl."

He nodded to Barnes who pulled Rachel up on her feet.

"Take her out to the front room," George instructed him. "And have Foster fetch some paper and ink from my saddle bags."

Barnes complied readily, dragging Rachel out the door.

"Why are you doing this?" Henry called after him.

"Why do most men turn to crime, Mr. Kohl? Money."

Henry shook his head. "You can't honestly expect to get any ransom from Michael Randolph that's worth all this?"

"I don't. My aims are far more ambitious."

Henry appeared dumbstruck.

"I can see you are confused," George continued. "But it's really quite simple. My son, Thomas, came out here to help Michael Randolph convince the town council to launch a major renovation of the town. Now, to finance such improvements, the council needs money, right?"

"I suppose so."

"But they don't have that much money on hand, so there is only one way they can get a large enough sum. That's to borrow it."

"From you?"

"Who else?"

"But how does lending money make you rich?"

"It doesn't in and of itself. But in order to secure a loan, most of the business owners will have to put up their stores and shops as collateral. Collateral, which I will own in exchange for my financial aid. So in essence, I will own the entire town once they sign their names."

"Only if every businessman goes along with the deal."

"Oh, they will. They will. You see that was Michael's job and, now with Rachel's help, I'm going to see he carries through with it and convinces his neighbors to cooperate."

"And if they still don't come around to your way of thinking?"

"Then Mr. Barnes and his friend Foster will earn their keep."

"You mean you'd force them into selling with violence."

"It's entirely up to them, Reverend. But with the exception of one old drunk, we have yet to run into any opposition."

"You know this doesn't make sense. Why would a rich man like you go to such lengths to take the measly receipts from a small town like Copper Creek?"

"You disappoint me, Reverend. Evidently you can't see the larger picture."

"Care to enlighten me?"

"Gladly. It's like this. Copper Creek is about to live up to its name and become a boom town. Bigger than Sutter's Mill or Tombstone ever were."

"Impossible. Those towns had rich strikes of gold and silver to draw prospectors. There isn't any ore like that around Copper Creek."

"Isn't there?"

Henry furrowed his brow. "You mean…"

George nodded. "There is at least a fourteen mile shelf of copper just waiting to be harvested right underneath the main thoroughfare of Copper Creek."

"Rumors!" Henry insisted. "No one has ever been able to find any proof."

"Until now," George replied. "And it's irrefutable."

Henry gave him a skeptical look.

"I don't know if you are aware of it, Reverend," George continued. "But I lived briefly in Copper Creek some twenty years ago, before Michael was married and we went our separate ways. During that time, I discovered a pocket of rich copper ore near the creek. But back then, I didn't have the resources or knowledge to go about claiming the land and mining the copper. Before I left, I concealed my discovery and made thorough notes on its location.

With the wealth I've managed to accrue since then, combined with the recent high demand for copper and my son's expertise in geology, I finally have everything I need to capitalize on my discovery. And according to my son's assaying results the wait has been well worth it."

"And by owning the town," Henry said. "You'll be free to mine the copper and keep all the profits for yourself."

"I knew you'd catch on."

"And Copper Creek? What happens to the community…to all the people who've staked their livelihoods there?"

George shrugged. "It isn't my problem, Reverend. Truth be told, some towns have rallied to become great capitals of industry. Others just dry up with the dust."

"You've done this before," Henry realized.

"Naturally. How else could I be sure it will be so successful?"

"Then this is how you've made your fortune… Through deception and theft."

"It's a living."

"Have you no morals?"

"I can't afford them. Now, if you'll excuse me. I don't want to keep Miss Randolph waiting."

"You won't get away with this," Henry called after him.

"Mr. Kohl, apparently you don't realize, I already have."

The last dim rays of afternoon sun were fading behind the horizon when Jane, Michael and Olivia came in range of an old homestead. They dismounted a few yards from the abandoned house and prepared to journey the rest of the distance on foot.

"Isn't this the old Richmond place?" Jane asked.

Michael nodded. "The idea of launching his plot from an old miner's cabin appealed to George."

"How are we going to get in?" Olivia asked.

"I figure we can just walk through the front door," Michael replied.

"What about the guards?" Jane cautioned.

"As far as they know, I'm still one of them. There shouldn't be any problem."

"What if Mr. Mason has told them about your change of heart?" Olivia asked.

"There doesn't seem to be any sign of him," Michael said.

"Do you think we could have passed him on the road?" Olivia asked.

"It isn't likely, with the head start he had," Jane observed. "Still…"

"Look, whether he's here or not my plan is the only option," Michael insisted.

"You could be walking right into a trap," Olivia warned.

"It's a risk I'm willing to take. That's my daughter in there."

Olivia looked as if she'd been struck. "Yes," she uttered. "You couldn't be expected to abandon your only child."

Her brave resignation cut him to the quick. "I would have done the same for our child, if I'd known." Michael said.

"Who told you about our son?"

Embarrassed, Jane admitted she was the culprit. "I did," she said.

"Olivia," Michael pleaded. "I never meant…"

Olivia raised her hand. "Now isn't the time to dredge up the past."

"No. I suppose not," Michael agreed.

At that moment, they heard a woman scream from inside the cabin.

Jane felt chilled to the core. "My God," she gasped. "That sounded like…"

"Rachel," Michael finished. "I have to get in there."

"Wait," Jane cried. "What do you want Olivia and me to do?"

"Stay here and keep out of sight. If I'm not back in say…ten minutes…"

"We'll have to think of another plan," Jane finished.

Michael nodded.

"Good luck," Jane said.

Bravery was a new phenomenon to Michael Randolph. Never before had he been so bold in his thinking or his actions. Then, he had never before realized what truly mattered. To protect his family and take responsibility for a lifetime of selfish cowardice, he discovered an infinite reserve of courage.

He approached the front door and opened it without hesitation.

"Well, what the hell are you doing out here?" Foster demanded, as Michael barged in.

"I want to see my daughter," Michael demanded.

"She's a bit tied up at the moment." He smiled and started to snicker at his own bad humor.

Insulted, Michael pushed his way past the thug and, as he did, he noticed Barnes emerging from the back room with Rachel. His face grew hard as stone at the sight of his daughter. Her hair had been mutilated and her face was a picture of agony and terror. She saw him standing in the center of the room and cried out.

"Papa…papa!" She managed to wriggle out of Barnes' grip and flung herself on her father's chest.

He embraced her and fingered the severed ends of her hair. "What have you done to her?" he demanded sharply.

"That was your doing," Barnes replied. "All 'cause you wouldn't cooperate with Mr. Mason."

Rachel continued to sob uncontrollably.

"Who did this!" Michael persisted.

"I suppose you could say, I did," Barnes tossed off.

Consumed with rage, he gently set Rachel aside and lunged out at Barnes, knocking him to the ground.

"Aw hell!" Foster said.

"Father!" Rachel cried, watching helplessly as Michael scuffled with Barnes.

Foster rushed over to keep Rachel from interfering. He didn't doubt Barnes ability to handle an old man like Michael Randolph, but it didn't keep him from shuddering when he heard George Mason swearing from the other room.

"What the devil is going on out there?"

Inspired by the sound of the struggle, Henry realized this was the distraction he had been waiting for to try to escape. When George turned to storm out the door, Henry grabbed him. He spun George around and belted him in the mouth. Stunned a bit by the blow, George staggered back, but didn't fall. He collected his wits and returned the punch as fiercely as it had been delivered. Henry answered with a jab, a hit in the gut, and a miss. His last failed blow allowed George to regroup and respond with two more punches. They continued to spar, oblivious to the uproar in the front room.

Michael had gotten in more than his share of punishing blows. But with his last hit, Barnes spun onto the table, and fell to the ground as it collapsed under his weight. Panting, he wiped his mouth. "You're gonna be sorry for that old man," he rasped.

Ignoring his insults, Michael closed in again just as Barnes drew his trusty knife. Michael stopped in his tracks, missing the point of the blade by inches. He backed up as Barnes got to his feet.

"C'mon old man! Where's your fight now!"

Michael kept his eyes fixed on the knife, as Barnes bandied it from one hand to the other.

A mighty crash distracted both men, when George and Henry came tumbling into the front room.

Outside the sounds of a brawl were clear. Olivia and Jane took that as their sign to intervene. They ran up to the house and looked through the window. From what they saw, it didn't seem wise to barge inside. They stayed out on the porch, watching helplessly.

Stunned to see George and Michael locked in combat, Michael failed to realize Barnes wasn't so preoccupied.

"Father, look out!" Rachel screamed.

Roused by her warning, Michael moved just as Barnes took a swipe at him with his knife. However, his movement wasn't swift enough to avoid being struck in the shoulder.

He cried out in pain and lashed out with his good arm. Barnes took hold and together, they spun into George and Henry's path. Michael gathered all the strength he had left and hurled Barnes away. The force sent him tumbling over some empty crates and he fell, landing on his own knife. After that, he didn't get up.

At the same moment, George broke free from Henry's grasp and braced himself against the wall.

"All right," he gasped. "That's enough." He pulled a small derringer from his vest pocket and took dead aim at Henry.

"I've had enough meddling fools!"

Michael could see that George was ready to squeeze the trigger.

"No!" he yelled. He pushed Henry out of the way just as the pistol fired. Instantly, his face went pale and the light went out of his eyes as they closed for the last time. Rachel screamed as her father fell to the floor.

"The damn fool!" George sneered.

Unapologetic, George tossed aside his empty weapon and reached down to pick up Barnes knife.

"I would have preferred it quick and simple," he said, glaring at Henry. "But it seems Michael has robbed you of the easy way out once again."

"Stop it!" Rachel screamed. "Leave him alone!'

George ignored Rachel's warnings and closed in on Henry, who was still lying on the floor where Michael had pushed him. George tightened his grip on the weapon with one hand and reached out with the other to grab Henry. He raised the blade with deadly aim. Just then, a rifle exploded leaving a wide, oozing hole in George's back. He dropped instantly. Henry looked passed his lifeless corpse, amazed to see Olivia standing in the doorway holding the smoking gun.

"You. Let her go and stand over there," Olivia ordered Foster.

He obeyed without hesitation and held his hands high.

Jane rushed inside to embrace Rachel who was shaking with horror.

"Olivia?" Henry uttered. "Where…?"

"Never mind that now," she scolded.

"Where on earth did you get that gun?" Henry persisted.

"One of these men was kind enough to leave it out on the porch," she replied.

"Shoot!" Foster exclaimed at his own forgetfulness.

Olivia turned sharply towards him aiming the rifle. "No! I didn't mean you," he corrected himself.

"I never knew you could shoot like that," Henry told his sister.

Olivia shrugged. "I guess that's just something else we need discuss. But right now, get some rope for Mr. Mason's friend over there."

Henry nodded and hunted down some old strips of rawhide. "I guess this will have to do," he said.

"I don't want no trouble," Foster assured him.

"Just turn around," Henry said.

"Sure...sure."

Henry started to tie Foster's hands. "Seeings how I've been so cooperative," Foster began. "Don't you think we could work out some kinda deal?"

"I'm afraid any deals will have to be made with Sheriff Simms," Henry replied.

"Now, what kind of attitude is that to have? There's no cause to bring the law into this. Listen to me...I can make it worth your while...."

But Henry had ceased listening. He watched as Olivia set aside the rifle and stooped down to sit beside Jane. She was still cradling her cousin and he couldn't help but admire Jane's selflessness and poise at such a moment. His growing regard for her swelled inside his heart. But he was forced to abandon his admiration to contend with Foster. Meanwhile, Olivia had bravely determined to offer a tenuous gesture of kindness to Michael's daughter.

"There now, sweetheart," Olivia said softly. "Your father wouldn't want you to grieve so...."

Chapter Sixteen

There was so much Jane wanted to say to Rachel. Words of apology, consolation and reconciliation all came to her mind, then died upon her lips, as too inadequate to meet the needs of the present situation. Rachel was so traumatized that words could not reach her. Jane knew the best thing to do would be to get her home. But in going home, she realized they'd have to face Ruth and try to explain what had happened. Once the facts were known, her aunt would be devastated; a circumstance that would only exacerbate Rachel's condition. However, Jane's concerns over her cousin's welfare soon crumbled with Olivia's gentle ministrations.

Jane was moved by Olivia's generous compassion for a girl she had every right to resent. What's more, Rachel seemed calmer in her presence. Relieved by that fact, Jane allowed her thoughts to wander to Henry. She wondered how he'd fared in all this commotion. As she looked across the room, she noticed he'd just finished tying up Foster. She took the opportunity to go over and speak with him, leaving Rachel in Olivia's capable hands.

"You're bleeding," she said, noticing the penetration of blood through his makeshift bandages.

Henry gently probed his head and sighed. "I think I'll live."

"I'm sorry about all this."

"There's no reason for you to apologize."

"But if it hadn't been for my family…"

"Your family had nothing to do with my ego. I'm the one who should apologize to you, Jane. You warned me and I rode straight toward the trouble. I even surrendered to it. Just for a chance to confront your uncle and then he goes and …."

Jane could see he was deeply troubled by Michael's sacrifice. "I guess you can never tell about people," she offered.

They both looked at Michael's lifeless body.

"Why did he do it?" Henry asked. "I hated him and he knew it."

"I think he must have finally decided to take responsibility for his past."

"That's something else, Jane. I was wrong to disparage your uncle. I never should have told you about his connection to my family in such a cruel way."

"You were angry and afraid. I understand that."

"Still, you were only trying to help me and I thanked you by destroying your perceptions of a man you obviously respected."

Jane sighed. "I'm glad you told me. It's always better to know the truth."

"You're taking it easy on me."

"We're friends aren't we?"

Henry smirked. "We must be for you to be so eager to forgive me."

Jane smiled. "C'mon, you'd better let me change that bandage."

"No. It can wait. We'd better get Rachel out of here."

"Yes. Of course but...."

"I'm afraid all of this was too much for her. The best thing for her now is to get her to her mother."

Jealousy burned in Jane's belly at Henry's sudden show of concern for Rachel.

"I'm not sure Aunt Ruth will be much help," Jane ventured.

"Why not? Who would know better how to comfort Rachel than her mother?"

"No one of course, I mean…I just think Aunt Ruth will be too upset herself to help anyone, when she finds out what's happened to Uncle Michael."

"I hadn't thought of that."

"I just don't know how I'm going to explain all of this to her," Jane went on. "I scarcely understand it myself."

"To be honest, neither do I." Henry paused to look over at Michael and George. "It escapes me how some people can be so consumed by greed that they allow it to destroy their lives…their very souls, and others escape its grip only to end the same way."

"It's not quite the same," Jane said gently. "Is it?"

"Perhaps not," Henry agreed. "That brief moment of reprieve; that short glimpse of goodness may make all the difference."

"I'd like to think so," Jane replied

Henry nodded and looked back at her. "Jane," he began, "we've both uncovered some ugly truths in this business, which might be best to forget."

Jane visibly balked at Henry's unexpected suggestion.

"Little good can come from telling your aunt, her husband was party to a plot to ruin the town," Henry added.

"But Uncle Michael changed his mind. He was only cooperating to protect Rachel."

"I know, still I wouldn't like her to know about his involvement in anything criminal."

"But what about the town…the sheriff? What'll we tell them about all this?" Jane asked.

"I don't know," Henry admitted. "If the townsfolk were to discover the truth about the copper and George Masons plans for it, I fear what may happen."

"So that's what they were after," Jane replied.

"Didn't you know?"

Jane shook her head. "I guessed that somehow the Masons were after money, but I never managed to discover any particulars."

"It seems they wanted to buy out the town so they could mine all the copper underneath it," Henry explained.

"You mean there really is copper in Copper Creek?"

"According to George Mason. And he was prepared to do anything to get it."

"I can believe that. But if what you say is true, then, the copper…"

"Can stay just where it is," Henry interrupted.

"You mean, don't tell anyone it's there?"

Henry nodded.

"I would hate to see the land torn apart and everyone's homes destroyed," Jane admitted. "Still, isn't it a bit high-handed for us to decide for everyone what should be done about it? It seems rather selfish."

"Only if you don't consider the fact a mine could do more than destroy the land," Henry replied. "It could destroy lives. We've already seen proof of the kind of decimation greed is capable of bringing about. As pastor, it is my responsibility to safeguard the souls of my congregation from the insidious mania money can create. For centuries that copper has been hidden beneath the ground. Why not let the earth keep her secrets and allow life to go on in Copper Creek as before?"

"Because I doubt Thomas Mason will allow it."

"That's right," Henry said. "He does know about it too."

"And I don't think he'll just forget about collecting a fortune and walk away because we ask him nicely."

"Maybe not. But we might be able to keep him from spreading the news around, if we can find him before he gets word about his father. Then we can turn him over to the law and, once he's incarcerated, there'll be little chance he'd spill the beans."

"I don't know," Jane said. "He'll likely have a trial and if it comes out then, there could be enough folks who will start looking for the copper. And what's to keep them from stumbling on the same spot the Masons found?"

"It's our only chance," Henry pointed out. "Besides, Thomas worked too hard staking out this claim to let it slip in court or anywhere else that there's copper for the taking. He'll bide his time and wait for another opportunity. Just like his father did."

"And then?"

Henry shrugged. "Who knows what could have changed by that time. Maybe even Thomas Mason."

"I hope you're right."

"In the meantime, we'll tell the sheriff the Masons were preparing to swindle the town with a sketchy financial deal and, when Michael objected, they kidnapped Rachel. Then when her father tried to rescue her, he was killed. Agreed?"

Jane nodded. "Agreed."

"We'd better start after Thomas then."

"There's no hurry," Jane answered. "Before we left the store, Uncle Michael and I tied him up in the parlor. We left a note for Aunt Ruth warning her not to release him and with any luck, he should still be bound and gagged right where we left him."

"That's the first good news I've heard all day," Henry replied. "I'll go outside and hitch up that team to the wagon that brought me and Rachel here. We can load the bodies in the back and Foster can ride up with me on the box. Then as soon as we're ready, you and Olivia can ride out ahead of us with Rachel."

"Are you sure you should? You've taken quite a beating and your head..."

"In this instance, my thick skull has been a blessing."

Jane appeared unconvinced and her eyes pleaded with him to reconsider.

"Don't worry...I can hold out long enough to get back to town and get this trouble settled once and for all. Keep an eye on Foster while I'm gone."

Jane nodded and Henry made his way outside.

The sun had set, but there was still enough afterglow for Henry to make out the silhouette of the barn beside the house. His head felt a little swimmy, as he walked toward it, but he was determined to get the women back to Copper Creek and out of danger. The barn door had been left slightly ajar. Henry pushed it open the rest of the way and stepped inside. The bellied glass of a lamp shone in the dim light. He reached out to take it down from its peg and then lit it with a match from the tinderbox mounted below it. The amber light spread out in a small circle all around him. As he held it high, its illumination startled the two horses corralled in their stalls. One of them neighed in protest at being disturbed. Now all he needed to do was hitch them up to the wagon outside.

Suddenly the barn door slammed shut. Henry whirled around to see a familiar, young man emerge from the darkness. He was holding a gun.

"Going someplace, Reverend?"

Henry instantly recognized the intruder as George Mason's driver.

"Your name is John, isn't it?" Henry replied.

The man inclined his head. "I'm surprised you remembered."

"How could I forget? You left quite an *impression* on me," Henry finished, rubbing his bruised chin.

John smirked. "Then I suggest you do as I say and get back inside or..."

"Look," Henry interrupted. "There's no need for this. It's all over."

"If you mean your life, you're right."

"Your boss is dead."

"Mr. Mason?"

"Yes."

John seemed a little taken aback.

"It's true," Henry assured him.

"Or else it's some kind of trick."

"I promise you, it's the truth. Now, won't you put down that gun and let us go?"

"If I do and you're lying, Mr. Mason will have my hide."

"You don't have to be afraid of him anymore."

"Who's afraid?"

"I only meant you don't have to let him control you."

John pulled back the hammer on his pistol. "No one tells me what to do. I'm my own man."

"I believe you," Henry replied.

"I don't answer to nobody. To no family...no woman...no god...and definitely no man."

"Then why worry about Mr. Mason?"

"Because he's paying me for services rendered. And I take pride in my work."

"He can't pay you anything anymore."

"We'll just see about that."

John leveled his pistol and Henry could see in his eyes that he intended to fire.

"You don't want to do this," Henry said. "You don't want to be a killer."

"Too late, Reverend."

The next instant Henry hurled the oil lamp at John's face. In trying to deflect the lamp, the gun misfired and the lamp fell, shattering at John's feet. The hay and fodder on the ground was ignited immediately by the exposed flame, which fanned up and caught John's pant leg. He began to scream in agony as the fire consumed his flesh. He ran out of the barn to try to extinguish the flames in the water trough, but it was empty. Skirting around the flames fanning the doorway, Henry chased after him.

By the time he reached John, his clothes were aflame as far up as his torso. Henry took off his own coat and shoved him down into the dirt. He covered John's body with the coat and tried quickly to smother the flames. John's continued cries brought Jane and Olivia out of the house. Jane rushed down the porch steps and reached Henry just as he finished extinguishing John.

"Quick," Henry shouted at her. "The barn. Get the horses out."

Jane ran towards the barn. High, hot flames were belching from the doorway so intensely that Jane staggered back.

"Let's try 'round the back," Henry said, running up behind her.

They hurried around the barn and found a few loose panels in the back wall. Together, they clawed and prodded them out of the way to make a large enough portal to rescue the poor beasts stomping in fright on the other side.

Henry made his way inside first and released the horse from the farthest stall. Jane followed close behind and led the second beast out. As they came around the barn with the horses, flames ripped up through the roof. Henry tried to steady the mares, but the stench of smoke fanned from the barn in great black columns made them skittish.

They led the horses up to the house and Henry called out to his sister.

"Livy…get Rachel. We have to get out of here now!"

He turned to hand Jane the lead rope in his hand. "Stay here. I'll go in for Foster."

Henry had barely taken one-step up on the porch, when he heard a crash from the side of the house. Foster had taken advantage of the confusion to burst through the window. Within seconds of his escape, he was on his feet and running with his hands still tied behind his back.

Henry cursed under his breath, as he watched Foster disappear into the nearby woods, and proceeded inside to help Olivia.

"Livy, c'mon we need to go!"

"I can't, Henry," she called back. "Rachel won't move."

"All right," he replied. "Get outside with Jane and mount up."

"But…"

"Go!" Henry yelled.

Olivia tarried just long enough to see her brother gather Rachel into his arms.

She hurried out to Jane.

"Henry said to get mounted up," Olivia said.

"What about Rachel?"

The necessity for Olivia to answer was eliminated, when Jane saw Henry emerge from the house with Rachel. She was unconscious and draped across his arms. The sight stirred a mixture of relief and despair in Jane's heart.

She turned and released the mares they had rescued as Olivia rode up behind her. Olivia handed down the reins of Jane's horse to her and she saddled up. Then Henry handed Rachel up to her. With a little difficulty, they arranged her in Jane's arms and finally Henry mounted Michael's horse.

"Wait," Jane protested. "We can't leave the bodies here."

"We don't have enough time to get them out," Henry replied.

"But Uncle Michael…"

"We'll come back for him once we've made it to town and gotten some help."

The angry creaking of boards preceded a loud crash, as the barn finally collapsed in on itself.

"C'mon," Henry added. "Let's ride."

The horses needed little prompting to fly the scene of the blaze. As they galloped away, the sky behind them was as brilliant as noonday. Jane held fast to Rachel as her horse navigated the terrain. Her cousin's shortened hair and strained features stirred her sense of loyalty and compassion. There was no more room in her heart for bitterness or self-pity. She would never deny Rachel anything again, least of all her love, no matter what. At that thought, Jane glanced at Henry up ahead and considered the ironies of the heart. How very odd to lose a man just when one discovered how very much he mattered.

"I can't make sense of this at all, Sarah."

"Not being a mind reader, ma'am, I can't help you unless you tell me what the note says," Sarah replied calmly.

"What it says is my husband is gone! Again!" Ruth vented.

"I'm sure he'll be back in a jiffy."

"He prattles on about regrets over dragging me into a dangerous situation and says that neither George Mason nor his son is to be trusted! It just doesn't make sense."

Sarah set down her full basket of herbs on the kitchen table and picked up a key that was lying there.

"What's this then?" Sarah asked.

"It looks like the key to the parlor," Ruth snapped, still fretting over Michael's note.

"What's it doing down here?"

"Honestly, Sarah! Is a stupid key all you can think of at a time like this!"

"Sorry, Mrs. R. I just thought it might be important."

"Well, it's not!"

Ruth tossed down the crumpled missive in her hand.

"Here, give me that!" Ruth said, snapping the key from Sarah's hand. "I'm going upstairs to get an explanation from somebody."

Ruth stormed out of the kitchen, leaving Sarah to roll her eyes. She was more than accustomed to Ruth's temper. Still, Sarah found with each passing year, it was harder to keep from slapping Ruth silly during her fits of hysteria.

Mumbling to herself, Sarah stopped to pick up the note Ruth had left behind and noticed a second sheet on the floor that was blown down by the breeze from the open window. Picking it up, she casually perused the last few lines.

> *...I'm leaving the key to the parlor for you.*
> *Whatever you do, do not go inside until Sheriff*
> *Simms is with you. When he arrives, you must*
> *instruct him to arrest Thomas Mason. I'll explain*
> *further when I return....*

Panicked, Sarah raced out of the kitchen after Ruth.

"Mrs. R!" she yelled. "Wait!"

She made it to the top of the steps just as Ruth inserted the key in the lock.

"Don't open the door!" Sarah yelled.

Ruth was distracted just long enough for Sarah to reach her and extract the key.

"What are you talking about, Sarah? I have a perfect right to open the door to my own parlor."

Gasping for air, Sarah leaned back against the wall still clutching the key.

"Read this," she said, holding out the second page of Michael's note.

Ruth quickly read the last few lines. "Arrest Thomas Mason? This still makes no sense."

"Sense or no, I think we better do as Mr. R asked."

"Well, how can we? Sheriff Simms hasn't been around all day. He's too busy running after phantoms in the woods with that crackpot, Curtis Webber."

The sound of a man groaning came from the other side of the door.

"Mr. Mason," Ruth said. "Mr. Mason are you in there?"

Another groan was the only response.

"It sounds like he's hurt," Ruth said.

"So what?" Sarah replied.

"We have to help him."

"No."

"Sarah. Give me that key."

Sarah shook her head.

"I will not be told what to do in my own house. Now give me that key."

"No one is going in there until either Mr. R or Sheriff Simms gets here."

"Sarah! That's enough. I won't ask you again. Give me the key!"

Sarah clasped the key firmly in her hand and put it behind her back.

Enraged by Sarah's defiance, Ruth lunged forward and grabbed at Sarah's arm.

"Stop it, Mrs. R. You don't know what you're doing! It isn't safe!"

Ruth wouldn't heed any of Sarah's warnings. Finally, after a considerable struggle, Ruth wrested the key from Sarah's grasp.

She hurried to the door and unlocked it before Sarah could stop her. In the next instant, Ruth swept inside the room. Her jaw dropped at the sight of Thomas Mason, sitting in her grandmother's rocking chair bound and gagged with the ties from her best curtains.

As she continued to survey the scene, Ruth noticed the entire room was in a shambles. Tables were knocked over and bric-a-brac was shattered in pieces all over the floor. Among them were the remnants of her favorite flowerpot, which was covered in dirt and the wilted leaves of her prize winning fern. Appalled, she marched over to Thomas Mason and pulled the gag out of his mouth.

"What has been going on here!" she demanded.

"Just a little misunderstanding," Thomas replied.

"I highly doubt that, Mr. Mason. My parlor looks like a battlefield. Where is my husband?"

"I couldn't say."

"And Jane?"

"I haven't seen her since she cracked my skull."

"Jane did all this?"

"No."

"Then who? And why do you say Jane hit you?"

"Who else could it have been? You and my father had gone. I was just talking to your husband and then everything went black."

"But Jane would have had to come home."

"She did."

"I thought you said you hadn't seen her?"

"I said I hadn't seen her since she attacked me. I did see her before."

"Before? Before what?"

"Mrs. Randolph, if you don't mind, I have a blinding headache and this conversation isn't helping it any."

"Of course. But if you'll answer just one more question."

"Yes?"

"Why are you tied up?"

"You're guess is as good as mine."

"Ah...well. No matter. We'll just untie you now and send for Doctor Owens."

"Thank you."

Ruth turned to the door where Sarah was still lurking. "Sarah, come in here and help me untie Mr. Mason."

"No, ma'am. Mr. Randolph said not to."

"Well, Mr. Randolph isn't here."

Sarah shook her head.

Fed up with Sarah's stubbornness, Ruth crouched down behind Thomas and started working on the knots herself.

"Just look at this," she complained. "My curtains are going to be absolutely ruined."

"I don't think you should," Sarah warned from the doorway.

"I'm well aware of that," Ruth replied. "But instead of your chastisement, I would prefer your help."

Ruth worked diligently to free the curtain tassels from their obscene contortions and finally the last of them dropped from Thomas hands.

"There," Ruth pronounced proudly.

Thomas stood gingerly and massaged his wrists.

"Now, Sarah. I want you to go and fetch Doctor Owens. Tell him...."

Sarah gasped suddenly and, as Ruth turned to look behind her, she realized why. Thomas had collected his gun from the debris on the floor and held it on them.

"I can't thank you enough for your help, Mrs. Randolph. Although I'm afraid Sarah was right. You shouldn't have untied me."

"What nonsense is this?" Ruth demanded.

"I'm deadly serious," Thomas replied. "Now, sit down."

Appalled, Ruth nonetheless lowered herself into the rocking chair Thomas had recently vacated.

"You," he said, looking to Sarah. "Sit down there, next to her."

Thomas' bullying tone irked Sarah. No duded-up pipsqueak was going to tell her what to do just because he had a gun. She came into the room slowly. As she did, she noticed Thomas was standing on a small rug Ruth liked to use to keep her feet warm during chilly evenings. She averted her eyes so as not to draw Thomas' attention to her discovery and continued into the room.

"That's right," he taunted. "We'll all take it nice and easy."

Now within striking distance, Sarah cried "I don't think so, sonny." She stooped down and pulled on the edge of the rug. Thomas teetered off balance and as he lurched forward, Sarah grabbed the only substantial piece of crockery still intact and shattered it over his head. Thomas fell on his face and remained down, unconscious once more.

Sarah hurried to pick up his gun and then looked over at Ruth.

"Shall we tie him up?" Ruth asked demurely.

Sarah picked up one of the curtain cords and handed it to Ruth.

"Must we use these?" Ruth implored.

Sarah glared at her.

"Oh, very well," Ruth grumbled. "Hold his arms together and I'll tie the knots."

Chapter Seventeen

It seemed to Jane as though they had been riding forever and the lights of Copper Creek still had not come into view. She began to fear the strain of the day was about to overcome her as a dreadful pounding filled her ears. Suddenly, she realized she was hearing the sound of riders approaching fast from the east. Within seconds, they burst into view and surrounded their little group.

"Hold up there!"

Jane released a sigh of relief. It was Sheriff Simms.

"Sheriff, we need your help," Olivia said.

"Aren't you Miss Kohl?" the sheriff asked.

"Yes. But...."

"Where in tarnation have you been woman!"

"Sheriff, there's no need to be so hostile," Jane intervened.

"Hostile! I've been out all day burning up horseflesh looking for this fool woman!"

"Sheriff, that's my fault and not my sister's," Henry said.

"Darn right. And you can expect there is going to be retribution for all the supplies and manpower wasted today on this wild goose hunt."

"Honestly, can't you think of something other than yourself!" Olivia shouted.

Simms was amazed at her show of temper and it turned his bluster into amusement.

"Now," she continued, "there is a hurt man at an abandoned cabin a few miles back. He's been burned and he is in bad shape."

"We saw the fire," the sheriff said.

"I'm afraid that's my fault too," Henry added. "I was attempting to defend myself against a gun...."

"And you decided to set the entire countryside ablaze," the sheriff finished.

"You'll also find three bodies, Sheriff," Jane put in. "As well as the remnants of evidence against the Masons, which I'm sure Mr. Webber told you about."

"He did," Simms replied.

"How'd you catch up with them, Janey?" Mr. Webber piped up from the ranks of the posse.

"It's a long story," Jane said.

"It's one I'll expect you to share in detail, Miss Randolph," Simms interjected. "Beginning with identifying those three bodies."

"George Mason and one of his hired men," Henry said.

"And the third?" Mr. Webber asked.

"My uncle," Jane replied.

"Michael?" Simms said in shock.

"I'm afraid so."

The sheriff looked around in frustration. "What happened to her?" Simms asked, taking note of Rachel.

"Well...," Jane began.

"I know. It's a long story."

Jane nodded.

"All right, you get your cousin back into town and we'll ride on to see what we can do about the fire and bringing in the bodies."

"It's the old Richmond homestead," Jane said.

"Fine. Men!"

Simms signaled for the men to ride on and as they filed passed, Simms rode up to Jane.

"I'll expect to see you at my office first thing in the morning. All of you. I want to hear this epic story of yours."

"Right, Sheriff," Henry said.

"I'll be there," Jane assured him.

Then with an authoritative nod, Simms rejoined the posse and headed towards the Richmond place.

When they had gone, the familiar calm of evening pressed in around them, as if Mother Nature neither knew nor cared about the horrific events of the past few hours. She was content to hum and sing with the peace of a soul untouched by evil. The song of a whippoorwill rippled through the air. Jane looked at Henry and, in the twilight, their unspoken understanding made her heart swell.

The next morning Dr. Luke Owens emerged from Randolph's General Mercantile bleary eyed and weary after a long night of mending wounded bodies and haunted minds. Rachel was his last patient and he regretted there was very little he could do for her. Ruth had taken to her bed at the news of Michael's death, a misfortune cruelly compounded by the state of her daughter. A sleeping powder had been the only relief Doc Owens could provide both women. He knew it would not be enough to mend Ruth's broken heart or Rachel's tortured thoughts.

Henry Kohl was waiting outside to meet him.

"How is Miss Rachel?" he asked the doctor.

"There's no way to know. Physically, there is very little wrong with her. But…I fear she's in a bad way."

"I'm sorry to hear it."

"Time is a great healer, Reverend Kohl. I think it's probably the best medicine Miss Randolph can take."

"And the rest of the family?"

"Coping as best they can. In that respect, I think you might be better able to minster to them than I am."

"Yes…thank you, doctor."

"Not at all. But if you would take some advice."

"Yes?"

"Go home and get some rest. You took a nasty blow to the head and I don't have any desire to have myself another coma patient."

"Thomas Mason hasn't improved?" Henry interpreted.

Luke shook his head. "I'm afraid he took a worse beating than you. Unfortunately, Sheriff Simms insisted on keeping him over in the jail."

"I expect that's best."

"A dark, damp cell is hardly the ideal place to convalesce, but when a man has committed crime on the scale Mr. Mason did…"

"Where else can you put him," Henry finished. "I expect he'll stand trial, if he does recover."

"'Fraid so. But this legal wrangle is well beyond my powers of comprehension. You be sure and take it easy now."

"I will. As soon as I've dropped in on the sheriff."

Henry watched the doctor stroll away and remained outside the store. Since they parted last night, Henry had been anxious to see Jane again. Their shared ordeal had strengthened his desire, even his necessity, to be near her. It made him feel strangely free and somehow safe to no longer have the secret of his past between them.

In that respect, Jane Randolph had become very important to him, in spite of all the barriers he had foreseen to such a connection. She was nothing like her uncle. Then again, last night Michael Randolph had proven he was nothing like the man Henry had loathed all these years. God had played quite a trick on Henry Kohl. But with the burgeoning feeling of happiness now ever present in his mind and heart, Henry couldn't complain. In fact, he was more delighted and grateful than he could say. He wanted Jane to know that.

He summoned all his courage and decided to go in to see her before stepping over to the sheriff's office. But as he reached for the doorknob, it drew back from his hand and he came face to face with Jane, as she emerged from the other side of the door.

"Oh! I'm sorry," Jane said. "I didn't know anyone was here."

"I was just on my way to see the sheriff," Henry replied.

"Me too."

Jane averted her gaze from Henry's face. A giddy rush of excitement had tied knots in her stomach the instant she recognized him and she was afraid to let him detect her delight at his arrival.

"I stopped by because…well I just wanted to…to find out how Rachel was doing."

"Rachel?" Jane's spirits plummeted. Henry's inquiry seemed confirmation of her suspicions he'd formed an attachment to her cousin.

"Yes. How is she?" Henry pursued.

"She's as well as can be expected. I managed to get her to eat a little something and she's sleeping now."

"Good. Good. I'm glad."

"Your concern for her is appreciated, I'm sure," Jane offered. "Though I suppose you'd rather hear that from someone other than me."

Henry furrowed his brow in confusion.

"I mean," Jane explained, "I'm sure that if Rachel was herself, you'd rather she told you how grateful she is to you for looking after her and saving her from the fire and all."

"Oh. Well…I…"

Jane mistook Henry's discomfiture and reached out to console him. She put her hand on his arm and said, "Just give her some time. I'm sure in a little while she'll be ready to… turn her mind to thoughts of romance."

"Romance?"

Jane blushed. She wished she had not brought up the subject at all, but she was determined to make the sacrifice. If Henry was in love with Rachel, she wouldn't stand in their way.

"Jane, I think there has been a misunderstanding," Henry said.

"Oh?" Renewed hope stirred in Jane's breast

"I think Rachel is a very sweet girl, but I'm not interested in starting a romance with her. I mean, I don't think of her in that way."

"In what way?"

"The way a man thinks about the kind of woman he hopes to marry."

"Have you thought about that?" Jane asked.

"Certainly. What man hasn't?"

Jane hesitated to press him but her curiosity would not allow her to remain silent

"Suppose," she ventured. "Suppose that sort of woman did come along. How would you know it?"

"I imagine she'd spark a kind of feeling no other woman could."

"Yes, but what would she be like?"

Henry turned away. Embarrassed to go on he stumbled over his words finally managing to say, "The particulars differ from one man to the next. But in my case, I've always envisioned her as a kind person. Someone who's gentle and thoughtful."

"Anything else?"

"She'd have to be loyal and strong in character."

"Beautiful?"

"Yes. But in her own way. More than that, she'd be wise and willing to stand up to me when I'm wrong. In that way, she'd be my equal, my companion and confidant."

"She sounds too good to be true."

"She sounds like you," Henry said gently.

Jane's eyes flew to Henry's face. "Me?"

"Jane, do you think you could ever love a man as riddled with faults as me?"

"Funny...Olivia asked me a very similar question. She seems to feel we could make each other very happy."

"I know. But what do you think?"

Jane turned and walked to the edge of the porch. As she looked out across the town, a warm glow seemed to be bubbling up from somewhere deep inside. She shuddered with delight at its awesome force and smiled at her sudden realization.

"I think..." she began, "she's absolutely right."

Still beaming, Jane turned to face Henry.

"Jane," he uttered. "Do you mean it?"

She nodded and he stepped forward to sweep her up into his arms. She thrilled at his embrace and was no longer able to hold back her tears of joy. Henry spun her around and, when he set her down, he tenderly wiped the droplets from her cheeks.

"Jane I never thought I could be this happy."

"Neither did I," she confessed.

"Somehow it seems wrong to feel like this when everyone around us is in such misery."

"Maybe. But I can't help it. The truth is I felt pretty miserable myself when I thought you were in love with Rachel."

"Why would you ever think such a thing?"

Jane shrugged. "You seem so concerned for her. And you *were* kidnapped together. How did I know what went on when you were alone."

Henry smirked. "You were really jealous?"

"Don't tease me," Jane said. "It was awful."

"I know. I wasn't too pleased seeing you with Thomas Mason either."

"Henry Kohl, no one has ever paid me a nicer compliment."

"Does that mean you were never really serious about him?"

"I never really thought about it until now. But I guess the truth is I always knew he wasn't the one for me. He never made me feel the way you do."

"And how is that?"

"I don't know if I can put it into words," she said, looking into his eyes. "It's like a kind of belonging I haven't felt since my parents died. I feel *home*."

"Jane…It's the same with me."

"Are you sure? After all, I am a *Randolph*."

"No," Henry corrected, smiling gently. "You're Jane…*my* Jane. If you want to be."

Jane smiled and reached up to caress his poor, beaten face. "I never wanted anything more."

Henry leaned in to her touch and seized her hand. He lovingly kissed her palm and her skin tingled at the warm sensation of his lips. Their fingers entwined as Henry lifted his head to gaze into her eyes.

"I can't pretend I've forgotten what your uncle did to my family," Henry continued.

"I can't seem to forget either," Jane admitted.

"But I intend to try to forget. I never expected I would ever fall in love and certainly not with a Randolph," he confessed. "But now that it's happened, I'm not going to let anything come between us, least of all the past."

"No," she concurred, tightening her grip on his hand. "Nothing could change our fate now."

Henry smiled gently. "I mean it, Jane," he said. "Last night what Michael did…his sacrifice, freed me from my mania for revenge. I'm just sorry my peace had to come at the cost of your family's grief."

"Uncle Michael made his choices. Aunt Ruth and Rachel know that."

"Yes. But they don't ever have to know the truth about Livy and me. I told Rachel it was George Mason I hated. Not her father."

"You did?" Jane marveled.

Henry nodded. "It was obvious how much Rachel loved her father. I couldn't destroy that."

"I couldn't tell Aunt Ruth that Uncle Michael and Olivia were married either. It just never seemed to be the right time."

"Well don't worry about it anymore," Henry replied. "With Michael gone, I can't see any use in robbing his family of their memories of him."

Jane was speechless. Even in the face of all his rightful grievances against her uncle, Henry Kohl was willing to shield her family from further pain rather than reveal the truth.

"Thank you, Henry."

"It isn't a hard thing to do…now," Henry replied.

"Still, I don't know how to repay you."

He smiled. "Perhaps you could start by walking with me to the sheriff's office?"

Henry held out his arm and Jane eagerly took hold.

As they made their way down the street, Henry added, "Perhaps after our visit with Simms, we should go tell Olivia."

"That we're in love?" Jane shook her head. "She knew it before we did."

"She did at that."

"But let's go to see her anyway," Jane replied. "There is an awful lot I'd like to thank her for."

On Sunday morning, all of Copper Creek gathered at the church. Two days had passed since the excitement at the old Richmond place and everyone knew about the Randolph's tragedy. Wide speculation regarding the narrow escape of the town from George Mason's greedy plot and the degree of Michael Randolph's involvement was rampant. Out of respect for Ruth and Rachel's grief, however, all gossip was suspended during the day of Michael Randolph's funeral.

Jane walked to the church alone, as Ruth and Rachel wanted to delay their arrival at church as long as possible. Though Rachel had shown a marked improvement since her ordeal, she was still as somber and broken-hearted as her mother. Both of them felt the well-intentioned, but overwhelming condolences of their neighbors would be beyond their capacity to endure for long. So, they would arrive in a private carriage just moments before services were set to begin.

In truth, Jane was somewhat relived to go alone. It would give her some time to herself. And though she felt surprisingly calm this morning, she couldn't deny she had experienced a jumble of emotions the last few days. Her sorrow over her uncle's passing and her concern for her aunt and cousin were tempered by her newfound happiness with Henry. Jane reflected on these shifting emotions, as she turned up the path outside the church. She smiled and waved when she saw Mr. Webber coming from the other direction, with Wes and Danny close behind him.

"Good morning, Janey," he called.

"Good morning, Mr. Webber…Wes. Danny."

"Miss Randolph," the boys said in unison, tugging at their caps.

"A fine day," Mr. Webber added, as he strolled up beside her. "Considering the circumstances."

"Indeed, Mr. Webber."

"How are the folks?" Curtis asked solemnly.

"They're taking it one day at a time."

He shook his head. "Quite a cruel thing. If I had known what we were really getting into, Janey, I might have reconsidered. I never would have guessed Michael would be involved in such a sneaky, underhanded, low-down, no good, rotten…"

"No, of course not," Jane interrupted. "Still, even if you'd known, I think your sense of justice wouldn't have permitted you to do anything differently."

He considered her assessment for a moment and said. "You're probably right. I guess it's an occupational hazard."

"Speaking of trouble, Mr. Webber, there was a very pressing matter I've been meaning to talk to you about."

"Oh?"

"Yes. It's about that letter of mine you printed."

"Funny you should mention that, Janey. The boys and I wanted to talk to you about that very thing. Didn't we, lads?"

Wes and Danny exchanged guilty looks, wishing they could disappear.

"Well, boys. What are you waiting for?" Curtis prompted them.

Danny shoved Wes forward. He gave his friend a dirty look before clearing his throat. "It was our fault, Miss Randolph," Wes said. "We put your letter in the paper."

"You?"

"We thought it was a test," Danny explained. "We hoped we'd make Mr. Webber proud of us, but I guess we were wrong.

"And?" Curtis said firmly.

"And…" Danny went on. "We're both sorry."

"Real sorry," Wes added.

"I understand that piece gave the reverend a good deal of trouble," Mr. Webber added. "So I've printed a retraction in the latest edition explaining everything."

"That is good of you, Mr. Webber."

"Not at all. It's my duty to set things right."

"If I may ask though," Jane went on. "When you boys printed my letter, why didn't you print both pages? It would have avoided all the trouble."

"We didn't know there were two pages," Wes replied.

"The other page must have gotten lost," Danny said.

"I see," Jane replied.

"I suppose I am to blame too," Mr. Webber added. "I never should have left that letter around for these two lunkheads to find!"

"We were only trying to use some init...initiative," Danny argued, delighted he got the word out.

"I know and I'm pleased," Curtis said. "It means you're starting to think like real newspapermen. But I wish you'd waited to try it until I was around. Frankly, I'm disappointed you didn't recognize the implications of your actions."

"Mr. Webber, the boys just made a mistake," Jane intervened.

"True. But by Jonah, they're going to learn from it!"

Wes and Danny looked cowed by Curtis' fierce pronouncement.

"Then with any luck, the next time they take the initiative it shouldn't be such a mess," he finished.

Relieved, the boys grinned.

"Now, inside with both of you," Curtis said, waving them off into church.

They ran to the door and pulled off their caps before stepping inside.

"They're good boys," Jane noted, watching them go.

"Don't think I didn't already know that," Curtis replied. "Let's hope with a little luck they'll grow-up to be good men."

"It won't take luck," Jane assured him. "They're in good hands."

Jane smiled and Curtis laced her arm through his to lead her into the church.

Inside, the pews were almost filled to capacity. Jane saw Olivia sitting down in front and she excused herself from Mr. Webber's company to go to join her.

"Everything all right?" Olivia asked her.

"Fine. I just wanted to have a word with Mr. Webber."

"About your letter to the editor?" Olivia guessed

"Yes. And it was good of you to forgive me."

"What else could I do for my future sister-in-law?"

"Olivia Kohl!"

Olivia smiled indulgently.

"Henry and I haven't made any wedding plans," Jane insisted.

"Why ever not? You're in love aren't you?"

"Well, yes, but Henry and I feel we should wait a bit. Out of respect...."

"Jane Randolph that's the silliest thing I ever heard."

"It is not. It's what Henry and I want. We need time to get to know each other."

"Take all the time you like," Olivia replied. "It won't change a thing."

"I hope it doesn't."

"Then why postpone your happiness? Take it from me, Jane, time passes much more quickly than we realize and time with someone you love... is even more fleeting."

Olivia's words were choked off by a sudden rush of emotions.

"Don't mind me," Olivia continued, as she dabbed at her eyes with a handkerchief.

"I'm so sorry, Olivia," Jane replied gently. "As if it wasn't bad enough for you to lose Uncle Michael again, you can't even take comfort in grieving openly as his widow."

"It's not that bad. Really. I haven't seen him in more than twenty years. I guess you could say I did my grieving long ago and now...I can have closure."

Jane reached out to squeeze Olivia's hand. Just then, Ruth and Rachel arrived. They came in quietly by the side door and sat in the empty pew reserved for them down front. Once they were seated, the pianist began to play. Everyone rose to sing along and a few moments later, Henry entered from the side door. He stood serenely behind the pulpit until the hymn had finished. Then he began his sermon.

"Today, I want to talk to you about sacrifice,... duty,...loyalty....*love*. And how one man in this community used his final hours to exemplify all four..."

A few weeks later, the last days of summer slipped into the crisp embrace of fall. This change meant it was time to begin preparations for the annual Founder's Day picnic. It had been suggested that the festivities be suspended this year since the celebration came so close on the heels of the Randolph family tragedy. However, Jane assured the planning committee that neither herself, Ruth, or Rachel, would want the town to abandon the tradition for their sake. So plans went ahead, as usual, and when the day finally came, a veritable feast was laid out before the citizens of Copper Creek.

Beer and barbecue, cakes and pies, smiles and good spirits were found at every table. By the time the sun started to sink below the distant hills, a full day of games and official presentations was winding down and the musicians started to tune-up. As the lanterns surrounding the marquee were lit, eager couples stepped out on to the dance floor for the first square dance of the evening.

Jane, Olivia, and Henry had spent an idyllic afternoon together, but Olivia was tired and ready to head for home. With a few well-chosen words, she urged Henry and Jane to dance and watched with a blissful heart, as they made their way to the floor.

Before the first reel ended, she strolled down the street leaving the strains of frivolity to fade behind her. Even in her relief to have her brother back, Olivia's heart was still heavy over Michael's death. Though she had lost him over twenty years ago, a part of her never stopped wanting him, missing him, loving him. To have found him again and received his apologies was more resolution than she ever expected. Even if he had lived, she knew she couldn't ask for more. Still, sentiment made her yearn for some part of him. Something that would be hers alone to remember about the first and only man to have won her heart.

The sound of a rider approaching drew Olivia out of her musings. He was coming from the west and the setting sun obscured his face as he pulled up beside her.

"Pardon me, ma'am," the young man said. "Is this the way to Copper Creek?"

Olivia held up her hand to shield her eyes. "Yes," she began "You just go…"

Her tongue was paralyzed as she got her first clear glimpse of the stranger. He was the image of Michael Randolph's clever, blue-grey eyes and beguiling smile and her own smooth straight nose and gentle sloping cheeks.

"Are you all right, ma'am?" the stranger asked.

"Yes," Olivia stammered, feeling a strange tug of familiarity.

"Ma'am?"

"Forgive me. I just thought…you look so much like…" Olivia stared at the stranger in wonder. She felt an undeniable connection to him she could not explain.

"Sorry?"

"Just follow this road and it will take you straight into town," Olivia said.

"Much obliged." He tapped the brim of his hat.

"Your most welcome, Mr.…."

"Kohl, ma'am. Ben Kohl."

Shock and disbelief consumed Olivia, as she watched the young man ride away. *It couldn't be him. It couldn't be…my Ben.*

Olivia massaged her temples, fearing the stress of the past few weeks was finally causing her to hallucinate. If this is what came of wishing for a memento of her past, she would never wish for anything ever again. Still there had to be something to this. *I couldn't have dreamed him up?* she thought. *Could I?* As she continued down the road, she realized there was only one way to find out.

Filled with an irrational sense of hope, Olivia changed her course and followed the cloud of dust left behind on the road by the stranger. She was going into Copper Creek to discover for herself if this Ben Kohl was really a figment of her imagination or her own flesh and blood.

If he was real, it would mean God had somehow restored the son she thought she'd lost in answer to her most fervent prayers. If he had been just a momentary vision, she would still be grateful for the encounter because it proved her heart was not empty and buried in the past, as Henry had feared, but very much alive and willing to love again.